LPF WEST BOG

ROCH

"Matthew Johnson, US
Marshal"/"Boggs,
Johnny D."

Mar 2021

3318700480 0344
FULTON COUNTY PUBLIC LIBRARY

D1711326

Fulton Co. Public Library
320 W. 7th Street
Rochester, IN 46975

MATTHEW JOHNSON, U.S. MARSHAL

Center Point
Large Print

Also by Johnny D. Boggs and available from Center Point Large Print:

The Killing Trail
The Raven's Honor
The Fall of Abilene
The Cane Creek Regulators
Buckskin, Bloomers, and Me

This Large Print Book carries the Seal of Approval of N.A.V.H.

MATTHEW JOHNSON, U.S. MARSHAL

Johnny D. Boggs

CENTER POINT LARGE PRINT
THORNDIKE, MAINE

This Circle Ⓥ Western is published by
Center Point Large Print in the year 2021 in
co-operation with Golden West Literary Agency.

Copyright © 2020 by Johnny D. Boggs.

All rights reserved.

First Edition
March 2021

Printed in the United States of America
on permanent paper.
Set in 16-point Times New Roman type.

ISBN: 978-1-64358-847-6

The Library of Congress has cataloged this record
under Library of Congress Control Number: 2020950556

*For Vicki Piekarski, my agent,
editor (willing to say, "Rewrite this!"),
sounding board, and friend
for more than twenty years.
One last time down the trail.
Good luck, and thanks for a great ride!*

CHAPTER ONE

Denver, Colorado
Late Spring, 1894

Stepping onto the depot platform, he cringed at the loud voices of children singing—or rather screaming—the way they always did, no matter the town, state, or territory.

Matthew Johnson,
United States marshal,
Strong as an ox,
And sly as a fox.
Matthew Johnson,
United States marshal,
He put Jeff Hancock
In that big pine box.

He hated that damned song.

But, being a politician again, Matt removed his hat and stepped away from the train before walking toward the temporary bandstand where those schoolchildren sang. Not much of a welcoming committee, Matt thought, but that would come later, at the Capitol, when he was sworn in as federal marshal.

"Matt."

He turned right.

"Marshal."

He looked to his left, then right again. From the right came a man wearing a gray suit of worsted wool, covered with a double-breasted heavy blue coat, unbuttoned. He might have passed for a local businessman except for the wide-brimmed, high-crowned, peaked cowboy hat and the shining black boots.

On his left hurried a much younger man, slim, tall, solid, with sandy hair down to his shoulders, a well-trimmed mustache and goatee, and a good deal of beard stubble covering the rest of a wind-bronzed face.

The kids went on trying to outshout each other with those dreadful lyrics.

Matt jerked his right hand out of the trousers pocket, retrieving the pack of sweet-fern chewing gum he had bought from a vendor before changing trains in Colorado Springs. He popped the gum in his mouth. Six cups of railroad coffee might have reduced any chance that some ink-slinger or Republican would smell the liquor on his breath, but those rumors of Matt's drinking had been dogging him a long damned while. *Rumors?* Matt tensed, feeling the weight of his flask in his inside coat pocket.

Reaching Matt first, the older man laughed, extended his hand, and looked at the younger man, who slowed his pace. "The old man beats the young kid." He grinned at Matt. "Us old-timers still got plenty of starch, don't we, Matt?"

Matt slipped the gum pack back into his pocket, and shook the gray-mustached man's hand. He knew why this well-dressed fellow won that foot race. Despite those cowboy boots and hat, this gent was used to the ankle express. Whereas, the long-haired man's bowed legs, like Matt's own, revealed a man used to riding, not walking.

"Marshal, allow me to be the first to welcome you to Denver City and the state of Colorado on a glorious afternoon," the race winner said. "Luther J. Wilson, at your service."

"A pleasure." Matt started to greet the younger man, but Wilson kept right on talking, so he pulled his hand back and concentrated on the gum.

"I have a small place on the Pine River east of Durango. Like you to come see it some time. I also dabble in real estate, what you might call a speculator. Made my pile investing in all sorts of things, but not . . . thank God . . . silver. But I'm here on this glorious day as a member of our state General Assembly. Only in the House, though, till the next election." Luther J. Wilson chuckled, and leaned closer to whisper: "I'm aiming for the Senate."

"Too bad the Utes can't vote."

Matt stopped chewing gum, and turned his attention to the younger man.

9

Those striking eyes, a pale blue, practically translucent, seemed hypnotic. Jeff Hancock had eyes like that, but nothing else—other than those bowlegs—reminded Matt of the friend he had killed at Rattlesnake Station seventeen years ago.

With his left hand, the long-haired man pulled back his Mackinaw and grinned. A badge hung loosely from a frayed vest.

"I'm Liberty Rawlings," he said. "Deputy marshal. Work out of Durango." The accent, Matt placed, somewhere down South. Not Texas. Not strong, either, just noticeable. Like Matt's own.

As they shook, Matt liked Liberty Rawlings's strong grip. "Durango." Matt looked back at Luther J. Wilson, whose smile had been replaced by a dark frown. "Then you know . . . ?"

"Yes," Wilson said hollowly.

"In passing," Rawlings replied.

A smile reappeared below Wilson's mustache. "We run with . . . different crowds." The voice contained no friendliness.

Matt tried to think, found himself talking. "Durango. There was a little trouble there with that railroad strike, wasn't there?"

"We put those anarchists in their place," Wilson said, but Matt kept his eyes on Rawlings.

"Some. Trinidad got the worst of it. And there are bigger troubles around Durango than the railroad strike."

Wilson put a hand on Matt's shoulder, leaned

in, and said: "Matt, I should get you to the Capitol. Before your admirers turn ugly."

Matt let himself be turned away. The children were on the last verse of their song. Wilson had managed to get him about ten feet from Deputy Rawlings before Matt stopped. When the kids screamed the last lyrics of the song, Matt clapped his hands.

After she curtsied, the buxom, young band-leader announced to the boys and girls: "Class, this is Marshal Matthew Johnson, the man who brought law and order to Idaho . . ."—Matt started to smile—"before you were even born, and when I was younger than you children are today."

Still, he chuckled, thinking how old Bounce McMahon would have given him hell for a week had he been here to hear that.

The kids jumped up and down, and Matt pulled away from Wilson to shake hands with the youngsters, and the young woman. He kept remembering that he was a politician. *Things would be different this time,* he told himself. *It wouldn't be like it had been in Idaho. I'm smarter. Know how to handle things.*

As the lady gathered up her singers, Matt slipped his right hand into the pocket of his woolen coat, feeling the coolness of a pewter flask. He felt his nerves start to fray, but after sneaking a couple of discreet swallows in the

11

smoking car on the ride north, Matt dared not risk opening that flask again—not in front of a handsome schoolmarm riding herd on her loud-voiced children. And a state assemblyman. And . . .

He whirled back to find that Rawlings had not moved.

"Levi," Matt said, "are you based here in Denver?"

"Durango," the deputy said. "And it's Liberty. Liberty Rawlings."

What did I call him? Levi. Jesus, you're an idiot. He told himself never again to take two swallows of bourbon in the morning without having breakfast, but he remembered how to laugh off a mistake. "Yes, yes, yes. Of course." He chuckled in that self-deprecating way he had perfected over the years. "Durango. Well, Liberty, maybe one day I'll learn to keep my mouth shut until I've secured my land legs." He gestured toward the locomotive. "Never have gotten used to trains."

Without attempting to hide his impatience, Luther Wilson cleared his throat.

"Will you be in town tomorrow morning or will you be heading back to Durango?" Matt asked.

"I leave on the two-thirty," Rawlings replied, "tomorrow afternoon."

"Good. I'd like to meet with you and any other deputy marshals in my office at nine o'clock."

"I can do that," Rawlings said as Wilson put his arm around Matt's shoulder.

"Really, Matt, we have a tight schedule," Wilson reminded him. "Allow me to escort you to your constituents and maybe a few future felons." His grin revealed new dentures. "Judge Perelman will swear you in, and your appointment as U.S. marshal will be official. Afterward, we shall see how well you can dodge bullets from the members of our press."

Matt nodded, only to remember his luggage. He called out to a porter, but Wilson took control.

"Oh, boy," the assemblyman said, and Matt noticed the wicked gleam in Wilson's eyes. He was talking to Deputy U.S. Marshal Liberty Rawlings. "Can you take your boss's luggage and things to Missus McBride's boarding house? You know the place?" He gave the address. Matt turned quickly, as the deputy nodded.

"It'd be a privilege," Rawlings said.

The bourbon in Matt's stomach soured, but he let Wilson turn him around, and steer him toward a waiting hack.

As the carriage moved away from the noisy depot, Wilson leaned forward and whispered: "After these shenanigans, Matt, I'd be honored to escort you to the lodgings we've arranged for you, and, after meeting Missus McBride, I can take you to sup with some of Denver's . . . and the state's . . . best men to know."

"All right." Matt nodded, and leaned to spit his gum out the window.

"The party members and I were concerned you might not get the appointment," Wilson said. "But we prevailed. Just don't expect to find the governor watching you be sworn in."

That came as no surprise. The governor was a Republican, and President Grover Cleveland, a Democrat, had picked Matthew Johnson to be a U.S. marshal, an appointment unanimously confirmed by a Democratic-controlled Senate. Lucky timing. The opening for the U.S. marshal for the state of Colorado came while Democrats still controlled the federal executive and legislative branches of government. With the crash of the silver market, Matt doubted if any Democrat stood a chance at being elected to office come November.

"I'm glad we got the votes." Laughing, Wilson nudged Matt. "Glad you got the votes, I mean to say."

Matt said: "The last time I voted in any election was back in 'Seventy-Six in Idaho Territory. Voted for myself, and, months later, I vowed never to make such a mistake again." He smiled. "The one promise I've never broken."

Wilson laughed.

He thinks I'm joking.

Matt looked out the window, feeling the bite of winter even in April, trying to recall what Denver looked like when he had arrived back in 'Sixty-Five, as Wilson kept talking.

"When we reach the Capitol, well, you know what it'll be like. Kissing babies, making a speech, shaking hands, and talking to those newspapermen." He leaned closer for another conspiratorial whisper. "The *Clarion* editor you won't have to worry about, Matt. I pay his damned salary." Wilson found his cigar case. "Marshaling isn't like it used to be, is it, Matt?"

It never was, Matt thought.

"Cigar?" Wilson asked.

Matt shook his head.

"I imagine every man, woman, and child at the Capitol will want to meet you," Wilson said, lighted his cigar, and tossed the match out the window. "Hell, who doesn't want to shake hands with the man who killed Jeff Hancock?"

Or spit in his face, Matt thought.

Standing at the top of the marble steps at the Capitol, Matt raised his right hand, placed his left over the preacher's Bible, and repeated the oath given to him by U.S. District Judge Warren J. Perelman. More claps and cheers, a prayer by the preacher, and finally Matt stepped to a lectern lined with red, white, and blue bunting. A young boy held up one of those speaking trumpets, but Matt shook his head.

15

He shoved his hands deep into coat pockets, cleared his throat, and looked at the people. The crowd wasn't that big. And he didn't see any Winchesters aimed in his direction. Forty degrees, windy, cloudy. Maybe fifty people had gathered to hear him talk.

He had never gotten used to this kind of speaking, though he had tried. After killing Jeff Hancock, he spent about six months speaking at packed opera houses, mostly in the East, and that cured him of any aspirations of becoming some new Edwin Forrest.

He opened his first speech as federal marshal of Colorado by retelling that joke he started using during his theatrical tour: "I told a city fellow I was a cowpuncher, and he said that he had never punched a cow. And I told him . . . 'I never *punched* any either, but I branded quite a few . . . some might have even been owned by the ranchers paying me.' "

A few people even laughed.

Most of what he said, he didn't remember—the usual horseshit any federal marshal, solicitor, or judge would have spewed out—flapdoodle, his ma called it. Yet Matt knew he could read about it in the *Evening Post, Republican, Morning Herald, Rocky Mountain News*, or Luther Wilson's paper, the *Cattlemen's Clarion of Colorado*. He thanked the children for their fine rendition at the depot, the best version of that

16

song that he had ever heard—which was saying something, because that song had been haunting him since 1877.

The speech ended, and polite applause died quickly. With the sun starting to dip behind the Rocky Mountains, Matt came down the steps to meet the throng of ink-slingers. "It's cold, gentlemen," he said, "but I can take a few questions from you today. If you have more, I'm sure I'll see you at the federal courthouse."

Evening Post: "Don't you think you'd be better suited as the U.S. marshal in the state of Idaho?"

A shout from the back of the crowd: "Like Idaho would have him!"

Answer: "As far as I know, there was no opening in Idaho. President Cleveland said I was needed in Colorado, and here I am."

Evening Post: "Did you actually talk to President Cleveland?"

Answer: "Just exchanges over the telegraph."

Republican: "There has been talk about opening the Southern Ute reservation to settlement. How would you handle it?"

Answer: "I don't deal in hearsay. That's one thing I learned in my past service as county, territorial, and federal peace officer. Judges and lawyers don't care much for hearsay . . . unlike newspaper reporters." (Laughter from crowd, politicians; smiles from the journalists.) "Right now, that's all talk. When it becomes more than rumor, I will meet with the Ute Indian agent, and the deputies I have in that region, and talk to my superiors in Washington City. Then we will formulate a plan of action . . . after, gentlemen, I also confer with the governor. But . . . remember . . . the United States Army policed those recent land runs in Oklahoma. Most importantly, for the time being, the Ute reservation has not been opened up to settlement."

Republican: "A shipment of weapons bound for Fort Logan here was stolen off a train last week. Do you have an update?"

Answer: "My deputies and the Army are investigating. That is all I can say at this moment."

Rocky Mountain News: "What do you think of Pat Garrett?"

Answer: "I've never met the man."

Rocky Mountain News: "But you are aware of the similarities between you and Garrett. He was a sheriff in Lincoln County, New Mexico Territory. You were a county sheriff in Idaho Territory. In Eighteen Eighty-One, Pat Garrett shot an outlaw called the Kid, and some people say Garrett and the Kid had been on friendly terms. In Idaho Territory in Eighteen Seventy-Seven, you shot and killed Jeff Hancock at Rattlesnake Station, and you yourself later admitted that Hancock and you were saddle pals."

Answer: "I believe I already answered your question. I don't know Pat Garrett. Nor did I ever meet this Kid from New Mexico, whatever his name was."

Morning Herald: "But how does it feel to earn an appointment as a federal lawman by putting a bullet in the back of a pard . . . a pard who was unarmed?"

Answer: "I wouldn't know, since Jeff Hancock had a gun, and since in one of President Cleveland's speeches, our President said I had earned his trust from my years serving as a lawman across the frontier."

Morning Herald: "*Years* as a lawman? By my record, you were elected a county sheriff in Idaho, and briefly served as the U.S. marshal in Idaho Territory. What other qualifications as a lawman have you, sir?"

Answer: "Enough to satisfy our President and the Sen- . . ."

Rocky Mountain News: "Who says Hancock had a gun?"

Answer: "The grand jury in Idaho seventeen years ago. And me."

Evening Post: "But speaking about Jeff Hancock . . ."

Answer: "I'm not speaking about Jeff Hancock. I don't see any point in answering questions that were answered seventeen years ago. He's dead. I'm alive. If you're interested in Hancock, there are about two dozen half-dime and dime novels, one alleged factual story, that wasn't, which was serialized in the *Idaho Tri-Weekly Post*, or you can ride up to Boise and talk to those who were around in those days."

Morning Herald: "Including your wife?"

No answer.

Cattlemen's Clarion: "Marshal, a lot of my colleagues appear bent to reprint the same old tripe that has been dogging you for years. But the *Clarion* respects what you've done in your career for cattlemen and . . ."

Rocky Mountain News: "Speaking of tripe."

Cattlemen's Clarion: "And we respect your work in Idaho in the 'Seventies, and look forward to seeing . . ."

Republican: "Do you respect his getting fired as U.S. marshal six months after his appointment?"

Cattlemen's Clarion: "But the West is changing, Marshal. The frontier, many believe, is even closed. But there are other challenges. You are replacing U.S. Marshal Grant Hayes, who lost his job by bungling his way when these railroaders went on strike. What is the situation with the strike now?"

Answer: "Trains are running. Tempers have cooled. The courts will sort through the rest of it, but it's relatively peaceful. I don't know how long that will last. But my deputies and I will be ready for anything."

Republican: "With the silver market destroyed, do you think the current condition of our weak economy will make your job more difficult?"

Answer: "I'm not an economist." (He pulled his vest forward, showing the badge Judge Perelman had pinned to the lapel.) "And this job is tough enough."

The laughter from the crowd and even the newspapermen convinced Matt to end the festivities. The handsome woman with the schoolchildren stood on another makeshift bandstand, and Matt knew those kids were ready to scream again.

"Gentlemen," Matt said, "I am here, appointed by the President, confirmed by the Senate, as marshal for the federal district of Colorado. If the press . . . or the general public . . . have inquiries regarding that subject, I will be glad to answer such pertinent questions . . . at the federal courthouse Mondays through Saturdays, from eight in the morning until five in the afternoon."

The kids started up again.

Matthew Johnson,
United States marshal,
Strong as an ox,
And sly as a fox.
Matthew Johnson,
United States marshal,
He put Jeff Hancock
In that big pine box.

Luther Wilson had his arm around Matt's shoulder, urging him through reporters who wanted answers to more questions, and helping him into another hack.

"Damn," Wilson said, removing his cigar, and grinning. "You're not the thirty-a-month cowboy I figured you for. You're an educated man. The way you answered those questions. I bet you even read books."

Matt nodded. "I've read a few."

Wilson tossed the cigar out the window. "Only book I ever read was *Matthew Johnson, On the Trail of the Vigilantes; or, The Last Stand of Jeff Hancock*." The look on Matt's face made Wilson laugh. "I'm just joshing you, Matt."

The coach turned off the main avenue.

"I'll introduce you to Missus McBride," Wilson

said. "Then we'll visit the Social Club. It's an exclusive club, but you'll be welcomed with open arms. Best chefs in town, wine from France, and this keg of bourbon from Pennsylvania that slides down one's throat like honey."

"Luther," Matt whispered, "you speak the language of my tribe."

CHAPTER TWO

The sign on the wrought-iron fence read:

Lodgers Taken
Weekly or Monthly
Meals Included
Smoking on Porch
Or Back Yard Only
Sunday Brunch: 9:30-Noon
All Welcome

Matt liked the look of the house, one that seemed familiar to him, even though his previous trips to Denver had been brief, and as far as Matt knew, he had never set foot in this neighborhood. In fact, this part of rapidly growing Denver might not have even existed when Matt had last passed through. In twenty years, Denver's population had grown from under five thousand to more than one hundred thousand. Only San Francisco boasted more residents in the western United States.

"My understanding is that you are not partial to the weed," Luther Wilson said after paying the driver of the hack. "So Missus McBride's tyranny won't be an inconvenience." With a casual oath, Wilson tossed the cigarette onto the sidewalk and ground it out with the toe of his boot.

Matt nodded, though he had not heard a word Wilson said.

Wilson nodded at the sign. "My understanding is that she doesn't care much for tobacco-chewers or snuff-dippers, either."

Matt heard that. "I chewed tobacco once," he said. "No, twice. My first *and last* time."

Wilson didn't even smile at Matt's joke, so Matt kept admiring the boarding house. It was two stories, perhaps three—or maybe just a windowed attic—well, a man didn't see a home like that in Tucson, and certainly not in Idaho all those years ago. It reminded him, though, of Tennessee.

A fence surrounded the front yard, but the gate must have been removed—too much of an inconvenience for paying guests, Matt reasoned— and a cobblestone path led to the steps, with two statues—green, or bronze turned green—of lions at the top. The porch wrapped around from the front to the corner street side, with four columns, also green, except for the carved, curved tops of gold. The trim was also green, blending well with the red paint, and the towering red brick chimney that ran up the street corner side. One of the second-story windows was gabled, and light shone from all the windows, giving the house a warm, cozy feel.

The house had the appearance of newness. Not brand new, but no more than a few years old. Close to the business area of Denver for convenience, far enough from the railroads to muffle the noise. He could walk to the federal courthouse from here, providing he remembered the way—they had driven past the building on a quick tour of central Denver—as long as the streets weren't covered by a foot of snow. This altitude and this cold would be something else he would have to get used to after four years in Arizona Territory.

"Is this where you stay while in Denver?" Matt asked.

"Heavens, no." Wilson gestured to the northwest. "Henry Brown opened a wonderful hotel a couple of years ago on Broadway. Tallest building in town. But you, old friend, couldn't afford that on a government salary." He patted Matt's shoulder, letting him know he was kidding when Matt knew he wasn't. "Well," Wilson said, "let's make our introductions because . . ."—he turned and winked—"the Social Club is waiting, and that fine bourbon I promised you."

Walking beside Wilson, Matt noticed as he reached the steps that the statues were of dogs, not lions. That made him feel somewhat more comfortable.

As Wilson rang the buzzer at the door, Matt looked to the left. He smiled, trying to remember the last time he had seen a porch swing. Back in Tennessee, he had sat on a swing with Miss Tiffany Madrid—Matt in his new Confederate uniform, Tiffany in a hoop skirt and her red hair all curled—Mrs. Beatrice Madrid frowning while pretending to prune the flowers around the gazebo. She wouldn't have been able to spy on Tiffany and Matt at this house, however, for the shrubs and latticework gave a hint of privacy for anyone on the swing. The other side of the porch, with the rocking chairs and a settee, had a clear view of the street.

Heels on hardwood made a pleasing sound, and Matt turned back and waited. When the door opened widely, a petite woman smiled broadly and pushed open the screen door. "Marshal Johnson." She spoke softly, but the Southern accent came clear, as she held out her hand. "Welcome to my home. I am Jean McBride."

Her eyes were blue, lovely, her shoulder-length hair a curly blonde. He doubted if she stood much taller than five feet, but she smelled of lavender—and that accent, like the house, took him back home to Franklin. Accepting her hand, while sweeping off his hat, Matt bowed slightly, and said something he hoped sounded appropriate and sincere. After lowering her hand, Matt's new landlady nodded at Wilson. "Good evening, Mister Wilson."

"Ma'am." He bowed slightly and removed a cigar from his inside coat pocket. "I'll let Missus McBride show you around, Matt, while I test out one of these rocking chairs, or maybe that swing, and enjoy a fine Havana. Don't worry, Missus McBride, I will be careful with my ash."

"I know you will." She stepped aside, allowing Matt to enter, and closed the door behind him without giving another glance to the assemblyman.

He saw the stairs to his right, a long hallway bathed in light from wall sconces; the sliding door on his left remained open, revealing a modest but wonderfully decorated parlor, with an ornate fireplace. Matt didn't know what that tall hotel on Broadway had to offer, but the McBride home seemed certainly fine for an old Tennessee boy. Matt turned back to Jean McBride. Her dress was warm yellow calico with blue, red, and green patterns of flying birds, folded collar, two flounces on the bottom of the skirt. He couldn't see her shoes.

She gestured, and he stepped into the parlor, twisting the hat around in his hands.

"A deputy named Rawlings and two men arrived with your grips and trunks, which I had put into your room," she told him. He kept twisting his hat. "There's a rack in the corner if you'd care to hang it."

He stopped fidgeting, smiled, and found the hat rack.

"Mister Wilson said you would be dining with him this evening, so we did not save you any supper, but . . ."

She led the way across the handsome rug, past the piano, and opened another door, and he followed, stopping briefly at the piano before stepping into the dining room.

"Do you play?" she asked after she closed the door behind her.

"Ma'am?"

"The piano," she said.

"Oh. No, ma'am. Mama tried to get me to play, tried to teach me, tried to get a fellow in town to teach me." He sighed. "I should have listened to her."

"I should have listened to mine." She waved at the table.

Matt pursued this part of the conversation. "So you don't play?"

"No, I play. Fairly well. I should have listened to other things my mother tried to teach me."

Which ended this part of the conversation. Matt turned into one of those silent dog statues on the porch.

"Breakfast is served at six-thirty till eight-thirty Mondays through Saturdays, and from eight to nine-thirty on Sundays. Dinner is available on request, between noon and one-thirty, for an extra charge, but I need to know a day in advance. We are open to the general public for Sunday brunch, and sometimes we fill up quickly. Supper is six-thirty every evening."

"That sounds fine, ma'am."

"If you are late for any meal and there are no seats, you must wait till one is vacated."

He thought about saying something like: *My job as federal lawman might cause me to miss quite a few meals, ma'am, but I shall do my best to give you as much advance notice as possible so as not to trouble* . . . He merely said: "Yes, ma'am."

"I imagine Mister Wilson told you about my intolerance for smoking tobacco . . . pipe, cigar, cigarettes . . . or at least you saw the sign."

"Both, ma'am."

"I wish you wouldn't *ma'am* to me, Marshal. You make me feel old."

"Habit," he said with a smile.

"You're not in Tennessee anymore, Marshal."

He cocked his head. "I didn't know it came out." He liked her smile.

"It comes out. Maybe not as thick as mine, but it's still there, sir. Some things we can never escape."

"Yes, ma- . . ." He stopped himself. "If it's all the same to you, ma- . . ." This time he laughed, and she echoed that. After inhaling deeply and exhaling, he told her: "If you wouldn't call me *sir*. When I hear sir, I want to look around for my pa or someone famous."

"My understanding is that you are a man of renown."

He felt that tension. "Well. Not really, ma- . . ."

30

"The name is Jean, Marshal." She held out her hand again. "Why don't we try it that way, Marshal?"

"Could you make it Matt?"

"Matt."

"Jean."

They shook again. "Franklin, Tennessee," he told her.

She curtseyed. "Why we are practically neighbors, Matt. Gallatin."

"Well, it was a long time ago," he said. "Haven't been back in years."

"My story is the same."

She led him back to the parlor. "The parlor is open for all guests . . . I have two schoolteachers, a clerk, and a worker at the Denver Telephone Dispatch Company, and an apothecary letting rooms. You will meet them at breakfast. The remaining room is available for nightly guests . . . occupancy varies depending on the season . . . and the other room is mine." She moved back through the sliding door and into the hallway.

"There is also a library here, likewise available to all my guests." She pointed up the stairs. "My teachers and the apothecary reside upstairs. That's also where the nightly room is. There is also an upstairs facility."

She led him down the hall, pointing at the wall. "We've been in this home for almost three years now. I detested that device, but it comes in handy

31

when you are forced to rent out rooms." He studied the telephone.

"Should you have any questions about how to operate that thing, I will refer you to Mister Childs. That's his room. He works for the Denver Telephone Dispatch Company."

Matt nodded.

"I can answer the device and I have made a few calls, but I am no expert at technology." The tour continued. "Down the hallway before you reach the kitchen is the other facility, and in the back yard, northeast corner, you will find an old-fashioned privy. The kitchen is off limits, but I generally have coffee and tea available during daylight in the library and parlor. This is your room." She pushed open the door, and stepped back.

Smiling, he stepped inside. A lamp on the bedside table had been lighted. His trunk and grips were stacked at the foot of the bed. He saw a wash basin, a pitcher, four glasses, two dressers, armoire, rocking chair, mirror, desk, and high-backed chair. Yet he figured he still had enough room to move around in. He wondered if all rooms were so spacious. It was actually more than he figured he would ever need.

"Our streetlights might be electrical these days, but this house is not. The lamps are all gas. Turn them down. Don't blow them out. We wouldn't want you to asphyxiate."

"No, ma'am."

She frowned.

"I'll break the habit somehow, Jean," he said.

For that, he earned the fleetest of smiles. "That's another reason I don't allow smoking inside the house," she said. "Four blocks over, two years ago, a tenant blew out the lamp, retired for a while, awoke, lighted up his pipe, and blew himself and Mister Lawrence Moore's brick home to pieces."

"I don't smoke," he said. He pulled out his pants pockets. "I don't even carry matches."

"Then I think we shall get along, Marshal."

Now he frowned.

"Matt," she corrected.

Damn, he thought, *you son-of-a-bitch, you are flirting with her, and without one ounce of shame. And that's a wedding band on her finger. And don't forget, Marshal, about that wife of yours in Boise and the two kids.*

"I trust the arrangement is satisfactory."

That made him straighten. He didn't even know he had a room in a boarding house until Luther Wilson told him, had figured he would stay in a hotel near the courthouse until he found a place to hang his hat.

"Well . . . if you . . . could refresh my memory regarding the terms?"

She told him.

He must have blanched.

33

Fulton Co. Public Library
320 W. 7th Street
Rochester. IN 46975

"Is there a problem?" she asked.

His head shook quickly. "No. No, not at all." He found a way to smile. "I just have to remind myself that I'm not in Denver anymore."

"But you are in Denver."

He laughed. "I meant Tucson. Or Franklin, Tennessee."

"Well, I must set batter for the morrow's breakfast, so you will find a key to your room on the nightstand, beside the Bible. I wash the sheets and towels twice weekly. You are responsible for your own laundry, though I can recommend several businesses. If you have any requests, within reason, I am willing to listen, and I believe that your guide, Mister Wilson, is waiting for you outside. So if you will excuse me . . ." She offered her hand.

He liked the way her hand felt in his, and as her heels spanked the hardwood floor, he closed the door, reached inside his coat, and found the flask. Quickly he twisted off the lid and drank.

He found no comfort, for the flask was practically empty. Hell, he realized, no wonder he had been so out of sorts when he arrived in Denver. Two swallows on the train ride? By thunder, he had almost emptied the entire flask. But the remaining swallow warmed him, steadied him, so he dropped the flask inside a drawer, found the key, and stepped into the hallway. After locking the door to his room, he walked past the telephone, and slipped inside the parlor, fetched his hat. A moment later, he stepped into the chill of the evening and found Wilson finishing his cigar.

"Nice lady," Matt said, as he tightened his coat around his waist.

"I suppose." Wilson dropped the cigar in a spittoon.

"What's her husband do?"

"Drummer," Wilson said. "Used to be a silver man. He's rarely here. Has a fondness for the bottle, and I think that's why she takes in boarders. Though if she'd open it up to another line of work, she might do better. Hell, for a sassy old bitch, she ain't bad-looking."

Matt straightened. He might be a lot of things, but some of that upbringing in a hard-shell Baptist family from Tennessee had failed to lessen its grip. He realized his hands had formed into fists.

As he moved down the porch, Wilson laughed. "Matt, at the Social Club, pard, you'll find much younger, much lovelier, and much more willing lasses. And tonight, Marshal, everything is on Luther J. Wilson. I am at your service."

The hack was waiting.

Reluctantly, Matt followed Wilson down the steps, down the pathway, and into the cab.

CHAPTER THREE

"Marshal Johnson?"

The voice came from somewhere down a long tunnel.

"Marshal Johnson?"

He rocked on that damned train as it climbed through Raton Pass. No, he realized dully, someone was softly nudging his left shoulder. He remembered the station at Colorado Springs, Denver, the boarding house. His stomach also rocked, and as his lips peeled apart, he tasted the remnants of bourbon on his tongue. The voice came again, louder, and suddenly he felt chilled. He wanted to brush the hand off his shoulder, but the eyes opened to a silhouette that at least blocked the blinding orange ball of fire off in the distance.

Christ, he was freezing.

The porch swing rocked as he jerked erect, the ghost with the soft voice lurched backward, and now the flames of hell leaped at him. He turned away, squeezing his eyelids shut and, for a second, thought he might puke up the *consommé vermicelli*, fried scallops in tartar sauce, oyster plant, squash, cold cornstarch pudding with currant jelly, brie and crackers, and how many damned gallons of Kentucky bourbon?

36

"Marshal Johnson."

Turning his head gently to reduce the pounding against his skull, he wet his lips and saw her, the tiny blonde woman with the mesmerizing blue eyes, wrapped in a thick robe. She stepped away, and the porch swing bucked like a rank mustang. Planting his boots on the flooring, he kept his seat, lowered his head, and when the eyes reopened, he saw Jean McBride's slippers.

"You'll catch your death out here," she said in a tone neither condescending nor angry. Just stating the facts.

Matt tried to think. The hack had stopped after that drinking bout at the Social Club with Wilson and others of the Colorado elite. He had made his way to the steps, up the steps, to the door, and . . . ?

His head rose, and he tried to smile. "Ma'am . . ." He got that much out before her eyes turned colder. Matt looked around, seeing only the glow from the gas lamps on the porches and a few streetlights in the distance. It remained pitch black. He had left the Social Club at . . . a quarter past two.

"Jean, I mean," he said, somehow remembering their agreement from . . . *hell, just a few hours earlier.*

"Ma'am is fine, Marshal."

Well, at least that was settled. *You can't get through one night before turning your landlady against you.*

"Lost my key," he explained.

She held it in her hands. "You dropped it on the porch by the door." That damned toneless statement again. He would feel a lot better if she'd just rip his head off. That would have been a blessing. "The front door remains unlocked. This is a peaceful neighborhood. The Denver police patrol it routinely, so there is no crime to speak of. But I encourage guests to keep their rooms locked when not occupied. I cannot guarantee the honesty of the guests who come to dine here on Sundays." Her eyes hardened. "Or even pay for room and meals."

After taking the key, he found enough strength to push himself out of the porch swing, which slipped back about a foot or so before coming back to bump against his thighs. At least that didn't knock him to his knees. "Would you happen to know what time it is . . . ma'am?"

"A little after five," she said, and showed him the newspapers. "I just came outside for these before getting started on breakfast." She turned toward the door. "Will you be joining us this morning?"

He managed to move one foot forward, keeping his eyes on the door. As long as the damned thing did not move, he might be able to make it. "I don't reckon so," he said, realizing he had not answered her. "I have a lot of work awaiting me, you understand. First day on the job and all."

"Oh," he heard her say, and this time she did not disguise her disgust. "I understand all too well."

He pulled the screen door open, tried the handle, felt the door open easily. *Stupid son-of-a-bitch. That's all you had to do three hours ago.* He started inside, remembered his manners, and stepped back, holding the door open for his landlady.

Inside, after closing the front door, he watched Jean McBride move down the hallway before disappearing inside the kitchen. She did not look back. Now all Matt had to do was find his room. Yes, he remembered which one was his. The one tucked in slightly underneath the slant of the staircase. Next to the telephone. Now, all he had to do was get this little key into the lock on his door, find his way to the bed in the dark, and try to sleep off another wasted night.

The chimes would not stop. Once the low *dongs* stopped, high-pitched *dings* started. Once. Twice. Finally, silence, but that's what caused Matt to open his eyes. He sat up, threw his legs over the side of the bed, and staggered to the dresser where he grabbed the Waltham repeater and used his thumb to press open the hunter case. Ten-thirty.

Swearing, he quickly poured water into the basin and washed his face. He had slept in his clothes, not even bothering to pull back the blankets or sheets. His hat lay on the floor. Maybe he could at least change his shirt. Somehow he had managed to take off his tie, but not his boots. Letting the suspenders fall over his shoulders and dangle against his legs, he bent forward—which might have been a mistake, though he somehow managed to keep everything in his stomach—and jerked the shirt off, tossed it aside.

That was a mistake. Because he had not unpacked anything. But there on the top of the trunk rested his saddle, with the bedroll still strapped behind the cantle. He loosened it, threw it on the bed, and unrolled the old sugan, reminding him of those old days—before he even thought about pinning metal on his vest. The shirt he had wrapped up wasn't fancy, just a collarless number of colorful calico, but it looked relatively clean. That went over his head, he tucked it in his pants, brought the suspenders back up, and found his coat. Somehow, he kicked the hat and it landed on the bed. Matt had to stifle a laugh. He couldn't do that again in a hundred tries, but he picked up the hat, pulled it over his head, and gathered the watch and his pocket knife off the counter.

He stepped to the door, remembered his key, fetched it, and opened the door. That's when his stomach and head started bothering him again. He peered out, saw no one, heard nobody, and moved onto the wooden floor. Softly he closed the door, locked it, and made his way to the rug, which muffled the sound of his boots. When he reached the parlor, the smell of coffee overpowered him, so he stepped inside, filled a cup, and drank greedily. After refilling his cup, he took it with him to the door, opened it, returned to the porch where he had slept for a couple of hours in the freezing predawn Colorado morn. He closed the door, glanced at the rocking chairs and the swing, all empty, heard the bustle of Denver beyond this neighborhood, and sipped more coffee.

Cup in hand, he moved down the steps, across the path, to the sidewalk, and made a beeline for the federal district. Four blocks away, he hailed a hack. By 10:58 he had found the courthouse.

Boise had been a bustling city when Matt served that brief stint as U.S. marshal after killing Jeff Hancock, but the courthouse had been nothing like the one in Denver—towering more than three-stories high of stone and marble, Denver's took up half a city block. Despite the frost, Matt found a handkerchief to wipe his sweaty forehead, and waited for his breathing to steady. As the Waltham repeater began to chime, Matt made his way inside. For a federal office in the federal courthouse in the state capital of one of the largest cities in the Western states and territories on a business day, Matt expected to see a stampede of activity. He was not disappointed. Weaving through rushing men and women, Matt eventually found the stairs, and hurried up to the second floor. His boots echoed as he walked down the hallway, past people hurrying to meetings while he looked at doors on both sides of the hall before finally seeing **U.S. Marshal's Office** in large black letters.

He stepped inside, closed the door, and saw two men. The one sitting behind a desk the size of a schooner he did not know, but the man standing by the window, peering outside, his grip by his boots—that one he remembered.

"Good morning, Levi," Matt said, closing the door behind him, and making a quick study of his new office. Enormous, it still made him claustrophobic, for he had never much cared for being cooped up inside. Several chairs and tables filled the waiting area, with doors to other offices on the west and south walls. He realized he still carried the coffee cup, now empty, taken from Jean McBride's boarding house.

Now she thinks I'm a thief and a drunk.

The bald man in a plaid suit rose from behind his desk, and marched quickly to Matt. "Marshal, I am your secretary. Carter Bowen the Third. It's a pleasure." The voice came out like a train whistle, which did not help Matt's hangover. The little gent extended his hand. "And, Marshal, an honor." Matt wouldn't have been surprised if the bald man broke out singing "Matthew Johnson, U-ni-ted States Ma-arr-shal."

"The pleasure's mine, Mister Bowen."

He handed Jean's cup to Bowen, who stared at it in complete confusion, as Matt made his way to the long-haired deputy.

"Thanks for meeting me this morning." He looked at the wall clock. "I guess I'm a few minutes late."

"It's Liberty," the deputy said. "Liberty Rawlings."

Matt shook his hand, offered the young man his best sheepish grin. "I'm going to get that right at some point."

"And the meeting was supposed to be at nine."

Jean McBride's coffee began roiling in Matt's stomach, as he looked again at the clock. "Nine? I thought it was eleven."

The scowl on Rawlings's face made Matt realize how wrong he was, but he looked across the office, the doors, the window, the cabinets, bookcases and even a telephone. "Which one's my office, Mister Bowen?"

Still holding Jean McBride's cup, the secretary grinned, and walked to the big door, pulled it open, and waved his hand.

Matt glanced back at Rawlings. "Do you have a few minutes, Liberty?" he said, relieved that he had gotten the name right. "I know you have a train to catch."

He let the deputy enter the office first. He started to follow, but turned back and asked Bowen: "Is there any chance we can get some coffee here for Deputy Rawlings and myself?"

"Yes, sir," the little man said. "There's a café across the street. Judge Perelman gets coffee there all the time. As long as we bring the cups back, they seem to like the business."

"Good." Matt turned to find Liberty Rawlings with his hat in his hand, waiting patiently. "Sugar? Milk?"

"Black," Rawlings said.

"Two blacks," Matt told his secretary. "And whatever you want." He handed the man a Morgan dollar. "Use that cup I brought with me. But don't break it or there'll be hell to pay."

Matt left the door open as Mr. Bowen went about his duties. He looked around, found the hat rack, set his on the closest hook, and stared at the desk, then stuck his head back through the open doorway and looked left, then right. Turning back to the deputy, he asked: "Did you tell any deputies about our meeting?"

"No, sir." The man stood with his hat in his hand, twisting it around by the brim. "Reckon I guessed you would have after taking the oath."

"No." Matt sighed and moved to the big desk. "I had to get settled in." Someone had put penny peppermints in his ashtray, so he picked one up and popped it in his mouth. He hadn't cleaned his teeth this morning, and that candy might remove the smell and aftertaste of bourbon, not to mention that *consommé vermicelli* which had not quite come to terms with his bowels.

"How was your first evening in Denver?" Rawlings asked.

"I survived." Matt motioned at one of two chairs in front of his desk. "Quite a get-together at the Social Club." He rubbed his temples. "Luther Wilson, some bankers, land speculators." The deputy sat, but Matt couldn't see himself sitting behind that desk—it was bigger than that Cumberland River sternwheeler Mr. Carter Bowen III had in the anteroom. So Matt settled into the other low-backed chair in front of the desk, cracked the remnants of the peppermint, and swallowed while crossing his legs. He kept talking about the celebratory gathering in honor of Colorado's newest marshal. "Railroad men. Entrepreneurs." His head shook. "Not exactly my kind of crowd." He uncrossed his legs. "I still think of myself as a thirty-a-month cowhand."

Liberty Rawlings just stared.

"How long have you been a federal deputy?" Matt asked.

"Three years and a few months," Rawlings answered.

"Before that?"

"Deputy sheriff in La Plata County."

Matt looked at the big map on the wall.

"The red one, more pink than red actually," Rawlings explained. "Bottom. If you flipped the top of Minnesota over, that's what it looks like."

"You a student of maps, Liberty?" Shaking his head, Matt laughed. "I wouldn't know what Minnesota looks like straight-up, sideways, or tilted."

"County seat's Durango," Rawlings said. The tone remained dull, impersonal, and probably seething mad.

"Right. You mentioned that yesterday. Narrow gauge railroad connects the mines, if I remember right."

"Yes, sir. D and RG."

"Which has been giving our government a fit lately."

The young man shrugged.

"Actually, the Denver and Rio Grande hasn't been that bad, and I supposed that railway union is to blame. . . ." He stopped, realizing he had been just repeating what most of the black suits had been saying to him last night.

"Did you like working under Grant Hayes?" Matt asked.

Another shrug. "He was all right, I guess. Better than the last sheriff I had in Durango. But to be honest, I rarely had much to do with Marshal Hayes."

Matt grunted. He tried to figure out why he had even wanted to meet with Rawlings, or his other

46

deputies. A glance at the open doorway revealed nothing, no coffee, no Mr. Bowen, and no other deputy marshals.

"Do you know Caleb Dawson?" Matt asked, turning around.

"He's chief deputy."

"Do you know him?"

"Not really."

"Little contact with Denver?"

"Since the silver market crashed, Durango and La Plata County don't get a whole lot of attention," Rawlings said.

"But there's that railroad strike."

Rawlings nodded. "But most of that action was in Trinidad."

Matt looked at the map again, saying: "That's the green one, right? Central? On the New Mexico border?" When he turned around, he felt slightly better to detect a slight smile.

"Sort of," the deputy said, "Connecticut without the rudder but a camel's hump."

Now Matt grinned. "I'll have to take your word."

Which was when Carter Bowen III entered the office carrying that dainty china piece that belonged to Jean McBride and a larger tin cup.

"Did you not get something for yourself?" Matt asked, as he took the china cup before the nervous secretary broke it.

"No, sir." Mr. Bowen handed Rawlings the

tin cup of coffee, and began reaching into his pockets. "Let me get you your change, Marshal."

Matt said: "Keep it for the peppermint candy fund." He sipped the coffee, disappointed that it was not as good as that served at his boarding house. "Have you seen Chief Deputy Dawson?"

"No, sir." The clerk straightened.

"Is he in the city?"

"I . . . I think . . . I think so, Marshal, but I'd need to check. . . ."

"Then check. And let him know that I'd like to talk to him when he has a minute. And any other deputies who might be in Denver at this time."

"Yes, sir."

"Mister Bowen."

The man stopped, turned, looked back.

"Close the door behind you, please."

They drank for a minute in silence, before Matt set the cup on the edge of his desk, and whispered: "You'd think a city of this size could serve better coffee."

"I cook pretty good coffee myself." Rawlings slid his cup on the desk, too.

Matt nodded. "I wrap the grounds in a bandanna."

"Put an eggshell in mine," Rawlings said.

"Mama did it that way. Eggshell, I mean." He leaned back, liking the young man. "How many federal deputies in Durango?"

"Just two now, though there's a deputy sheriff

who sometimes swears in for a temporary assignment."

"Who's your pard?"

"Strongo Stroheim."

"Strongo?"

"Stefan. He's foreign . . . at least his ma and pa were. Swede. Austrian. German. Something like that. Everybody calls him Strongo. If you meet him, you'll know why."

"You're not from around here either, are you?"

"Born in Louisville, Kentucky."

"Tennessee," Matt said. "Franklin."

"I know." Rawlings sipped, and Matt waited. "It's from the song, Marshal."

Oh, yeah, of course, that damned old song.

Matthew Johnson
Was wounded in Franklin

Both men picked up their cups and sipped.

"Yeah," Matt said. "I was born in Franklin. By the time John Bell Hood led those Johnny Rebs to their deaths, I was getting out of a Yankee prison camp. Took the oath to the boys in blue, got out of that deathtrap. Got sent up to Minnesota." He laughed. "But I still couldn't tell you what that damned state looked like."

The smile on Rawlings's face was fraudulent. Matt could tell that by the man's cold eyes.

Again, both men returned the cups to the

49

desk's edge. After clearing his throat, Matt said: "Yesterday, you said there were bigger troubles than the railroad strike in your jurisdiction."

"Did I?"

Matt nodded, and waited.

The deputy rose, found his hat on a bench, and said: "Marshal Johnson, I have a train to catch, I'm sorry to say." Though he wasn't a damned bit sorry. And not about to extend his hand.

"Like that line about me getting shot at Franklin," Matt said, "everything you've heard about me might not be true. And I'd like to know what's going on in my jurisdiction."

The silence settled as both men reached again for their coffee cups, sipping, though not enjoying the lukewarm, weak brew.

"Oh, I'm sure Luther Wilson gave you an earful last night."

He wondered how the conversation had turned cold.

"It would be nice if we could trust one another, Liberty." There. At least Matt had gotten the kid's name right. Again.

"It would be."

"I got the feeling you wanted to talk to me."

"Did you?"

Conceding defeat, Matt nodded at the door, but when Rawlings grabbed the knob, he tried one more trick.

"I didn't murder Jeff Hancock for a bunch of

cattle barons. That's not in the song, of course, but it's what most people say."

Rawlings turned. "I wasn't there."

"You weren't at the Social Club last night, either."

"Wasn't invited. But that's not my crowd, either, Marshal. You see, I still think of myself as a thirty-a-month cowhand, too. But I never shot a pard in the back."

"Don't believe everything you hear."

"I don't. That makes me a pretty good peace officer, I think. But I hear things, and some of those things I tend to believe."

"Such as?"

He opened the door. "That you took this job because you needed money."

"Everybody needs money."

"Yes, sir. But I also heard that you're a drunk."

"I'll take a drink, but no more than two," he lied.

"Yes, sir. I reckon your coat doesn't have the same limit as you. Because your coat reeks of whiskey."

CHAPTER FOUR

The rest of his day lacked stress. He met lawyers from the U.S. solicitor's office, two deputy marshals, and toured the federal courthouse. The best part of the day came when he walked through the jail cells, and found a powerfully built black man in a jailer's uniform smiling like a boy on his birthday.

" 'Afternoon, Marshal Johnson," the jailer said.

Matt stuck out his hand. "You know me?"

The jailer's grip cut off the circulation to Matt's fingers. When the handshake ended, Matt felt the way he had back when that broom-tail mustang had pitched him over its head, and planted a forefoot that shoved Matt's right hand a half foot deep into the mud.

"Never met till this day," the big man said, "but my boys . . . all five of them . . . will be grinning ear to ear when I tell them I shook Marshal Matthew Johnson's hand this afternoon."

Matt couldn't think of anything else to say, but the jailer said: "They been singing that song about you since the littlest one was in diapers, Marshal. When I got this here job, they started singing it. Drove my wife plumb crazy. It's an honor, sir, to meet you at last."

Matt shook his head. "I . . . well . . ."

"My name's Fletcher, Marshal," the jailer said. "I'm . . ."

"You're Matthew Johnson, Marshal." The big man grinned. "Strong as an ox. Sly as a fox."

"Well. Keep up the good work, Fletcher. Don't . . . well . . . if you need anything, come up to see me."

Walking back to the boarding house, he imagined what all his saddle pards, even Jeff Hancock, would have said about him. Being afoot. Years back—another lifetime ago—he would have swung into the saddle, and ridden his horse across the street, or down the street to another hitching rail, another saloon, rather than walk. No cowboy alive, not Jeff Hancock, not Matthew Johnson, not Rex Chesser or Kim Buchman or Bounce McMahon would have walked anywhere when they could ride. But that had been a different Matthew Johnson. This afternoon, he felt proud of himself, though, for he had lost count of all the gentlemen's clubs, saloons, dram shops, and buckets of blood he had passed without stepping inside a single one, not even for a pint of stout.

It had been a long day, not good, though not exactly bad. Most meetings went better than that one with Liberty Rawlings. Near the courthouse, he had found a laundry, which had gotten the odor of spilled bourbon out of his coat. He had been introduced to other lawmakers and lawmen, attorneys, and federal clerks. And he had signed his name on so many documents that his wrist and fingers hurt. Purposefully, he had not read a single newspaper.

Old Malcolm Adney, who had scouted for Matt back in Idaho, would have been proud, too. Matt made it back to Mrs. McBride's big house without having to ask for directions once. But seeing smoke rising above the hedgerow from the porch's corner gave him pause. A rocker creaked; a boot scraped on the floor. Boarder? Reporter? He sighed, remembering something Malcolm Adney told him more than once: *Never let 'em see your back.* Flee, find some hiding place in a Denver alley, or try to climb the fence and come into the McBride mansion through a back door, and he imagined the headlines in tomorrow's papers:

COWARDLY U.S. MARSHAL
HIGHTAILS IT FROM DENVER
REPORTER SEEKING INTERVIEW

"Hell," he whispered, and followed the path to the steps, thinking that maybe he should have stepped inside one of those saloons.

Besides, he told himself, a newspaperman wouldn't sit in that rocking chair. He'd sit on the other side of the porch, where a fellow on the street couldn't see him because of the Victorian trim and the taller bushes.

"Good afternoon, Matt." Luther Wilson flicked ash onto Mrs. McBride's floor instead of into the ashtray or receptacle near one of her flower pots. "Figured I would stop by and see how your first day in the office went."

Breathing a little easier now, smiling, Matt climbed the rest of the steps.

"Cigar?" Wilson had already pulled one from his vest pocket.

"No, thanks." They shook hands, after which Wilson motioned at the neighboring chair.

Matt checked his watch, slid it back inside the pocket, and settled into the chair as Wilson sat down.

"Get anything done today, Matt?"

"Just tried to figure my way around the courthouse . . . even my own office. Big place. Little more to it than what I had back in Idaho."

"Idaho was a long time ago." Wilson again flicked ash.

"You don't have to tell me."

Wilson chuckled. "Well, Matt, I'm older than you are. By quite a few years." Wilson set his cigar in the ashtray. "Did you have a chance to chat with Judge Perelman?"

"Just a few words. He had to get back to his office for pre-trial meetings with some attorneys."

"And Carter Bowen?"

"He's efficient." Matt smiled. "Told me he saves everything."

"Big admirer of yours." Wilson grinned. "Good man to have around. Knows the city, the courts, and he's got a memory like an elephant."

They rocked, but Matt stopped. He had mastered several horses in his day, but he could never get used to porch swings or rocking chairs. They weren't quite as bad as railroads, which made him nervous, and especially not the stagecoaches that left him seasick.

"There's some other folks I'd like to introduce you to, Matt," Wilson said. "How about having supper with me at the Social Club?" He winked. "Maybe a snort of a hundred and twenty-five proof?"

Matt wanted to say hell yeah. He wanted to stand up out of this god-awful chair, and he came close to doing both at the same time. Wilson would have laughed, made some joke about how fast the legendary lawman could move after all those years, that the lyrics to the song failed to capture the speed of Matthew Johnson, United States Marshal.

Instead, he gestured toward the front door. "I'll have to pass," he said. "Told my landlady I'd take supper here." He grinned. "Might as well. As much as I'm paying her."

"Her husband fancied himself as a silver baron."

Wilson picked up the cigar. "Think I told you something like that last night."

Matt couldn't remember much of anything from last night. He said: "Well, good for Mister McBride."

Wilson pulled hard, tilted his head back, tried but failed to make a smoke ring. "Up until last year, maybe. Lost his ass. Probably would have lost this house, if not for her." Pointing his cigar at the door, Wilson suddenly grinned. "It'll be interesting to see how long they can pay the mortgage on this monstrosity. But it's a fine home. Wouldn't mind having it myself . . . if I could get a good price on it. Which I might, economy being what it is these days."

The taste of gall settled over Matt's tongue. He tried to swallow it down, but it stuck with him, like that damned song always stuck with him, like Jeff Hancock's ghost.

"Maybe you could take supper here with me," he suggested, regretting that immediately. He hadn't touched a drop of spirits all day, yet he had just made the most asinine invitation.

Matt couldn't blame Wilson for laughing. The well-dressed man, now looking bemused, shook his head and again flicked ash onto the porch floor. "I'll have to pass on that courteous suggestion." The cigar again gestured at the front door. "You see, Matt, I am not allowed inside Jean McBride's house." He chewed on the cigar again, and reached inside his coat pocket. "You have enemies. I have enemies. That's always the case for successful men. The good thing for you is that your biggest enemy is dead."

My biggest enemy, Matt thought, *had been my best friend.*

So when he turned back to see the silver-plated flask in Wilson's right hand, Matt did what came naturally. He took it, unscrewed the cap, and drank. Just a swallow, although he felt like chugging all that glorious whiskey down.

"I know you'll probably have to pay a lot of attention to the railroad strike and everything . . . damn those anarchists, Matt." Wilson accepted the flask from Matt, but did not drink, just tightened the cap. "But, as your friend, I ought to warn you that the Utes are on the prod down south. The last thing you need, I need, or the state needs is an outbreak. Our nation, I dare say, will not stand for another Wounded Knee. If you know what I'm saying."

Matt didn't know what Wilson was saying, and it couldn't be from just one swallow of bourbon, but the businessman didn't seem to want Matt to say anything. He merely let the flask disappear inside his pocket. Wilson withdrew a handful of envelopes.

"But enough about politics." Wilson smiled broadly. "These are letters of introduction to some gentlemen in Denver, and you'll do well to make acquaintances of them. I wanted to give these to you before I take the train back to Durango. Duty calls, you understand."

Matt took the envelopes, glanced at the name on the top one, recognizing neither name nor address, but certainly understanding the power of the railroad and the title of vice president. Slowly, he put the letters inside his coat pocket.

"I'll look at these in my room," he said.

"Wise. Good bedtime reading." Wilson snuffed out his cigar, but at least he had the decency to do that in the ashtray. "Don't know when I'll get back this way, Matt," he said, after pushing himself out of the rocking chair. He extended his hand. Matt rose and shook. "But if you should need anything, feel free to send me a telegram. Or, hell, come down to visit. The Strater Hotel's excellent. Rivals the Brown Palace here. And with the silver crash, prices keep dropping for rooms, meals, horses, land. If Colorado doesn't watch out, the whole state might declare bankruptcy. Lucky for you, your pay comes from the federal government."

Wilson adjusted coat and hat, smiled, and slapped Matt's shoulder before he moved down the steps and pathway, and turned the corner to head downtown. Matt then looked at the porch floor. He used his boot to slide most of the ashes through a crack, and emptied the ashtray into the receptacle.

● ● ●

Laughter came from the dining room. He smelled roast beef and the strong aromas of coffee and tea. Matt fished out the key to his room, and stepped inside. He removed his hat, washed his face, and stared at his reflection in the mirror.

You've been in stampedes. Had your ribs busted in horse wrecks. You've stared down gun barrels. Been caught in a blizzard. Survived Point Lookout and the Payette River War. Spilt more whiskey than most men have ever seen.

He wiped his face with the towel and whispered to himself: "You can survive supper, too."

The letters came out of his pocket, and he tossed them onto the dresser, looked at his watch, found his backbone, and stepped out of the room. Conversation and mouth-watering smells led him to the door, and he stepped over the threshold as all talk ceased.

"I am sorry for being late," he said.

The schoolteachers were easy to recognize. Young, trim, unmarried, proper, both brunettes. He guessed the burly, bald dude with the handle-bar mustache to be the man from the Denver Telephone Dispatch Company. The clerk and the druggist, he decided, were interchangeable.

Jean McBride rose, wiping her lips with a checkered napkin, and said: "This is our newest resident, Matthew Johnson, duly appointed federal marshal for the state of Colorado." She introduced those surrounding the table, but Matt knew he wouldn't remember one name.

"*The* Matthew Johnson?" either the apothecary or the clerk said.

"It's a common name," he said. "I'm just one of them." Which caused a thought to cross his mind: *Was Liberty Rawlings really that deputy's name, or did he take it the way Bounce McMahon had renamed, reinvented himself?*

"You are not late at all, Marshal," Jean said, and pulled out the chair next to hers. "As I've told all my guests, I am not your mother. You may join us for meals whenever convenient. We always start supper at six-thirty, but the food remains available until eight."

"Pleasure to meet y'all." Matt moved to the chair.

The telephone worker began singing softly: "Matthew Johnson, United States Marshal." The two other men chuckled. The two schoolteachers looked horrified. Jean McBride silenced the telephone man with a cold stare.

Matt found the beans and cornbread.

"Did . . . ?" The bespectacled schoolteacher wet her lips, found the courage, and made herself finish: "Did you really kill James Hancock?"

"His name was Jeff," the telephone worker corrected. "Shot down in the back in the prime of life for five thousand dollars. And a U.S. marshal's badge."

Matt let Jean McBride fill his glass with tea, and the man next to him—the one who hadn't said anything—passed the roast beef.

"Yes, ma'am." Matt offered the platter to Jean McBride, who passed it to the schoolmarm who didn't wear eyeglasses. He shook his head when offered the potatoes, but helped himself to a biscuit. "I shot Jeff." He smiled at the woman before turning to the Denver Telephone Dispatch Company employee. "Two hundred and fifty dollars, though. Idaho was a poor territory then, and Jeff wasn't Jesse James."

The older gentleman cleared his throat, but his voice remained squeaky and nervous when he asked: "Did you see the newspapers today, Marshal?"

"Not today." He turned to Jean McBride. "This cornbread is exceptional, ma'am. Reminds me of home."

Her face brightened, and she looked away from him, her attention on her other paying customers. "The marshal and I both hail, originally, from Tennessee."

"I'm from Kentucky," one of the men said.

"Indiana," said the inquisitive schoolteacher. Kansas, Ohio, and "right here in Denver" were also mentioned, the latter coming from the telephone man.

Matt washed down a piece of roast beef with tea while the big man pushed back his chair, wiped his thick mustache with the napkin, and shook his head.

"Shot a man in the back," he said, staring at Matt. "And now they make him the highest paid lawman in Colorado."

"Mister Childs," Jean McBride said sternly. "There are rules at my supper table, sir. Polite conversation is allowed, but let us not ruin our appetites with political discourse."

Childs, Matt decided. He could remember that name.

"My appetite, alas," said the teacher who wore glasses, "is already spoiled. If you'll excuse me . . ." She rose, nodded at those still seated, and bowed at her hostess. "The meal was exceptional, Jean. As always."

"I hope you feel better at breakfast, Alma," Jean McBride said.

"As do I." Her eyes locked briefly on Matt, who kept his head down as though inspecting the beans, but he saw her plain enough. He had seen that look many times before. She walked out and down the hall. The dining room remained so silent, Matt could have counted the steps she made, even those up the stairs, where a door opened. Closed. Locked.

The Kentuckian said: "From what I've heard and read, you did the country a favor by shooting that Hancock. He was stealing cattle from ranchers, killing innocent . . ." Catching Jean

McBride's eyes, the man fell silent, glanced up and down the table to find the cornbread, and muttered a soft apology to the landlady.

Matt tried the roast beef again.

"I just remembered I'm to meet a friend at McGillicuddy's," Childs said. His chair scraped the floor.

"No dessert, Mister Childs?" Jean McBride asked.

"Dessert'll be a porter, ma'am." He made a scene of balling up his napkin and throwing it on the plate. "I don't think apple pie will get the taste out of my mouth like one of Ainmire's brews."

Matt picked at his plate, while the druggist, the clerk, and the other schoolmarm made their excuses and left the dining room. He chewed, and did not look to his right until Jean McBride said: "I hope you are hungry, Marshal Johnson."

He wiped his mouth, turned, and saw her.

"The pie is peach," she said. "And we have all of it to ourselves."

"I don't know if I can eat half a pie, ma'am," he said. "But I'll do my best on your cornbread and beans."

She pointed at a side table, and he saw the newspapers. "I'm sure tonight was just because of the press this morning and afternoon."

"I'm used to it, ma'am," he said, "after almost two decades. Like tonight's *political discourse.*

I'm a hero. I'm a cold-blooded killer. But . . . if you'd like me to take my meals elsewhere . . . even in my room, if that's allowed . . . I can. . . ."

"I am sure," she interrupted, "that this . . ."— she struggled to find the right word—"this . . . ill-temper . . . will pass. It's probably . . . well . . . nerves."

"I know that feeling."

"They are just . . . scared."

"I've only shot six or seven men during supper, ma'am. Maybe you could tell them that at breakfast."

She stared, flashed a brief smile, and shook her head.

"I'm serious about taking my meals somewhere else," he said.

"Breakfast is at seven," she said, rose, and nodded at his plate. "Please finish your supper. I'll clean off these plates, and bring you back a peach pie."

She had not brought up this morning. He had not apologized for falling asleep on her swing.

"I can help, ma'am."

"Nonsense. You are a paying guest. Eat. But please save room for pie."

CHAPTER FIVE

He spent most of the evening working, unpacking, putting things away, trying to open and close the drawers as quietly as possible, even if part of him wanted to keep Mr. Childs of the Denver Telephone Dispatch Company awake as long as he could—only to remember that Childs had left for a dram shop.

What stopped Matt's progress was finding the book. He looked at the title, let his fingers run over the leather cover, then down the cut-edged pages, and he sat on the bed and let the book fall open. He read:

> That I could forget the mockers and
>   insults!
> That I could forget the trickling tears, and
>   the blows of the
> Bludgeons and hammers!
> That I could look with a separate look on
>   my own crucifixion
> And bloody crowning.

Remembering, he thumbed through the pages until he found the beginnings of "We Two—How Long We Were Fool'd", and he saw the faded ramblings he had written in pencil so many years earlier:

> Instead of the Styx, I crossed the Snake
> Instead of Charon, the ferryman was
> Jeff Hancock

Or was it? he wondered now as he closed the book, and slid it onto the bedside table. He went back to work.

The front door opened, footsteps tapped down the hallway, and the door opened to the neighboring room. The dresser butted up against the wall to where Mr. Childs bunked, and through the walls Matt heard the telephone man whistling that song some wandering minstrel had made up just weeks after newspapers across the nation told the stories about Jeff Hancock being shot dead by Matthew Johnson at Rattlesnake Station, southeast of Boise.

Shaking his head, Matt looked at the dresser, and found the envelopes. Those he brought back to the bed as he undressed. After turning up the lamp, he sat on the edge, frowning, turning the first envelope over and over before he started to tear one side. He swung his legs onto the bed, and pulled out a piece of stationery.

It was exactly what Luther Wilson said it would be, a letter of introduction to the vice president of the Denver, Leadville, and Gunnison

Railway. There was another letter to J.S.G. Early, chairman of the Citizens Alliance Committee on South Edith Street, and one to Curwood Scarth, who owned a surveying company on Clarkston Street, with locations also on Fourth Street in Grand Junction, and Main Avenue in Durango. The fourth letter, the thickest, was an introduction to an assistant cashier at the German National Bank of Denver. Lying in the folds of the page Matt withdrew five crisp twenty-dollar bills and five tens, all national currency, all printed by the German bank. **A U.S. marshal should be well-dressed** had been written on the back of the letter, so Matt wasn't surprised when he found the last letter of introduction came from a tailor on Larimer Street.

The hundred and fifty he slipped inside his copy of Walt Whitman's *Leaves of Grass*. The letters he stuck inside his trunk, which he had dragged beside the larger dresser.

Eventually, he turned into the bed and turned down the lamp. But he did not fall asleep until well past two in the morning.

When he stepped inside the dining room, he found Jean McBride sipping coffee.

"Am I early?" he asked, knowing he wasn't.

She set the cup on a saucer and shook her head. "Mister Friedrich left a note that he had to be at work early," she said, "and Mister Steuart said he would be late coming to breakfast."

Late, meaning after he hears me walk out, Matt figured.

"And our schoolmarms?" Matt asked.

She shrugged.

After I've gone, too.

"And Mister Childs?"

She frowned. "From the racket he made coming home after his porters, I suspect he shan't be joining us for quite some time."

"Well," he said, trying to find the words. "I must apologize for my stupidity, everything . . . sleeping on your . . ."

"I accept your apology, and we shall hear no more about it." She pointed, he found the rack by the entrance, hung his hat on it, and sat across from her.

"Well, I'll just have some biscuits and gravy, ma'am. And coffee."

"And the slice of pie you didn't eat last night."

He grinned. "If you insist."

"Would you care to look at the morning newspapers?"

"Oh, ma'am, I . . ."

"I've already flipped through them. There is no mention of your name anywhere that I saw, except for a glowing editorial in the *Cattlemen's Clarion*."

Matt smiled. "In that case, I'll take a peek at

the *Clarion*." That was the one newspaper whose reporter had defended him after he had been sworn in as federal marshal for Colorado. It was also the newspaper at least partially funded by Luther J. Wilson.

The ever-efficient Carter Bowen III greeted Matt at the door with a cup of coffee and a piece of paper.

Matt took the coffee with pleasure and surprise, but glanced at the paper with a degree of suspicion.

"What's this?" he asked.

"Your schedule for the day," the secretary answered.

In Idaho Territory, he remembered, men, women, judges, newspaper correspondents, and deputy marshals just came in unannounced. There were no schedules at the territorial capital, except stagecoach schedules, which were hardly reliable. Matt scanned the list of appointments. Warren Perelman and Caleb Dawson were the only names he recognized—the federal judge and Matt's chief deputy—but others at least had titles. State senator. Editor. Well, that would be interesting. He looked the page over, top to bottom, then looked at the names demanding his attention.

"This Mister Tarleton," Matt said. "He's editor of which newspaper?"

"Not a newspaper, Marshal, but *Munsey's Magazine*. It's published in New York City."

"New York City," Matt said, sipped the coffee, weak but still coffee, and listened.

"It's a wonderful magazine, Marshal. With interesting articles, and photographs."

Matt arched his eyebrows.

"Poetry, too."

"You think they want me to write a poem for publication, Mister Bowen?"

He had at last cracked Bowen's façade. The secretary actually laughed. "Oh, surely, Marshal, you have sharpened your wit today. A marshal and a poet. That would be something."

"Yes, it would. Do you have a copy of the magazine? Any issue. I'd just like to see what I'm getting myself into."

"I shall have one on your desk within the hour."

"Excellent." *In case it's one of those muckraking sheets,* he thought to himself. Then he read down the list.

"Missus Hecker?"

"Temperance leader for the town of Highlands. That's just northwest of Denver."

He nodded. "Well, that should be an interesting meeting," he said, skipped past the senator and assemblyman, then asked: "Hugo Persson?"

"He's an assistant cashier with the German National Bank of Denver."

Hugo Persson's name had been on one of those envelopes Luther Wilson had given him, the letter of introduction that also contained the one hundred fifty in notes from the German National Bank of Denver.

"I see. Is Persson a German name, Mister Bowen?"

"I do not think you have to be German to work in that particular bank, Marshal. But, honestly, I cannot state his bloodline or heritage one way or the other."

"Very good." He held up the cup. "Thank you for this. And send Deputy Dawson in as soon as he arrives."

When he reached the door to his office, Matt turned back to the secretary. "Carter."

The man looked up.

"Could you give me a list of the scheduled meetings a day in advance?" He tried to give his most reassuring smile. "From here on out. Just so I'm not ambushed, so to speak. If I have an inkling about what the hell it is I'm supposed to be talking about, I might not come across as the ignorant thirty-a-month cowboy I used to be, and still am."

"Well . . ." Carter Bowen III looked flabbergasted. "Well, yes, yes, of course."

"Excellent. I know there will be unscheduled meetings, probably even telephone calls. But the better prepared I am, the better I'd feel. Suppose you have tomorrow's list of meetings to me when I return from dinner."

"Of course, Marshal. But I do not think you were ever ignorant."

"And one more item, Carter. Drop that 'marshal'. The name's Matt."

Caleb Dawson, unfortunately for the chief deputy, reminded Matt of Mr. Childs, the worker for the Denver Telephone Dispatch Company. Same build, same thick, well-groomed mustache. Same eyes, squinting, too close together. But Caleb Dawson had a mountain of thick, black hair, whereas Mr. Childs was bald on top, thin along the sides. Holding a black hat in his left hand, Dawson wore a gray Prince Albert, striped britches tucked inside his boots, and a vest of blue brocade. He had a firm handshake and a pleasant smile.

"Marshal Johnson," he said as he entered the office, closing the door behind him. "I heard a lot about you."

"Unless you heard it from me, it's the truth," Matt said. That always got a laugh, and Caleb Dawson did not disappoint.

Matt motioned to a chair, and the men sat across from one another.

"Since I'm new here," Matt said, "let's get to know one another. And because you know all about me, why don't you tell me all about you?"

Like most lawmen, Dawson was succinct. He had been chief deputy for two years, before that had been based in Trinidad, where he also served as a deputy sheriff. Before that, he had worked as a guard at the state prison in Cañon City. Did one hitch in the Army. Thirty-two years old. Born in Dallas. The Army sent him to Fort Garland. He had been in Colorado ever since.

"What's your opinion of Judge Perelman?" Matt asked.

"By the book. In court or on Arapahoe Street."

"My secretary, Mister Bowen?"

Dawson couldn't hide the smile. "He's a *secretary*." The last word was drawn out and laced with derision.

"There's a deputy I met when I first arrived. Liberty Rawlings?"

"Thinks he's Wild Bill Hickok."

Matt cocked his head. "In what way?"

"Ought to get his damned hair cut."

"And other than that?"

"Young, green. But I don't hardly know him."

Dawson had not lost that twang from those years in Texas. "Well," Matt said, figuring he had likely got about all the information he could, then asked: "Where do you bank? I mean, where is your account?" He shook his head, grinned, and added: "I'll need to open an account at some point."

"Only banks I ever set foot in was them that had been robbed."

Yes, here is a Texan.

"You don't save any money?"

"What's the point?" Dawson grunted. "I'm a lawman. Chances are I'll be killed. I just hope it's quick. My money goes to my rent, my horse, grub, tobacco, to my favorite faro dealer, and my favorite watering hole. Hell, there ain't much to save even before all that."

A brief silence followed.

"So," Matt said, "you're my chief deputy, I just arrived in Colorado, and I haven't had a federal posting in a number of years. But the Senate confirmed me, and here I am." That thought—*And I'd like to hold onto this badge longer than I held that one in Idaho*—raced through his mind so fast, he almost turned mute. He made himself drink more coffee, and found the words. "Where do we need to focus our attention, Caleb?" *That's right, use his first name. Make him relax, as though this man with the broad shoulders and stiff back ever relaxed.* "What's the biggest threat, that you see, to the safety of the citizens of this state and the federal government?"

The reply came instantly. "It's them damned anarchists with the D and RG."

"My understanding was that the strike was . . ."

"Nothing's been settled," Dawson said. "*Nada.* And Trinidad's where it'll all bust loose. Grant

Hayes couldn't do nothing, or didn't have the *cojones* to do nothing. He was a political appointee. I'm hoping . . . based on what I heard about you . . . that you're like me. The law comes first. Break the law, and we'll break your backs. With lead."

Which sounded, to Matt, like something one of those half-dime novelists would have written about Matthew Johnson.

"That's very interesting," Matt said.

"If I was you," the deputy went on, "I'd get in touch with the commanding officer at Fort Logan. Send troops to Trinidad. Get ready for a ruction and when it starts, show them the steel and lead."

After letting the man's face lose some of the redness, Matt asked: "What are you working on now?"

Dawson scoffed. "Damned counterfeiter. Passing money up in Greeley."

"Any leads?"

His head shook. "He'll slip up. Hope sooner than later. Ain't much excitement chasing down them kind of criminals."

"You're not working on the robbery of that shipment of Army guns?" Matt asked.

"Hell, there's a couple snot-nosed deputies workin' on that one, Hannah and . . . I disremember the other kid's name. Besides, let them soldier boys find their own damned guns."

Matt rose, smiled, and checked his watch. "Well, Caleb," he said, as he slipped the Waltham back inside his vest pocket. "I've taken too much of your time already. And I truly appreciate that you shared your concerns with me. If I need to be in Trinidad, I'll be in Trinidad." They shook hands, and as Dawson walked to the door, Matt called out one final question.

"What do you think about the Utes?"

He didn't know, exactly, why he had asked that, and Caleb Dawson's face and answer said that the chief deputy didn't know why he had been asked, either.

"Utes?" Dawson said. He snorted. "They're taking up a lot of good land that ought to be used for us white people. But, yeah, you gotta watch out for 'em."

The rest of the morning meetings dragged on with typical boredom. Judge Perelman instructed Matt on what would be expected from the deputies testifying in a trial next week, what he would tolerate, what would incite the wrath of a Lincoln Republican. Skipping dinner, Matt read a few articles and all of the poems in the copy of *Munsey's Magazine* Bowen brought him.

The temperance woman never brought up the allegations—*Is it an allegation if it is true?* Matt wondered—of his drinking, but invited him to speak at the meeting at the Methodist church on

Eighteenth and Broadway on Wednesday, May 23rd.

Carter Bowen III let Matt know the next meeting was canceled; Senator Germaine got stuck in his chambers, but would reschedule. That's what gave Matt the idea.

"Well," he told his secretary, "tell the senator that he has my vote . . . if he's in my district . . . come re-election. Since I failed to eat dinner, I think I'll grab something from one of the nearby vendors on the street. And some coffee. Where was that place you went the other day? And what time is my next meeting?"

Matt nodded when Bowen checked his desk and gave the answers, although this change of plans seemed to make the secretary break out in a sweat. "Excellent," Matt said. "I should be back well before three-fifteen." He grabbed his hat, left his office, stepped out of the courthouse, and found the café for a coffee. He wasn't hungry—not after the breakfast Jean McBride had prepared that morning—but he made himself pick at the baked batter pudding. He paid quickly, grabbed his hat, and found the saloon.

In every town he had known, no matter the size, territory, or year, a man could always find a saloon practically next door to the courthouse or jail.

CHAPTER SIX

"What poison can I get you?" the bartender asked.

Matt pointed. The bartender looked, then frowned. "The telephone?" he asked.

"That's right. Need to phone a couple of places." Matt pulled back his coat to reveal the badge. The beer-jerker frowned, but Matt pulled out a coin and tossed it on the bar, then tilted his head at the young man sipping a dark wine, or so Matt guessed.

"Blackburn's Dry Madeira," the bartender said.

"And the telephone," Matt said, dropping another coin next to the filthy bar towel, then another.

"Help yourself," the bartender said. "But two calls only. Then get out. We don't like lawdogs here."

"I don't like Madeira," Matt said. "But I'll be gone . . . after two conversations on that thing and . . . after the . . . Madeira."

When the wine came, Matt slid it toward the young wine drinker. "How'd you like to do me a favor, son?" he asked.

Now the bartender stepped back and waited.

The kid looked at the glass, studied Matt, glanced at the bartender, and wet his lips.

Matt pointed at the big wooden box. "That thing is as foreign to me as a bicycle, kid," Matt said. "The Madeira's yours if you'll help me work *that*."

That was all the bartender needed to hear. "He touches anything other than Charley's three-boxer, and both of you get thrown out on your arses, lawdog or not." He gave his meanest snarl, and moved down the bar to draw a better customer a pint of double-strong ale.

"Who am I calling?" the kid asked.

"The German National Bank of Denver first," Matt answered. "Then the federal courthouse, United States marshal's office."

When the boy frowned, Matt showed him the badge pinned to his vest. "There's no law that says you can't be drinking Madeira when you're fifteen years old, but there is a law that says I can arrest you for being drunk and disorderly."

The kid protested. "I'll have you know that I am not fifteen, but twenty, and I am also studying at the Colorado Seminary."

"Then you're breaking all kinds of laws," Matt said.

The boy drained the glass he had been sipping, moved down the bar to the oddly shaped contraption of dark wood nailed to the wall near the back-bar. The bartender, now chatting with another customer, kept glancing at Matt and the seminary student. Seeing Matt still on the customers' side, the kid waved him over. "This won't reach you, and you'll likely have to yell into this hole here."

Matt obeyed, and listened as the boy—Matt would have recommended him for any job at the Denver Telephone Dispatch Company—explained the operations. "This is the magneto, and this is how you call up the operator." He held one piece to his left ear and quickly turned back to Matt. "You know what the number is?"

"No," Matt said.

Then the kid was speaking into a hole in the middle box, saying that he had an important call to make to the German bank.

That's all it took. The boy handed Matt the handle with the wire, showed Matt how close to hold it to his ear, and told him to step closer to the middle box. By the time the kid was sipping his payment of Madeira, Matt was talking to someone at the German National Bank of Denver.

"Yeah. This is Matthew Johnson, federal marshal. I'm supposed to meet one of your cashiers, a Mister Persson, but I'm way behind schedule. Could you give me a description of him, in case he thinks I've forgotten about our meeting and is heading back to your office while I'm running into mine?"

He listened, thanked the man for the information, and held the ear piece toward the kid.

"Just set it in its cradle," the boy said, like he was telling a new mother how to change her baby's diapers. "Then lift it out, place it near your ear, and press the magneto till the operator starts talking to you."

A minute later, Matt started talking to Carter Bowen III. "Carter. This is Matt. Matt Johnson. Yeah. Listen, I won't be able to make my meeting with Mister Persson. But reschedule him at another time that suits him, and you. And when I figure out how to end this telephone conversation, you send my apologies to that magazine editor. I'll be able to meet with him another time, too. But tell him I like his magazine. Especially the poems. And the photographs." He returned the ear piece to its holder.

Lifting the glass of Madeira, the Colorado Seminary student smiled. The bartender seemed relieved that Matt was heading through the front door.

His luck held. A hack happened to be trotting down the street, and stopped for Matt, who showed him the badge and climbed into the driver's box beside him. "Just wait here a spell. Then we're gonna follow somebody home, I hope."

Since the massive three-story structure served as courthouse and post office, Matt had to focus on the people leaving, but he figured the lanky, blond-haired man with the pale face, wearing duds that Matt could not have bought with two months' wages, coming out of the federal courthouse had to be Hugo Persson.

So Matt nudged the hack.

"See him?" Matt said. When the driver nodded, Matt said: "Let's make sure he gets home. Or to a bar, brothel, or his office. But let's make sure he gets there. And there's three Morgan dollars extra for you if he doesn't notice you, me, or your gray Percheron."

He pressed his lips together, and checked the time. Three-twenty-six. The German National Bank of Denver closed at four, but Persson could go back to work. Or he could find a saloon, restaurant, go shopping, or, hell, catch a train to Julesburg.

The blond man found a hack, and Matt followed along behind in the cold, spring wind for what felt like two hours, but was likely no more than two miles. Hugo Persson climbed out of the carriage, paid the driver, and walked gloomily to a stately house on Marion Street. Not as nice as Jean McBride's, but better than most of the places where Matt had hung his hat.

"Now what?" the driver said.

Matt wrote down Persson's address, stuck the paper inside his coat pocket, and gave the driver the address for Jean McBride's boarding house. "I'm going to pick up something there, then we'll come back here. That sound fine by you?"

"It's your money," the driver said. "What if he ain't here when you get back?"

Matt realized how naïve he was. "Then I turn you loose with your three dollars extra, and I wait for him to come home."

"What if he don't even live here?" The driver found a cigar in his pocket, and relighted it. "What if he's just visiting some chirpy? Or his dying ma?"

Matt looked at the old man, chuckled, and said: "You ever want a job as a deputy U.S. marshal, you come see me."

The driver spit over the side of the hack. "I got the job I want, buster. All I got to do is sit on my arse and let my draft horse do all the work." He turned to Matt and stared with cold, gray eyes. "And usually, I ain't got to talk to the customers I'm hauling across this cistern called a city."

He didn't find Jean McBride in the house when he got there, but grabbed the letter of introduction to Hugo Persson and the hundred and fifty dollars, sticking the envelope inside his coat pocket. Finding a piece of paper on the desk, he scribbled a note saying he had to work late, and might be late for supper, might even miss the meal, and wanted to apologize now and hoped he had not caused any inconvenience.

An eternity later, he knocked on the door of the boarding house on Marion Street, only to learn that Hugo Persson had left for the evening and that the short, elderly man with curly white hair and copper-rimmed spectacles had no idea when he would return.

"I'll wait," Matt said.

The man gave his fiercest scowl.

Matt had gotten used to showing men his badge. The man studied it, looked up at Matt, and asked: "You Johnson?"

"That's my name."

"Shit." The door closed, the latch bolted, and Matt moved to another one of those damned porch swings.

Not many people talked about Matt's eight months with the Pinkerton National Detective Agency—especially the Pinkertons. That one had come after that lecture tour and his stint as a bank guard in Omaha. Matt never had been much of a detective, and now he passed time counting all the mistakes he had made as the sun sank, and the temperatures dropped. He had failed to bring an overcoat or at least a blanket. He had no idea what the hell he was doing here, or why. Nor did he know what was going on in Denver, or Colorado. But Luther Wilson and Caleb Dawson had muttered similar phrases about that railroad strike with the Denver & Rio Grande. Anarchists. Damned anarchists, damn the anarchists. Something like that. Which, Matt knew without having to hear a lecture from Warren Perelman, meant absolutely nothing in a courtroom. None of that could put anyone in a courtroom. But there was something going on, and he was in the middle of it. Matt didn't like that. He had ridden that trail before.

After buttoning his coat, he pulled up the collar, and tried to keep the swing anchored.

The blackness thickened, the cold crept into his bones, but he laughed, making the swing buck like a skittish colt, and thought to himself: *Well, Jeff, you'd never believe this, but ol' Matt Johnson went through an entire day without even a taste of whiskey. I even bought a glass of wine . . . for somebody else.*

Damn. He could sure use a bracer right about now.

At some point, with only the street lamps on Marion Street to warm him, he realized he was shivering. It did not take him long to understand that the shakes came not from the cold, yet he told himself that this might help keep him warm. He saw Jeff Hancock, the way he usually did, imagined his own wife Darlene up in Boise, and his daughters who never wanted to talk to him, who—at least if Darlene was telling him the truth—refused to open any letter he sent them. He saw the others, too, the men from Boise— the publisher for that outfit in Salt Lake City, the one that started those half-dime novels—and the soldiers at Fort Sherman singing in drunken Irish brogues the first time he had ever heard, "Matthew Johnson, United States Marshal."

At some point, he wondered if he might be freezing to death, until the clopping of hoofs on Denver's paved streets reached his ears and his senses. A driver stopped the hack in front of the boarding house. Matt caught a word here, a grunt there, before the blur of the coach and draft animal moved down the street, and a tall, dark figure approached the house, the occasional red glow from a cigar alerting Matt of the nearness of the man.

The shoes tapped the wooden steps, and the man reached the porch before trying to find the keys in his pants pockets. When the porch swing squeaked, the tall man spun around, gasping as Matt stood.

"Hugo Persson," Matt said, hoping he came close to the right pronunciation. "Sorry I couldn't meet with you this afternoon, but I'm here now. I'm Matthew Johnson, U.S. marshal."

One foot had fallen asleep or maybe, Matt thought, it was frostbite. Yet he managed to cover the eight feet until he could smell the pungency of the tobacco, and see from the glow of the cigar that Hugo Persson was scared out of his wits.

"You did want to meet with me, didn't you?" Matt said.

"I . . . *Ja självklart.*"

Matt didn't know what to make out of that. German? What did Matt know about German? Well, Hugo Persson sure didn't come from Franklin, Tennessee.

"What did you want to talk to me about?" Matt asked.

He understood the awkwardness. A dark porch. Late at night. He smelled whiskey on the tall foreigner's breath, and wished he had some whiskey on his own breath or tongue.

"I assure you," Matt said, and once more pulled back his coat to show the shiny new six-point star pinned to his vest's lapel. "I am Matthew Johnson. I know I might not look like the fire-breathing devil in black, but here I am, flesh and blood, and cold as hell."

The man blinked. He finally remembered to remove the cigar from his mouth.

Too shocked to invite Matt inside, but that had never been Matt's plan. Like he had a plan. Like he ever planned anything out. What happened at Rattlesnake Station in 1877 had not been planned. Matt had just taken a wild stab that Hancock would show up.

"Here's my bona-fides," he said, and reached inside his coat. "This is my letter of introduction. From a wealthy entrepreneur named . . ." Hell's fire, he was so damned tired and cold he couldn't remember his benefactor's name. So cold and worn out he almost said Jean McBride. "Wilson."

The name, thankfully, came to him at last. "Luther Wilson." He waved the envelope. After a long while, Hugo Persson eased the letter from Matt's numb fingers.

"Hugo," Matt said, and waited till the man's wide eyes finally steadied and focused on Matt's. "You tell your friends, your bosses, or the men who work for you. You tell them this . . . Matthew Johnson might damned well be the kind of man who'd shoot his best friend in the back for a puny reward of two hundred and fifty dollars. He might be a stove-up rapscallion closer now to sixty than thirty, and he might be a drunk, an idiot, and as dishonest as the Whiskey Ring. But what's left of his integrity is not for sale. You savvy what I'm telling you, Mister Persson?"

The frightened man managed to nod quickly.

"Good." Matt straightened, wondering if he would be able to recall any of this conversation when he was in the courthouse tomorrow morning, or in his room at Jean McBride's boarding house. Of course, there was also a decent chance that he'd be dead by tomorrow, with his body found frozen in some alley between Marion and Race Streets.

He made his way down the steps and onto the sidewalk. Lacking any idea of how he could get back to his boarding house, he followed the street lamps, the way he thought the hacks had headed. His teeth clattered, and he had halfway decided that if he saw a church, to head inside the sanctuary—providing a door wasn't locked—and sleep on floor or pew until morning came. Instead, another hack came clopping down the street, and Matt realized how lucky he was to be in a city as vibrant, populated, and greedy as Denver. That got him back to the fancy home with the gate and the gables and the two dogs guarding the front porch.

Whispering praises to the name of Jean McBride, he opened the door, walked down the hall, found his key that gave him entrance to his room, and crashed onto the bed, wrapping himself in the blanket and falling asleep, still in his boots and coat.

He slept fitfully, waking up about every forty minutes. He prayed that he would remember what had happened this night, but wondered if anything would make the slightest bit of sense come morning.

CHAPTER SEVEN

The Waltham chimed, his eyes opened, and the hall outside his room came alive with the pattering of feet. Doors opened, closed, nobody talked, but the smell of coffee spoke loudly enough. Matt groggily slipped out of bed, silenced the repeater, and eventually found the wash basin to splash cold water onto his face.

The mirror reflected the image of a pitiful man, needing a shave, bloodshot eyes, wearing wrinkled clothes that looked as though he had slept in them—which he had . . . again. He looked at the watch, whispered a curse, and did his best to comb his hair with his fingers. Another blast of cold water helped a little, so Matt grabbed his hat, folded the coat over his arm, and left his room.

No one sat at the table in the dining room, and one plate setting remained, but Matt was already late for work. He wolfed down a biscuit, filled a cup with coffee, and stepped back into the hallway. Dishes clattered toward the back of the house, and Matt followed the trail. Sleeves rolled up, rubber gloves on her hands, Jean McBride bent over the sink, pumping water to rinse off dishes. In a house like this—a business—Matt expected to find a servant, not the owner, doing a menial chore. The image of his mother flashed through his mind. He recalled her voice as she complained: *I am just a scullery maid for you, your sister, and your pa.* Matt tapped on the wall.

Jean stopped working the pump's handle, and turned. Her face looked like stone, her blue eyes hard. Without speaking, she removed the gloves and found a towel to dry her arms.

"I'm sorry I missed supper last night," he said. "Hope you found my note and I didn't put you out or anything."

"I saw the note," she said. "Thank you."

"Slept late. Missed breakfast. I was out all night," he said. "Playing detective."

He smiled. She didn't.

"There's a plate in the dining room," she told him. "Food's cold, but I can heat it up."

"No need, ma'am. I grabbed a biscuit." He showed her the cup. "Got coffee. I supposed I should be off to work. But I hope to be back for supper."

"Very good." She began pulling the gloves on, and although the kitchen remained hot, Matt felt her coldness.

He might have failed as a Pinkerton operative, but he solved this mystery. He looked like hell. She had probably heard him stagger in early this morning. Besides, who wouldn't have expected Matthew Johnson to be drunk again. Retreat, he decided, seemed prudent, so he bid her good day and left her to the chores.

At 10:30, he reached the federal courthouse to find a crowd surrounding Carter Bowen III's desk. He figured those men had meetings scheduled, that some of these were those he had neglected yesterday, but when they turned, he recognized Judge Perelman, Chief Deputy Caleb Dawson, and a few other clerks and attorneys he had seen around the building.

" 'Morning." Matt's greeting prompted a few mutters as the men scattered like a covey of quail after a shotgun blast.

After stepping to Bowen's desk, Matt spotted a man in a plaid suit sitting in one of the uncomfortable chairs reading the *Morning Herald.* "What's my day like?" Matt asked Bowen.

Always ready, Carter Bowen III handed Matt papers. "Your schedule for the day, and tomorrow, a report from Deputy Marshal Stroheim in Durango." The secretary didn't even look at Matt.

Glancing at the top sheet, Matt found several names scratched out, although the 9:15 name remained. "I suppose," Matt said, "you'll have to reschedule the meetings I missed this morning, too." He tried his best grin. "Overslept."

"Most canceled of their own volition," the little man said. "Except him."

Matt stared at the man who kept his face hidden by the *Morning Herald*. "I should get this over with," he said. After a long sigh, he cleared his throat and called out: "Mister Tarleton?"

The *Munsey's Magazine* scribe folded the newspaper and stared. Dark-haired, cleanly shaven—if he ever needed a straight razor—wearing glasses and a suit that showed its age, Lawrence Tarleton of *Munsey's Magazine* did not look like the editor Matt expected. Meaning: no cloven hoofs, horns, or pointy tail. "If you'd care to join me." Matt gestured while moving toward his office, boots sounding loudly on the floor, as though the entire courthouse had emptied.

After closing the door, Matt gestured to a chair in front of the desk. The journalist, still carrying the Denver newspaper, found his seat, and Matt leaned against the desk, laid his schedules and the deputy's report on the top, covering them with his hat.

"Why does a New York City magazine have any interest in me?" Matt asked.

"*Munsey's* is a national magazine," the young man said, "and you arc a man of national interest."

"Not in ten years or more," Matt said.

"You're in the news today."

Matt grinned. "I was sworn in as federal marshal. Maybe that's news, but I don't think you shall see my name in the newspapers much.

Since my deputies do most of the hard work, I'd rather . . ." The change in Tarleton's face stopped Matt cold. What had he said that was so wrong?

"You have not seen this morning's *Herald*?" Tarleton unfolded the copy, and started to rise, but Matt covered the distance quickly. He snatched the newspaper from the man's hand, and found the item—at least it was on page four, not the front page, and had been buried at the bottom next to an advertisement for Royal Baking Powder.

DRUNK ON DUTY
New U.S. Marshal For Colorado
Up to His Old TRICKS!
Maathew Johsnson
SHOULD BE SUSPENDED AND TRIED

Well, he could take some comfort that the editors had misspelled both of his names. He read the article.

> MATTHEW JOHNSON, who reported earlier this week to take over the vacancy in the United States Marshal's Office for the district of Colorado, left work early yesterday for an important engagement.
> Yes, the murdering hero who made a name for himself by shooting down an old friend, outlaw Jeff Hancock in Idaho Ty.,

more than a dozen years ago, crossed the street and found a perch at the bar at Magawley's nefarious establishment when the hour was hardly past noon.

Since our new U.S. marshal hails from Kentucky, we assume he ordered a "Kentucky Breakfast"—a steak, a bottle of rum, and an Irish setter. The dog, of course, is there to eat the steak. We don't know how much aguardiente Marshall Johnson consumed, but he certainly partook of enough that instead of crawling back to the U.S. courthouse and post office, he hired a hack to take him home.

Perhaps he's still haunted by the ghost of the friend he shot for bounty all those years ago. Join us as we sing the chorus to that popular song:

Matthew Johnson,
United States marshal,
Drunk as a skunk,
Bullyragging punk.
Matthew Johnson,
When his pistol sounds CRACK,
Bet you all he sees
Is an old pard's back.

Perhaps it is not so disgraceful as the act Matthew Johnson performed at

Rattlesnake Springs, but there should be consequences for the highest ranking peace officer in this state to go about rinsing his tonsils with the extract of hops.

Maybe the attorney general will take note.

He folded the newspaper and returned it to Tarleton, trying to remember something he had said to himself, or maybe just a thought that raced through his mind yesterday afternoon or evening. Something about Matt Johnson making news again, going into a saloon and not drinking a thing. Well, the joke was on him. He rubbed his face, feeling the beard stubble, and recalling the wrinkles in his clothes and along the corners of his eyes.

I look like the walking whiskey vat I usually am. He sniffed. *Smell like it, too. Not whiskey or beer, maybe, but . . .*

Tarleton cleared his throat.

"Looks like the *Morning Herald* got the story you wanted first," Matt said.

"That's not what I want, sir," the journalist said.

Matt studied him. "What is it you want?"

"Justice."

So, Matt thought, *this is how it ends. Here's some young kid who grew up listening to songs about Matthew Johnson, heroic songs, then the songs that mocked the legend. Here's where some kid pulls out a hide-away pistol and pops Matthew Johnson in the belly. Jesse James had his Bob Ford. Bill Hickok had his Jack McCall. Billy the Kid had his Pat Garrett. And Matthew Johnson has . . . Lawrence Tarleton.*

But the man made no move to find any sort of weapon. He was a kid, at least to Matt. Maybe twenty years old, perhaps still in his teens. The pale face fit with Tarleton's flaccid handshake. Pencils and quills did not leave calluses on the fingers and palms like ropes and leather reins. Lawrence Tarleton looked to be the type of boy who put his nose into a book, who couldn't hurt Matt any more than that anonymous reporter for the *Herald*. That fool had said Matt came from Kentucky, when even that damned song mentioned Tennessee. But the song didn't get sung so much these days. Matt hadn't heard it in years until a few days ago with that choir of schoolchildren at his swearing-in ceremony.

Matt backed up to his desk. "You don't work for *Munsey's Magazine*, do you?" It was a wild grab, but Matt knew he had guessed right when Tarleton's face paled even more.

Tarleton suddenly stared at his city shoes. "I had a poem published in the magazine two years ago," Tarleton said.

"Prove it."

Whatever Lawrence Tarleton was, he was not

used to being challenged like that. He looked at Matt, then at the walls and windows, and stuttered: "I . . . I-I . . . I d-don't have . . . a . . . copy. That w-was . . . two years . . . ago."

"If a magazine like *Munsey's* published one of my poems, I would remember every word I wrote," Matt said. "Hell, boy, I still recall poems I made up sitting around a campfire with . . ." He swallowed down the names and those memories.

The man smiled nervously. "Oh, I don't think a rugged man like you, a lawman, a legend in Western annals . . ."

"The smell, the noise, the smoke, the dust," Matt said. "I sweat, I swear, I clinch, I curse. The iron is hot, I feel the heat. Slap the brand, hard yet neat. The calf, he rises, runs off to mother. His pain subsides, but not mine, brother. The days are long come branding time. Burn fifty a day, not one of them mine."

Lawrence Tarleton's eyes revealed amazement, perhaps shock. After wetting his lips, he asked: "Did you write that?"

"I can't say I ever wrote it down on paper or anything," Matt said. "And it certainly never showed up in some fancy magazine like *Munsey's*, but . . ." He shrugged. "The words are mine, all right." Shaking his head, he laughed at the memory. "Friend of mine, a long time ago, we'd get into what we called poetry duels. He'd try one out, I'd fire another back. On and on.

That's how we entertained ourselves at camps, in the bunkhouse, sometimes even at saloons. Work cattle long enough, Mister Tarleton, and, well, you go sort of . . . loco."

Damned if the gent didn't bob his head like he understood.

"Your turn." Matt nodded at Tarleton.

"Sir?"

"Your turn. Just like me and . . ." He stopped, swallowed. "Just like those poetry duels. I gave you one of mine. Now you tell me one of yours."

Tarleton fidgeted for a long time, and Matt did not rush him. At length, the man summoned up enough courage to speak.

If I were a chemist
I would bottle up
her voice
laughter
the lavender in her eyes
and even the gray
(sometimes)
The gentleness
Kindness
Respect
The way her hand
fits into mine
ever so . . . naturally
If I were a chemist
I could uncork a bottle

of
Her stories
More laughter
The boats to build
and the scent of her perfume
on my pillow
But
If I were a chemist
I would know that
science cannot replace
reality
And even with a
magical bottle
of memories
I would
still miss
someone

"Jesus, God Almighty." Blinking rapidly, Matt shook his head, and moved behind his desk to sit in his chair. "What the hell am I doing trying to write poetry?"

"You *liked* it?"

"Better than anything I read in that issue of *Munsey's* that my secretary showed me yesterday." Now he leaned back. "All right. You got into my office. You might not be Lord Byron, but you're closer than I'll ever get. Justice. What kind of justice?"

The nervousness returned, and Matt glanced

at his schedule, seeing what time his next appointment was—but most of those conferences had been canceled, and the next meeting would be at 1:45 that afternoon—if Carter Bowen III had not already scratched it out on that sheet in the waiting area. Which, at the rate Lawrence Tarleton kept fidgeting, might be about the time the young man had gotten to the point.

"I believe . . . ," Tarleton finally began. "I think . . . I'm pretty sure that . . . my brother-in-law was murdered."

Matt leaned back. "That's a serious allegation."

"I know." The boy seemed dead serious, and dead certain.

Matt searched for something to write with, before realizing one of those fountain pens was right in front of him. He pulled a piece of paper over, and asked: "Who was your brother-in-law?"

"Cole Stevens."

Matt had the boy spell the name.

"Give me some information about him."

"He worked for a newspaper. The Pagosa Springs *Weekly Item*."

"Forgive me," Matt said. "But remember, I'm new to Colorado. Where's Pagosa Springs?"

"In the San Juans. About three days' ride east of Durango."

"Pagosa Springs. There's a town marshal . . . constable?"

"Cole wasn't murdered in the town. He was found dead outside of Durango."

Durango. Matt stared at what he had just written. He cleared his throat, leaned back in his chair, and studied Tarleton. "Found dead and murdered are not necessarily one and the same."

"I know what you're getting at, but Cole was murdered. Near Ignacio. Over gold."

"Gold?" Matt stared at the visitor. "As in robbery?"

Tarleton did not answer, and Matt tried to read that nervous face, finally sighed in defeat, and said: "Well, there's also a matter of jurisdictions. Murder, usually, is a state or territorial crime that does not fall under federal law. You'd need to reach out to the county sheriff or the . . ."

"Marshal Johnson, Ignacio is on the Southern Ute Indian reservation. That's where Cole was murdered. And that does fall under your dominion, I believe."

CHAPTER EIGHT

"Why didn't you just report this to the deputy marshal in Durango?" Matt tried to read Tarleton's face.

"I . . ." The kid seemed even more scared.

"Then why this ruse? Pretending to be a writer, editor, for a magazine?"

Tarleton stuttered. "I wanted to see you. In person. You're Matthew Johnson. I read all about you when I was a little boy."

"You also read about me in today's *Morning Herald*. And that still doesn't explain this pretend business."

"You were my hero. I don't believe . . ."

Matt held up his hand. "I just don't savvy why you'd make up a story about wanting an interview for *Munsey's Magazine* to tell me about your brother-in-law's murder."

Tarleton focused on the floor. More than a minute passed before the kid spoke, and when he started talking, he still did not look up.

"Cole was doing something. That's what got him killed. An Indian woman told me that much."

"Something . . . meaning newspaper reporting?" Matt asked.

Tarleton didn't answer.

"Did this Indian woman see Cole murdered?"

"I don't know."

"Well . . . what about the gold?"

"I found some in his room."

"In Pagosa?"

Tarleton looked at the closed door. He was sweating now, fidgeting like an expectant father, and hammering out a string of words so rapidly Matt barely caught what the boy was saying. "I didn't want anyone to know that Cole was my brother-in-law. I didn't want anyone, except you, to know that I knew that Cole was murdered. Cole taught me never to trust a lawman. Any lawman. But . . . well . . . I figured . . . I mean . . . I had to trust Matthew Johnson. I remember all those stories. And the song."

"Jesus." Matt shook his head.

Tarleton didn't give Matt much information after that, not about Cole Stevens, or why he had been murdered. The boy was flummoxed, and Matt figured that Tarleton had a wild imagination. Some poets did. Like Jeff Hancock.

He studied the kid, finally deciding that the boy, right now, was scared out of his wits. "Did you tell my secretary where you're staying in town . . . how I can get ahold of you?"

Tarleton nodded, and paled even more. "You won't . . . he won't . . . let anyone know . . . will you?"

No, Tarleton's not scared out of his wits. He's petrified. "What are you afraid of, Tarleton? Who are you afraid of?"

"Everybody," the boy said, and Matt had to smile.

"I know that feeling." Still, Matt said that Carter was safe, and that Matt would look into the killing of Stevens and let him know what he found out. He asked the young man to return to his office in a few days. "Schedule an appointment with my secretary."

After Matt walked Tarleton outside and shook his hand, he watched the young man walk, head down, to Carter Bowen III. While the nervous poet scheduled a meeting, Matt moved to the map on the wall, found Durango, found Ignacio on the Southern Ute reservation.

By the time Matt returned to his open door, Lawrence Tarleton was heading toward the exit like a man heading for the gallows. The chairs around the office were empty. Matt walked to Carter Bowen III, who, always ready, raised his head and reached for an ink pen. "Yes, sir?" he asked.

"Do I have any more meetings?"

The little man sighed. "Your other meetings canceled as well," Bowen said.

"No court appearances?"

Shaking his head, Bowen verbalized that answer too, and after being asked, announced that there were no meetings or appointments on the schedule for the following day, either.

"Messages?"

"Not . . ."

Matt finished for Bowen. "Yet." His head shook. "The *Republican*, the *Rocky Mountain News*, *Frank Leslie's*, *Harper's*, the Nashville *Daily Union* . . . if it's still around?"

Carter Bowen III seemed befuddled.

"Well, if someone happens to ask, you can tell them that the *Morning Herald* was wrong. I'm not from Kentucky, as any damned fool who ever heard some idiot singing that god-awful song in a saloon or a street corner knows. And if anyone had bothered to go inside that dram shop to ask the bartender, he would have said that I ordered a glass of wine . . . for a seminary student . . . which, I reckon, should damn my soul. But I wasn't drunk."

He pulled the hat he brought out of the office onto his head. "And since I don't have any appointments, I think I'll wander the streets in search of counterfeiters or Army deserters."

There was no mistaking the Union Stock Yard Company. Anyone with a nose could have found the way to the sprawling stockyards bordered east-by-west by the railroad tracks and the South Platte River, and north-by-south by Fifty-Second Avenue and Forty-Sixth Avenue. The sound of bawling cattle took him back to Idaho Territory, but the stockyards in the northwestern United States paled in comparison to the monstrosity in Denver. He had overheard someone say that folks kept talking about erecting an Exchange Building at some point, and wouldn't that be something?

"Hey, mister."

Turning, Matt saw six school-age boys, all wearing straw hats and denim britches, probably not yet in their teens, hanging in front of a pen. One of the kids held a lariat. Two others were blowing big colorful bubbles, and a fourth tried to roll a cigarette but had trouble getting the right amount of tobacco onto the paper. The last two kids had climbed up the wooden fence, paying attention to whatever livestock ran about inside. Matt walked toward them.

The leader of the group pointed to the pen. "Can you show us how to rope a cow?" He nudged the freckle-faced one, who remembered the lariat in his hand, and held it up for display.

"Shouldn't you boys be in school?" When Matt started walking toward them, the gum-chewers tried to run, but the leader stopped them with a quick bark, though Matt wasn't sure how long that kid could keep his command from disintegrating.

Towering over the youths, Matt stopped, stared at the lariat, then at the leader. "You boys are pretty young to be starting a career in rustling, aren't you?"

"We ain't cow thieves," a gum-chewer sang out.

"And he ain't no cowboy," said the big kid on the top rail of the fence. "Look at 'im. Other than that banged up ol' hat, he looks more like a drummer."

He wasn't sure if pride or resentfulness made him reach over and take the lariat, but, hell, it was something to do. After slipping the lariat over his left shoulder, he held out his hands to the would-be tobacco smokers, took the paper in his left, and shook off the tobacco, and brought the pouch up in his right hand for closer inspection.

"You boys never heard of Bull Durham?" he asked.

"We couldn't afford . . ."

"Ain't nothin' wrong with what we got!" shouted the blow-hard on the railing.

Matt sprinkled tobacco onto the paper, tightened the pouch by pulling the cord with his teeth, and pitched the Kentucky Standard to one of the gum-chewers. He licked and sealed the cigarette, and stuck it in his pocket.

"You ain't gonna smoke it?" asked the other gum-chewer.

"I don't want to get sick, which you boys will be if you smoke that shit."

Their mouths hung open at the profanity, and

Matt moved to the fence, looked for a gate, gave up, and climbed the rails to peer over the side. His audience of boys quickly joined their two cohorts on the fence.

"Black Angus," Matt said. "They brought those over from Scotland years ago." He dropped over the side.

"Ewwwwww," one of the kids said. "He stepped in cow- . . ."

Matt grinned. "Happens all the time."

The big Angus, alone in the pen, lifted its head, snorted, and moved to the far side.

"What do you want me to do with him when I'm done?" Matt asked.

"Rope the bull again," said a new, squeaking boy's voice.

"Steer," Matt corrected, "not a bull. Though I wonder why he's in here by his lonesome."

"What's a steer?" said one of the kids, and Matt had to remember that these were city boys, not ranch kids or farm boys. Which reminded him of just how big Denver had grown.

"An unfortunate bull," Matt said, "like a capon's an unfortunate rooster."

"What's a capon?" the leader asked.

"He just tol' you," said the big kid with the bigger mouth. "An unfortunate rooster."

Shaking out a loop, Matt moved through cow droppings, and the kids fell silent. The steer, which had to weigh fifteen hundred pounds or more, ducked its head, and started moving toward the far side. "This is why cowboys ride horses!" Matt called out, and moved toward the steer. When it bolted toward the fence, Matt let the loop sail. It bounced off the steer's head, but the big black kept running, and Matt laughed when the gum-chewers and two others leaped off the fence before the Angus stopped, turned, and snorted.

Unfortunately, the jackass of the kids kept his seat. "See," he said with a harsh laugh. "I told you he ain't no cowboy."

Matt started gathering the rope. "Problem is," Matt said, "back in my day, the cattle we roped had horns." He stretched his arms out to give the boys a sense of length, and history. "Huge horns that'd tear chunks out of your horse's hide and your own legs if you weren't careful." He got a smaller loop on the hemp, and moved through the muck and hay as the steer trotted back from the kids. He let the animal pass without wasting a throw. "Kim Buchman said over and over you always missed your first throw just to let the son-of-a-gun get overconfident," Matt said, smiling now, remembering and liking the feel of a lariat in his hands, even without gloves. "Kim also said that if nobody saw you get bucked off, you weren't bucked off." The steer darted, and Matt's eyes followed the big Angus. "Always liked the way Kim Buchman thought." Matt remembered that he wasn't on a horse, and that the Angus didn't have horns, and he let the loop fly again, reading the animal better, giving it a bigger lead. The loop connected, the animal snorted, turned, and Matt let his end of the long rope drop.

The steer circled around, dragging the lariat, past the stunned boys, past Matt, and stopped at the back of the pen.

"You didn't catch him," the big punk said.

"You didn't say catch him. You said rope him. I did." He brushed his hands on his trousers. "There's no saddle horn for me to make a few dallies. And if I wore a suit covered with cow dung into my landlady's house, she'd throw a hissy fit."

"What's a horn?"

"What's does dally mean?"

"What's a hissy fit?"

"That's my pa's rope."

That comment caused Matt to smile broadly. He nodded at the loudmouth. "Well then, I guess you better go fetch it. Otherwise, you'll have a lot of explaining to do to your old man."

From down the alleyway, a voice bellowed: "What are you damned kids doing up there?"

The boys, even the big one, leaped off the fencing and tried to run.

"Stop! Stop or I'll shoot."

That prompted a few sobs, gasps, and one: "We

ain't doin' nothin', mister." Matt looked at the steer, at the rope, and decided his boots and pants were messy enough. He moved to the fence, climbed up, and saw the back of a thick-armed man in rubber boots who had four of the six kids backed up against the fence on the other side of the alley. The two gum-chewers, the fastest of the lot, were beating a path toward the river.

When Matt cleared his throat, the big man, who held a small club but no gun, turned around and froze as Matt climbed over the fence.

His Adam's apple moved a few times before the man pushed back his railroad cap and said: "What the Sam Hill is you doin' here?" He gestured at the boys. "With these street rowdies?"

"Showing them how to rope." Matt hooked his thumb toward the pen containing the Angus steer. "See for yourself."

"That's trespassin', mister, and I'll have the law on you and these hoodlums."

Matt pulled back his coat. The man's eyes bulged as he saw the badge. The kids saw the star as well, and that's when they got their legs to work and thundered after the gum-chewers.

"Hey!" the big man shouted. "Stop or I'll . . ." He looked over his shoulder at Matt.

"Let them go," Matt said. He fished out the cigarette he had rolled and offered it to the stockyard worker. "They meant no harm. There's a lariat around the neck of the steer in there. One of those boys'll likely get his hide tanned by his pa for losing a good lariat. That'll be punishment enough."

The man's fingers almost dropped the cigarette. "You roped a steer?"

"Haven't lost my touch after all."

"Afoot?"

"Didn't have a cow pony handy." He nodded, and found his way down the path. By then, all six boys had disappeared.

He tipped a shoe-shine man outside the Brown Palace two bits for the job the gentleman did on his boots, grabbed his dinner at a café on Larimer, where he was pleased to see not one patron reading the *Morning Herald*. He smiled at the memories his adventures in the cattle pens at the stockyards brought, and he thought about Lawrence Tarleton and his dead brother-in-law. Reluctantly, he returned to work, but stopped at a telegraph office and paid to send a wire to Liberty Rawlings in Durango.

TELL ME ABOUT COLE STEVENS STOP FOUND ON RESERVATION NEAR IGNACIO STOP EARLY MARCH STOP

He signed it, let the telegrapher figure out the cost. The man's eyes widened behind his bifocals, and he looked up and said: "Marshal, you could have this sent from your office."

"I know," Matt said, though he couldn't figure out quite why he did not want Carter Bowen III to send this particular telegram.

"When I get the reply, do I bring it to the federal courthouse?"

"Yeah," he said reluctantly, trying to dismiss any suspicions he had about Bowen . . . Perelman . . . Dawson . . . and Luther J. Wilson. Nor did he want to send it to the boarding house, and become a bigger nuisance to Jean McBride.

Heading back to the office, Matt glanced inside the windows at Magawley's as he walked past the saloon, and defeated the urge to go inside—curse the *Morning Herald*—and treat himself to something stronger than Madeira.

At the office, Carter Bowen III handed him the messages and telegrams, which Matt read while standing over the secretary's desk. The U.S. attorney general's said simply: **DO NOT EMBARRASS THE PRESIDENT OR ME.** That was clear enough. Luther Wilson was a bit more cheery. **DENVER HERALD PRINTS NOTHING BUT LIES. READ THE CATTLEMEN'S CLARION.** There was a hand-scribbled note from Caleb Dawson that said, if Matt could make out the scrawl, the chief deputy was on his way to Fort Collins to chase down that counterfeiter. And a woman at the *Morning Herald* wanted to know if he cared to comment on the article from this morning's edition. Matt took a pen off Bowen's desk and wrote: *You didn't think to ask me last night, or the barkeep, what I drank. Did you?* Changing his mind, Matt dropped the notes into the trash, even the one he had written for the reporter.

"You don't want to send that?" Carter Bowen III asked.

Matt shook his head. "I gave up battling windmills about a year after Jeff Hancock died," he said, and stared at the coffee cup on the secretary's desk. He had forgotten all about it.

"What is the maximum sentence for stealing a coffee cup?" Matt asked.

The secretary remained befuddled, and Matt lifted the cup, empty and clean. Yes, Carter Bowen III was efficient. "Oh," the little man said before he began stuttering until Matt thanked him for washing his landlady's cup. Matt retreated to his office, where he spent the rest of the day reading *Munsey's Magazine*, hoping to find a poem by Lawrence Tarleton.

Even though the shoe-shine man had worked magic on the boots, Matt wiped the bottoms furiously before he entered the McBride home, and looked down the hallway.

"Marshal?" Jean McBride called out from the

formal parlor, and Matt turned to find her sitting next to a pudgy man with silver hair and the eyebrows of a Scot. She rose, and turned toward the man who brought a tumbler of whiskey to his lips. "This is my husband, Marshal, Reginald McBride. Reggie, this is the new federal marshal for our state, Matthew . . ."

The silver-haired man slammed the empty tumbler to his thigh, laughed, and began singing.

> **Matthew Johnson,**
> **Was wounded in Franklin.**
> **Powder and ball,**
> **But he gave his all.**
> **Matthew Johnson,**
> **Rode west from his kin,**
> **But war followed him.**
> **His legend grew tall.**

Reginald McBride had trouble standing, but he managed, and extended his hand after shoving the flask to his left. "A pleasure to . . ." The train of thought was lost as Matt briefly shook the drunk's hand. "Are you . . . enjoying . . . your accommodations?"

"You have a beautiful house," Matt said. "And your wife is a wonderful cook."

"Yeah?" He looked down at Jean, who focused on the designs in the parlor rug. Matt felt her shame, and wondered if this was how he made

Darlene feel all those years ago. He didn't think about his wife too often, mainly because when he did think about her, he also pictured the two daughters he had not seen, or heard from, in years. And the only time he heard from Darlene was when she needed more money. "Well . . ." Reginald McBride raised the hand holding the flask. "How about a snort, Marshal?"

He had shoved both hands inside his trousers pockets after shaking with Mr. McBride, and it took all he could do not to jerk out the right hand, snatch the flask out of Reginald McBride's fingers, and drink the liquor down.

"Thank you, but I have some work to do in my room, and a clear mind is in order." Which was a lie. He didn't have a damned thing to do, but he had made it days without a sip of even a beer— which had to be a record.

"Let me fix your supper." Jean finally looked up, but Matt could not meet her gaze. The dampness in her eyes hurt him too much.

"No need," he heard himself saying. "You should visit with your husband. I can fix my own meal . . . if the other boarders do not mind."

"There are no other diners tonight, 'Matthew Johnson, United States Marshal,'" Reginald said, singing the last words. "Everybody decided to eat out."

"We could dine with you," Jean whispered.

"Only if the bastard has a drink with me first."

The flask shot out again, and Matt gripped the lining of his pockets tightly.

"Reginald . . . ," Jean said tightly.

"No, thank you again," Matt said. "It was a pleasure meeting you."

"The pleasure, like the Scotch, is mine, 'Matthew Johnson, United States Marshal.' " Again, Reginald McBride sang the words to that damned song, then added: "You are a Southern gentleman, deep down, that's a fact. I never would have suspected it."

He might have said more, but Matt nodded again at Jean, and started out of the parlor, only to stop, reconsidering that look in his landlady's eyes. Turning slowly, he looked at the couple and said: "Well, maybe I could visit with y'all a spell."

"Delightful." Reginald McBride shoved the flask toward Matt, who again shook his head. Jean gave Matt a look of thanks, as if he had ridden to her rescue like the Matthew Johnson of the early dime novels.

He found the coffee pot, and slowly retrieved the cup he had borrowed from his overcoat pocket, showing it to Jean. "Just," he said, "so you don't think I'm a thief."

"Huh?" the drunkard said. Matt couldn't tell if Jean recognized the cup. Giving up, he removed his overcoat, draped it over the back of the chair, and finally sat down with coffee he didn't want.

119

Listening to Reginald McBride tell incoherent stories, he kept glancing at his landlady, but her blue eyes were focused on the rug.

He sipped coffee. Jean still stared at the rug. Reginald McBride talked and drank, but not for long—not after all he had consumed before Matt reached the boarding house. Thirty minutes later, the man's head fell back, and he started snoring.

Jean McBride let out a sigh of relief.

"I'm," she said, still looking at the floor, "sorry."

"You have no need to apologize, ma'am." Matt rose. His gut tightened. *I've lost count of the number of people I should apologize to. Darlene. My daughters. The people of Idaho. Jeff Hancock.* "I can take him to your room, ma'am."

"No." She looked strong and frightened at the same time.

"You can't leave him here. You have other guests."

"But . . ."

"Missus McBride," he said, "if you knew how many times people hauled my drunken arse . . . pardon the language . . . to bed or jail or just off the sidewalk and into a ditch . . ." He frowned, looked at the flask Mr. McBride had dropped, and wished it weren't empty, that he could take it to his own room and forget about this day. Just as he knew Jean McBride wished she could forget this evening.

"I wasn't exactly . . . sober . . . when I wound up on your swing," he said. "I apologize for that, ma'am. It was disrespectful. It was stupid. And . . . I haven't had a touch of liquor since."

She did not meet his stare. "Thank you," she said, then whispered more to herself. "Reggie never apologizes."

"I'll get him, ma'am. Follow you, put him on the . . ."

"Sofa," she said, standing now, and she stepped into the foyer.

In his room, Matt undressed, and read Walt Whitman for an hour before finally drifting off to sleep.

The ringing in his head made him groan, but he swung his legs over the bed, and reached for his Waltham before he waked enough to realize the sound did not come from his repeater. Footsteps rose above the damnable racket, followed by a woman's voice that must have silenced those bells.

More footsteps, then a tapping on his door, and the soft voice of Jean McBride: "Marshal?"

By then he was coherent enough to speak. "Yes, ma'am."

"It's for you, Marshal."

What's for me? he thought, but Jean McBride answered: "The telephone."

CHAPTER NINE

Barefoot, and dressed in pants and a coat over his nightshirt, Matt felt his face flushing as he found the damnable monstrosity in the hallway. Thankfully, Jean hurried away, leaving Matt alone as he struggled to understand what the hell somebody was saying into his ear.

He quickly woke up, listened, trying to fathom everything. "All right," he said when the voice stopped squeaking. "I'll get down there on the first train available." When he hung up the ear piece and turned around, Jean, in a robe over her nightgown, held out a cup of coffee.

Taking it, he smiled. "Thank you, ma'am."

"Thank you." She gestured at the cup Matt held. "I didn't even know it was missing."

While Matt looked down at the cup, she asked: "Bad news?"

"Railroad trouble in Trinidad. I have to get down there."

"I'll make you some breakfast."

"You don't have to."

"I want to."

He sipped the coffee, tried to smile, and said: "What time is it?"

"A little after five." She smiled. "I was up

122

before the telephone began making that racket. I'll fix you breakfast."

"Not much, ma'am," he said, and watched her head down the hall, thinking: *You stupid son-of-a-bitch. Don't look at her that way. She's a married woman, you're a married man . . . at least according to the law and the church . . . and her damned husband is sleeping off a drunk just a few doors down.*

"Call me Jean," she said before she disappeared.

Late that night, he stepped down onto the platform of the railroad station in Trinidad, finding a horde of Army soldiers, most of them green as June mint, all of them shivering in the cold of a late spring freeze.

"What's your business here, ma'am?" one demanded of a woman in black.

"A funeral," she said.

"The son-of-a-bitch got what he deserved, ma'am," the soldier barked.

"My mother," the woman said, her voice strong, "was eighty-two years old, but I still do not believe that she deserved the cancer that called her to Glory."

The man blinked, but his attention changed when Matt stepped out of line and approached a rough-hewn fence that had been erected around the depot. Nervous, freezing soldiers unlimbered their rifles without orders, and pointed them at

Matt, who did not stop, even when the leader of the greenhorns stepped away from the woman, and barked: "Stay in line, mister."

The bluecoat reached to unfasten the flap on his holster when Matt stepped underneath the street lamp, and pulled away his coat to reveal the badge. *This,* he thought, *is getting to be a habit.*

"I'm Matthew Johnson," Matt said, "United States marshal."

The hand froze on the flap. The soldiers quickly brought their rifles back to their shoulders.

Turning to the woman, Matt removed his hat and said: "I am sorry for your loss, ma'am, and I apologize for the witlessness of today's youth. It was a long train ride, ma'am. Can I hail you a hack?"

"None's running, Marshal," the leader of the soldiers said. "Suspended. We got a curfew."

Matt turned to the bluecoat. "Well, then, Corporal. I guess that means you and two of your troopers will have the honor of escorting this woman to home or hotel."

Someone left the saloon across the street, his boots clopping on the cobblestone road as he made his way over to the depot.

"But . . ."

"That's an order, mister." He looked back at the woman. "If that's all right with you, ma'am."

"I'd rather be escorted by a gentleman such as

yourself, Marshal," she said, and her eyes flashed venom as she considered the soldiers.

"It would be my honor, ma'am, but I think it best for me to stay here and keep some semblance of dignity and honor in Trinidad for the night."

By then, Caleb Dawson had stopped at the gate of the depot's makeshift fence.

"Move, soldier," Matt told the corporal.

"But Capt'n Reagan tol' us . . ."

"I'll explain to your commander where you are, after I explain to your captain how the federal government will handle the rest of this situation."

Grinning, Caleb Dawson opened the gate and let the three bluecoats escort the lady down the boardwalk. Matt waved the four other passengers through. "You'll have to get where you're going by ankle express," he told them. "There's a curfew because of the strike, so get to your homes or hotel quickly, and do not stick your nose out the door until dawn."

"How 'bout that saloon?" one man called out.

"Deputy Dawson was closing that establishment. Go home."

After the passengers had moved on, Dawson grinned. "You ain't bad at hoodwinking greenhorns," he said, staring as the soldiers escorted the woman. "I wonder what he'll do when he learns that you ain't supposed to give orders to no troopers."

"I am in charge of keeping the peace." Matt

nodded at the groggery. "Why isn't that place shuttered?"

"Figured you'd want it open after that long ride from Denver. The mayor, Captain Reagan, and the station manager for the D and RG was convening at Bevans's."

That craving hit him hard, and he could taste bourbon already, but even his mother had nicknamed him Hard Head, and no one could ever question his will—although for the past decade or so, it has usually been his will to find a damned drink.

"I need to get my grip from the porter," Matt said, and he tilted his head to the station house. "Why don't you herd the captain and the rest over here? Then have Bevans, or whoever is running that place, close up for the night. Since Trinidad seems to be under martial law."

The coffee tasted like crap, but it was hot, and after Matt shoveled coal into the stove, the station house turned almost tolerable. Taylor Leach, stationmaster for the Denver & Rio Grande in Trinidad, explained the situation in town, but Matt had figured out most of that already.

Last summer, the American Railway Union had organized a work stoppage after the Great Northern Railroad had forced wage cuts on all employees. After two weeks with no workers, the union and the railroad went to arbitration,

126

where the surprise ruling sided with the workers.

"Never should have happened," said Leach, who had left Bevans's establishment with a full bottle of Old Overholt. "Got 'em all uppity."

Traveling on a series of trains all day and most of the night, Matt had read in the newspapers that the Pullman Car Company had started a wildcat strike.

"We put those damned fools in their place." Leach took a large pull from the bottle, coughed, and shook his head. "Thought we had everything under control. And now . . ."

"We don't want to see what's happening in Chicago happen here," Captain Reagan said.

What had happened in Chicago, Matt remembered, was that strikers had overturned a milk train in the center of town, and set fire to the cars.

"You can deputize every man I got working for me, Marshal," Leach said. "I can have them here in . . ."

Matt silenced him by lifting his hand.

"What happened to the telegrapher?" Matt asked.

Most of the railroad telegraphers were members of the American Railway Union, Matt knew, and, when Judge Perelman had telephoned the boarding house, he said a Union Pacific telegrapher had been shot and killed in Trinidad, and that rioting was imminent.

"The bastard came at me with a crowbar, Matt," Dawson said, putting his hand on the butt of his Remington revolver. "I had to defend myself."

Matt nodded but said: "Yet, in Pueblo, when I got delayed again, folks were saying you shot the man because he wouldn't serve you a drink."

"That's a damned lie, Matt, and you know it."

"Maybe." He sipped wretched coffee, and thought back to his cowboying days in Idaho— this coffee might have been just the way he liked, but after a short while in Denver, he had grown used to Jean McBride's fixings. He looked at the captain. "But who brought the soldiers in?"

"Colonel Schmidt ordered me here," the bluecoat captain said. "We're under martial law."

"Only the governor can declare martial law," Matt said.

"Well, I'm sure he must have. Colonel Schmidt did not . . ." Seeing Matt's head shaking, the officer fell silent.

"According to the telegram that reached me in Pueblo, our governor is furious that someone brought in the Army and suspended *habeas corpus* without even talking to him." Matt set the tin mug down. "The governor seems to think I issued those orders. When I happened to be in peaceful slumber."

He let the silence linger. "Maybe," Dawson said. "Well, it must have been Judge Perelman."

"Judge Perelman didn't say he did when he

used that damned telephone to wake me at five this morning and order me down here."

The quiet stretched to an uncomfortable level before Matt looked at his chief deputy and said: "I thought you were tracking that counterfeiter in Fort Collins."

"Trail turned cold," Dawson answered.

The door opened. Heads jerked, and a man in an overcoat and porkpie hat stepped inside. Tall, mustached, looked to be Mexican, or at least partly, the man spoke in a thick accent: "I am Porfirio Hernandez. Marshal of Trinidad."

"I'm Matt Johnson, federal marshal for Colorado," Matt said.

"It is an honor, *señor*."

"The honor is mine, sir." He gestured to the coffee pot, but the lawman shook his head. Matt's respect for Porfirio Hernandez grew. Nodding at the others in the room, Matt explained: "We were just trying to figure out our best way to handle things tomorrow."

"The best way to keep peace," Hernandez said, "would be to send him far away." His black eyes bore through Caleb Dawson.

"What brought you to Trinidad?" Matt asked.

"I'm chief deputy," Dawson answered quickly. "Deputy Lewallen telegraphed me about the ruction with all those strikers."

The railroad man went at it again. "And we can't let the Denver and Rio Grande follow with

129

the Union Pacific and . . ." Until Matt told him to shut up.

"How many federal deputies are here?"

"Twenty," Dawson said.

Twenty. Matt recalled Liberty Rawlings saying Durango had two. He remembered something else, too. "According to the accounting papers Carter Bowen the Third put before me, there were four on this month's payroll."

"I deputized the others. To keep the peace."

"Yeah," Matt said. "Next time you decide to do that, you might remember that only the U.S. marshal has the authority to deputize." Matt knew that was true for county sheriffs, but he could not recall the laws pertaining to federal lawmen. It didn't matter, though, because he said it as though it were fact, law, and he suspected that Caleb Dawson understood federal law less than Matt did.

"Here's the way we play out this hand tomorrow." Matt moved to the captain. He felt better now, acting, moving, thinking at the same time. It wasn't much different than herding cattle, he figured. You anticipated. Mostly, you just learned how to react. "As soon as the sun peeks over the mesa, you take your bluebellies just outside the city limits. If a war breaks out, you ride with guidon flying and trumpets blasting."

"We're infantry," the captain said.

"Then run as fast as you can."

He turned to the town marshal. "How many deputies do you have?"

"Three at most times. Tonight, ten."

Hernandez was a man with great dignity, pride. He was a man, Matt thought, who would have made an excellent chief deputy for the federal district of Colorado.

"Is Lewallen one of your deputies?" Matt asked. Most federal deputies added to their pay by taking on the job as a local lawman, too, either in the town or county.

"No, *señor*." His eyes again trained on Dawson.

"All right." Matt found his coffee. *Keep drinking coffee,* he told himself, *and maybe nobody will see how bad you're shaking.* "Post your deputies around town as you think best. At church for the funeral. Probably the graveyard." He looked at the deputies. "Caleb, you round up Lewallen and all the other federal deputies here and have them report to me, right here, by six in the morning." He checked his Waltham, and figured he would have to sleep on the train ride home later tonight—if he were still alive. "I'll swear them in. Make them legal." Letting the watch slip back into his vest pocket, he turned to Leach, and asked: "First northbound leaves here at six-twenty, right?"

The agent sighed. "If anyone's still working for the Denver and Rio Grande."

Matt stared directly at Dawson. "You'll be on that train."

"He should be in my jail," the town lawman said.

"You did not arrest him, Marshal," Matt said, "after the death of that telegrapher. But you get the grand jury to act, you get an indictment, and I'll bring my chief deputy back myself."

"You just try that," Dawson said.

Matt turned. "Your presence here is like coal oil next to a hot fire, and I'm not getting burned black if I can help it."

"Matt," Dawson said, "I'm your chief deputy, and I been here a damned long time. It's these damned anarchists . . ."

Anarchists. Matt was getting tired of hearing that word.

"You're on that train in the morning, or you're on a stagecoach, or you're riding north on the back of a horse, rented, bought, or stolen . . . I don't give a damn . . . but you're out of the Trinidad city limits or you're out of a job. Savvy?"

Caleb Dawson's head barely moved, but that was enough.

Matt thought: *I'm not half bad . . . when I'm sober.*

CHAPTER TEN

Mouths open quickly to release
Mists of white
200 men, women, children
Hands in pockets, heads bent down
No songs
Too cold to cry
No sound
For maybe the world has gone deaf

It was too cold to write, too, and probably not the thing to do as the funeral possession moved down the hilly street in Trinidad. Even the newspaper reporters kept their gloved hands away from pencils and paper. They watched, shivered, likely wished they were in Bevans's bucket of blood interviewing each other over Old Overholt or a pilsner. Which, Matt figured, would have suited him, too, even if everyone thought he only drank bourbon. Hell, Matt would shoot down the rankest liquor in Rattlesnake Station or tequila in Tucson. He longed to see one of those ink-slingers bring him something to warm his belly, and the rest of his body. He thought of the poem he had written in his head, wondering if it were any good, if he would remember it when his fingers, nose, lips, and ears had thawed out.

"What are all those white ribbons about?" a correspondent for one of the national magazines whispered, breaking the silence.

The older reporter next to him sniffed. "A.R.U. The union, you know." He snorted. "Like a workers' march, instead of a funeral."

Matt studied the ribbons pinned to the overcoats. White ribbons outnumbered black armbands. He remembered Boise.

• • • • •

"Where the hell do you think you're going?" Sam Beckwith demands.

"I figured I'd see Jeff buried," Matt tells the head of the Idaho Cattlemen's Association.

"You step into that street, any blood spilled will be on your hands." He reaches for the bottle, fills a tumbler, then another, sets the rye on the counter, and picks up both glasses. "Hell, boy, most of the blood spilled would be yours." The rancher turns, looks at Matt, disgust in his cold eyes. "For Christ's sake, take that black bandanna off your arm. You ought to be wearing an Idaho Cattlemen's Association red ribbon to celebrate that son-of-a-bitch's passing."

"Jeff and I rode together too many years. We were friends."

"And if you were still saddle pals, we'd likely be planting you alongside him." The glass shoves before Matt. "Have a drink. Watch the show from this window."

He takes the glass, kills half of it. Beckwith looks through the curtains, smiles, sips. Matt turns away, kills his drink, and refills his glass.

• • • • •

When the last of the mourners disappeared up the hill and around the corner of the red-bricked building, a white cloud rose like a locomotive releasing its steam. Everyone must have simultaneously breathed out sighs of relief.

Now the reporters talked, scribbled notes, opened their flasks to warm frozen tongues. They talked about the news, the violence in Chicago, the fact that the Denver, Fort Worth & Gulf Railroad was running now too, along with the U.P., the Denver & South Park, and the Denver & Rio Grande.

The young correspondent sighed. "I was hoping for something damned more exciting. My editor might not want me to write anything, now."

"Blame it on those two peacekeepers," a Denver reporter said, glaring at Matt and Porfirio Hernandez.

The Fort Collins writer laughed. "Matthew Johnson, peacekeeper. Ol' Jeff Hancock must be rolling in his grave."

"That's a hell of a line," another reporter said. "I'm stealing it."

"It'll cost you a round of Scotch."

"Is Bevans's place open yet?"

"Not till Matthew Johnson says so."

"Bastard probably closed it so he could drink all of Mike's rotgut."

Those pettifogging reporters were still at it when Matt and the town marshal stepped out of the cold wind, and inside the railroad station.

Leach, the stationmaster who had kept his shades pulled down and his head out of sight during the funeral procession, lifted his head and let out a sigh when he saw the two lawmen, then went about his business and stoked the fire in the stove.

"Did you notice how many of those mourners had bulges under their armpits or on their hips?" Porfirio Hernandez asked as he headed for the coffee pot.

"And those who figured crowbars and iron rods were fine to bring to a funeral," Matt said. The stationmaster frowned, closed the door to the stove, and moved back into his office. Matt found the coffee pot and a couple of tin cups.

"You were smart to keep your deputy and your soldiers away," Hernandez said.

Matt passed a cup to Hernandez. "They aren't my soldiers. And Dawson definitely isn't my deputy." He sipped, frowned, and shook his head at the awful coffee. "How many strikers were arrested yesterday?"

"Nineteen."

"If you want to transport them to Denver, now's the time to do it. We can put them on the train, be out of Trinidad before those men and women are back from that funeral."

"Is that your recommendation?"

"It's just an offer."

They drank more coffee.

"That could lead to more violence," Hernandez said.

"And if they are still locked up, those men with firearms, crowbars, and iron rods could try to break their pals out of your jail."

"Neither I nor my deputies made those arrests," Hernandez said.

"I know."

They finished their coffee. Neither wanted more.

"I have no authority to release them," Hernandez said.

"Nor do I," Matt said. "But the magistrate could release them on bail, or merely set a fine for disorderly conduct."

"They were arrested by a federal deputy. I am merely a town constable."

Matt's eyes brightened. "Yeah, but they're being held in the town jail."

Hernandez reconsidered a moment before his own eyes showed bemusement. "What you suggest could get us both fired and, quite possibly, jailed."

"I've been fired and jailed before."

The Trinidad marshal bit his bottom lip,

considering, before he sighed, and shook his head. "Those men would not have money to pay the fine."

"I would." Matt grinned. "And enough to satisfy the judge, too."

"And what if those men, upon release from my humble jail, decide to burn down this city?"

Neither man smiled now, and Matt shrugged. "It's a gamble." He breathed in deeply, and exhaled. "Either way."

"You are not like the United States marshal that you so recently replaced," Hernandez said. "Nor are you like the Matthew Johnson I read about fifteen years ago."

"I never met the marshal I replaced," Matt said, "and I'm not the Matthew Johnson I was fifteen years ago." After Hernandez stared at his empty coffee cup for several seconds, Matt added: "I don't think we should wait for that funeral to end."

The town lawman's head nodded, and he set the cup on the stove. "Yes, you are right. Our priest, he does not like the cold, but the funeral is a full Mass. We have some time. Let us wake up the magistrate."

The fines totaled ninety-five dollars, plus twelve fifty for miscellaneous court fees, and two double eagles to the judge. Which left Matt with about fifty-three dollars to get him back to Denver.

In the Trinidad jail, Matt stood next to Porfirio Hernandez's desk as the town marshal's two deputies brought the prisoners out of the jail, lined them up, and had them sign receipts as their valuables were returned. The law had changed since Matt had cowboyed. Back in Matt's youth, when the jailer turned him loose, he might have gotten his spurs, revolver, and gun belt back—but certainly would not have seen any cash or coin that had been on his person upon arrest.

After each man signed his name and pocketed his possessions, Hernandez told him to go home. Most left without a word. One asked about the funeral, but Hernandez shamed him, saying: "Look at yourself. Would you want to look down upon your own funeral and see a man who stinks of filth and whiskey, who has not shaven, whose shirt is ripped, and whose nose remains caked with dried blood? Go home, see your wife, and your sons."

He liked the way Porfirio Hernandez handled himself. This was the kind of deputy marshal Matt wanted operating in his district.

The next prisoner shoved his change purse into his trousers pocket, and when Hernandez handed him his pistol, the man deliberately thumbed back the hammer, and started to shove the Smith & Wesson in Porfirio Hernandez's face.

Matt moved without realizing what he was doing. His left hand gripped the revolver, pushing it down, as the burly man jerked the trigger. Pain shot through Matt's hand, but no gunshot exploded. He could feel blood already dripping down his fingers, as the heavy weapon ripped flesh and fell to the floor. By then, Matt had slammed his right into the big man's face, feeling the nose give way. His knee came up into the man's groin. The man gasped, groaned, and as he doubled over, Matt slammed his head against Hernandez's desk.

That sounded like a gunshot, and the railroad striker collapsed in a heap. Matt stepped away, gasping for breath, feeling his body begin to shake. He raised his left hand, seeing the blood, the ripped flesh. Finding a handkerchief in his pocket, he clapped the silk over the gash. His chest ached. His hands turned clammy.

Porfirio Hernandez rose like nothing had happened, like he had not come so close to getting his head blown off. The striker's revolver had been a .45-caliber Schofield.

"That is a nasty wound," Hernandez said softly, calmly. "I shall take you to my home. My wife has been a good nurse to me, and she charges less than the *gringos* in Trinidad." Seconds later, as the railroad man rolled over and groaned, Hernandez brought the Schofield up and held the weapon over the man's face. The eyes took a long time before they focused.

Hernandez cocked the hammer, aimed at the

ceiling, and touched the trigger. "I removed the cartridges, *señor*," the lawman told the battered bully. "I am not *un pinche idiota*."

The last sentence, Matt figured, had been aimed at Matt, not the bully. Matt didn't know what Porfirio Hernandez had said, exactly, but had a pretty good guess. "No," Matt said, still clamping the handkerchief on the torn flesh on the back of his hand below the pinky. "You're no *pinche idiota*. But I am."

The town lawman smiled, before nodding at one of his deputies to drag the man on the floor back into the cell.

At the depot that evening, after they shook hands, Porfirio Hernandez thanked Matt for all he had done to keep the peace, and apologized for the hand injury.

"I hope the pain is not extreme," the lawman said.

"Thanks to your lovely wife," Matt lied, "I hardly feel a thing."

He gestured to the hills surrounding the town. "Those soldiers are still out there, just in case. I telegraphed the commanding officer at Fort Logan, said he should withdraw his forces. When he'll do that, though . . ." Matt shrugged.

"Tempers have cooled," Hernandez said, "but these labor wars . . . they can be like a volcano."

"Yeah." Matt breathed in, out, and made

141

his decision. "I can always use a good deputy marshal here."

"I have a job already."

"It would be when you're needed. That might be fairly often till these railroad troubles are settled, but, generally, not often. I think you'd be a good deputy. You're level-headed, and you'd be protecting your people."

"I protect my people now. Which is why I have this job."

"You could still have it. Both jobs. One for Trinidad. One for . . ."

"*Los Estados Unidos*," Hernandez said.

Matt cocked his head.

"Your federal government does not always protect my people, *mi amigo*," Hernandez said. "It was your government that sent your marshals, your soldiers here. And it was your deputy . . ."

"Not my deputy," Matt said. "And if you indict him . . ."

"But he was a deputy for your government." He put his hand on Matt's shoulder, smiling. "You are a good person, Matthew Johnson. You have a kind heart. You are nothing like the stories they tell. But this land, this *estado*, this once belonged to Mexico. And Mexico was the country of my father and my mother. Till *Los Estados Unidos* took it." He squeezed Matt's shoulder and let his smile grow. "I work for my people, my friends, my family, my city. I am no different than the

Utes to the west of here, you must understand. Your country took away the country of the Utes, and the Apaches, and the Navajos, just as your country took away the country of my father. Now I hear that men want to take the land of the Utes, cast them out like Moses, to wander the desert."

The hand came off, and the arm went down.

"I think I understand," Matt said, though he wasn't sure what the marshal meant about those Utes getting cast off the federal reserve near Durango.

"*Bueno.*" Hernandez nodded. "You, Matthew Johnson, are welcome in my home and my town always." He pointed at the bandaged hand. "And if you leave your current position in Denver, gladly would I welcome you as my new jailer."

They laughed, and Matt watched Hernandez until the lawman rounded the corner. He looked across the street at that rawhide saloon, yet somehow found enough strength to board the train. Five minutes later, he stood, grip in hand, before Taylor Leach. "How do I get to Durango from here?" Matt asked.

The stationmaster frowned. "Well, usually it would be simple. Take the train to Cuchara. Then the westbound to Alamosa. Then the southbound to Antonito. And the westbound would bring you to Durango, Silverton, wherever you want to go. Even Salt Lake City eventually."

"Usually?" Matt said.

Leach's spit sizzled on the stove. "Till our boys get the snow cleared, you can't get through La Veta Pass. And there's a ton more needing to be cleared at Alamosa." He looked at the map on the wall, though, frowned, and shook his head. "There's a chance you could ride up to Pueblo, cut west, but if you could even get to Montrose, and I'm not sure you could even make it to Gunnison, you'd still have to get . . . well, sir, it's just been a wet, heavy spring. Maybe. Even if you could make it, that way would take you a long time. Crews figure two weeks before the tracks are all cleared. And it's costing all these companies a fortune. Ask me, that's why all them strikers are stirring up trouble. They . . ."

"Stagecoach?"

The man looked hurt that he could not continue explaining the railroad's legitimate concerns. "I . . . well . . . I don't know of no regular runs, no straight runs to Durango from here. Reckon you could take the stage to Chama. Got to be a stage that runs from there, I'd reckon."

That sounded good to Matt, until he remembered how much he loathed traveling by stagecoach, the rocking, the turning green, the puking over his fellow passengers. "Where's the nearest livery stable?" Matt asked.

"You're thinking about riding a horse to Durango?" Leach took a step back. "At this time of year? . . . when you got a railway pass that'll take you anywhere in this state?"

Apparently, Leach had not remembered all the words to that damned song.

Matthew Johnson,
Found work as a cowboy,
In Idaho,
Yip-yip-e-i-oh.
Rode fast, road hard,
Made friends in cattle camps,
One's name was Hancock
So the story goes.

"You'd never make it, mister," said a black porter eating his supper in the corner. "Can't ride a horse over the mountains. You'd have to go south a long ways . . . and getting over Raton Pass ain't easy. No, sir, only way that I can see is like Mister Leach says. Stagecoach to Chama. Then you can take one of our trains to Durango. Or wait till all the tracks get cleared."

"We got snow plows," Leach said, "but every time we get a track cleared, we get dumped on again. Damnedest spring I ever seen in the Rockies."

"Where's the stagecoach station?" Matt asked.

Since that particular stagecoach company had no messenger riding guard on the Trinidad-Chama run, the jehu let Matt ride on top. Matt figured he just missed frostbite by a couple of hours, and he only threw up six times.

At the Chama depot, when he looked at the map, he saw that the train would take him right to a water stop called Ignacio. So he paid twenty dollars for a horse, fifteen more for a rig, bought some jerky and crackers for himself, grain for the horse, and let the engineer and conductor know that he would be getting off at Ignacio.

If the maps and Matt's guesses were close enough, it would be about a day's ride to Durango, where, Matt hoped, Liberty Rawlings or Luther Wilson would loan him enough money to get back to Denver.

CHAPTER ELEVEN

At the train station in Ignacio, Matt saddled his horse, nodded at two Southern Utes, watched the train pull out, and asked an Irish railroad worker for directions to the trail to Durango.

"Mister," the heavy-set man said, "don't you know that train that just left goes to Durango?"

"I wanted to be horseback." Matt grinned at the expression on the worker's face.

"That's the damnedest thing I ever heard." The worker spit out tobacco juice, and gave him directions.

There wasn't much to Ignacio other than that adobe depot, a leaky water tower, three privies, a lean-to, and two hardscrabble shacks that reminded Matt of sharecropper homes back in Tennessee. The Indian agency consisted of a two-story cabin and three empty corrals. At the agency, the agent proved to be little help. No dead white man had been found in Ignacio in the six months he had been living in this godforsaken blight of the nation. He had never heard of Matthew Johnson or any Cole Stevens or Lawrence Tarleton, and had never seen anyone matching the descriptions Matt gave him. Matt flipped the old man a nickel.

"What's this for?" the agent asked.

"For not knowing Matthew Johnson," Matt answered.

He tried the two Ute men, but neither spoke English, and Matt had never mastered sign language. He glanced back at the cabin, but decided he didn't want the agent translating for him, so he thanked the Indians anyway, and rode back to the railroad men. Their faces revealed that they figured Matt to be the laziest fellow ever born and maybe the strangest. He knew what they were thinking: *What man in his right mind would saddle a horse, ride thirty yards to the agency, then ride back to the depot?*

"A man named Cole Stevens was found dead here in March," Matt said. "Murdered, according to an informant of mine." Matt let the railroaders see his badge, and his holstered revolver.

"Murdered?" The men glanced at each other.

One of the younger ones laughed. "You just getting down here to investigate a homicide that happened . . . in March?"

The tallest of the men elbowed the laughing boy. "Lots of saloons between here and Denver."

Matt's expression held firm. "I just got this job, boys. And I'm checking things out for myself." He gave the description of Cole Stevens, studying the faces, and slowly beginning to think he was the damned fool these men thought he was.

Again, the railroaders looked at one another, not speaking, some shrugging, others cocking their heads, but no longer smiling or laughing. Finally, the graybeard of the bunch turned back at Matt. "Marshal," he said in a respectful tone, "no offense meant, but I think somebody's playing a joke on you. Last man to die here was Packer Pechous . . . oh, sixteen, eighteen months back. Got bit by a rabid coyote while he was drunker than Hooter's goat." He pointed to the graveyard Matt hadn't noticed. "I wouldn't call that murder, and Packer sure didn't look nothing like that Cole Stevens you described."

Matt's shoulders sagged, and he wet his dried lips with his tongue. If he thought he could find a bottle of whiskey at the agency, he would have ridden over right then. A floorboard squeaked behind him, and Matt turned, staring up at the stationmaster who stood on the platform, smoking a pipe.

"How about you?" he asked.

"Mister," he said, pointing the pipe toward the now distant train, "up till today, ain't a body stepped off a train here other than to take a piss since last October." The pipe now pointed at the agency. "And that was Mister Gottselig, and I bet he wishes he'd stayed on that train . . . same as me. I never heard of no Cole Stevens, and if somebody got killed here, well, most of us would be celebratin', 'cause it would sure have broke up the monotony."

He had one last shot, for a Ute woman wearing

a heavy coat rode up to the agency on a dun mare, dismounted, and entered the building. Again, Matt stepped into the saddle and rode up the road to the agency, swung down, and waited until she came out with a wheat sack stuffed with whatever plunder she needed. Removing his hat, Matt stepped toward her and said: "Pardon me, ma'am, but do you speak English?"

The two Ute men Matt had tried to question earlier moved quickly to her side, their faces about as friendly as a wild boar's. Matt rushed his words, explaining that he was the federal marshal, that maybe there was nothing to this, but that he had a job to do, and he just needed to find out if Cole Stevens had been murdered. . . .

He stopped, wet his lips, and swallowed. The name had sparked a bit of recognition. He was sure of that. This woman spoke English. But she looked at the two and spit out guttural words. The taller Ute eventually looked away from Matt and down at the woman. He spoke sharply, briefly, and turned back to let his black eyes show Matthew just how welcome he was on the reservation.

The woman turned, swallowed, and did not look at Matt when she spoke. "I am sorry. I do not know of this Cole . . . Stevens."

Matt gave her that same description.

Her head shook before he had finished. "No," she said. "Sorry. I am sorry. I must go."

Still holding the sack, she climbed onto the back of the horse, and rode away. He let the two Utes and the men at the depot watch him as he watched her. She followed the trail to the fork at a hill, where she turned east. Looking back at the two Indians, Matt nodded at them, thanked them again, though for nothing, and mounted the horse.

"Son-of-a-bitch," he said softly, and let his eyes follow the railroad tracks. He could've been in a warm coach. The horse snorted, and Matt smiled. After swinging into the saddle, he left Ignacio.

When he came to the fork, he looked at the trail that turned east. He could still see the woman on her mare, and he figured every man jack in Ignacio, even Mr. Gottselig at the agency, was staring at him, waiting to see. The two Utes were likely moving to their horses.

But Matt fooled them. He turned his horse northwest.

In some ways, the country reminded him of Idaho. White-capped mountains in the distance, the wild flowing river, and a landscape that revealed the arid Southwest but sprinkled with pockets of green vegetation, and a wind that felt as though it had blown all the way from the North Pole.

He had not done anything like this since back when he had cowboyed in Idaho Territory. Once,

Jeff Hancock and Matt had saddled up, drawn their time from a ranch, and ridden over to a place called Craters of the Moon—just because Bounce McMahon said that was something a body should see. This time, Matt had been smart enough to send telegrams to Denver so people would know where he was headed—even if he didn't exactly give anyone a good reason that explained why he had taken off for Durango.

When he thought about it, Matt knew he didn't have a good reason himself.

After leaving the river, he followed a juniper-studded trail that paralleled a small stream, knowing he had at least pointed his horse in the northwesterly direction toward Durango—unless the railroad man who had told Matt how to find the Durango trail had sent him somewhere else. The idea of someone giving him false directions brought a long dormant memory.

• • • • •

"What the hell put you two loafers in such humorous spirits?" asks Lundahl, the brewer, beer-jerker, and owner of what serves as the only saloon in Long Valley. "Before you've even sampled my latest batch?" He splashes amber and suds into two tin cups. "First one's on the house."

Jeff Hancock raises his cup. "We met a wayfarer on the ride down." He drinks. Matt does the same, and smacks his lips, even though this

152

might be Lundahl's worst beer ever. The sourness is repellant, but, hell, this beer at least is free.

"He was lost," Hancock says after wiping suds off his mustache.

" 'Course he was lost. Who else would be in this circle of hell?"

"Oh, he wasn't lost," Hancock says. "He said he was on his way from Idaho City to see Liam Bergström. Asks if we know him?"

Matt finishes his beer, nods at Hancock. "Jeff says . . . ' 'Course, we know him. Who don't in this country?' " Matt laughs so hard sour beer comes out from his nostrils, and as he turns to snort, cough, and wipe his face, Hancock picks up the story.

"So we give the greenhorn directions." Hancock's mug slaps against the bar.

Lundahl has stopped wiping the bar with his rag. "Where to?" he asks. Several moments pass before Matt understands the change in the beer-jerker's voice.

"Here, of course," Matt manages to say, still trying to get his nose back in working order.

"Just," Hancock adds, "in a roundabout way."

"This fellow," Lundahl asks, "he give his name?"

"Nope," Matt says, turning around. "We sure didn't ask."

"He'll be paying you a visit." Hancock holds out his mug for a refill.

Lundahl does not move. His blue eyes have turned into narrow slits, and the remnants of his latest brew have vanished.

"When?"

Hancock laughs. "Well, if he don't stray into some badger's den, I'd guess . . ." He looks at Matt, but Matt won't take his eyes off Lundahl. "Oh, tomorrow morning. Maybe afternoon." He cackles in delight, until the beer-jerker reaches beneath the bar and comes out with the sawed-off single shot, and thumbs back the hammer.

"You two dumb-ass sons-of-bitches. Get out of my place, get down that trail, and you fetch my brother back here or so help . . ."

Matt has fallen off the stool. He sees Hancock standing, his hand stretched high over his head. "Brother," Hancock cries out. "But he said he was looking for a Liam Bergström."

"That's my real name, you stupid peckerwoods, and the only family I got that knows where I am is my brother, who was running a hardware store in Idaho City. Now get the hell out of here and don't come back till you got Edvin with you."

Hancock jerks Matt off the floor, shoves him toward the door.

"And when you come back, you're damned well paying for those two beers I just served you."

• • • • •

He realized he had stopped and let the horse graze. Bounce McMahon would have given him

154

hell for that, and Matt smiled at that memory, too, and he wondered how many times he had heard that stove-up cowhand complaining: *The horse eats when you want him to eat, not when he feels like it.*

Or how many times Matt had fired back: "You ever been hungry, Bounce? And when you were hungry, didn't you want to just eat?"

Miles later, he understood why he had decided to travel to Durango, and why he had opted to ride horseback northwest from Ignacio. It had nothing to do with a dead man named Cole Stevens, and it had nothing to do with being a lawman. He just wanted to be alone. To be horseback. Like he had felt all those years earlier.

Cowboying came about by luck. Bad luck, maybe. Joining up to wear the gray at age twenty-one in 1863, defying his parents, who had hired a substitute to take Matt's place in the Confederate Army. Matt told his folks he was no coward, and that talk around Franklin had it that Ol' Jeff Davis and the Congress in Richmond planned to get rid of the exemption real soon because of the way the war was going, that Tennessee would be conscripting men like Matt to fight for their country. He might as well join up. He had, and was trotting toward Chattanooga with other replacements when they happened to ride right into a Yankee patrol. So without a chance to see the elephant, Matt found himself at prison camp on the Maryland coast. The prison's name was Camp Hoffman, but nobody called it that. At Point Lookout, better than ten thousand prisoners crammed into thirty acres at right about sea level. Fifteen men living, sleeping, dying inside a tent meant to hold five. Getting soaked by rains and high tide. Catching, eating rats to survive. Freezing in winter, sweating to death in summer. And learning all about things called dysentery, typhoid, smallpox, and scurvy but mostly—what everyone called "the itch".

Just thinking about it made Matt want to scratch.

So when that bluebelly captain came in to announce this opportunity for prisoners to get out of Point Lookout alive, Matt waited. Damned if he would be the first to desert the army. Damned if he would be the first Tennessean to quit. The first man stepped forward, though, followed by two kids probably not yet sixteen. An old man was next. Karl Stotz, a bunkie who Matt had managed to keep alive after Stotz came down with an awful bowel complaint, was next. Then two fellows captured with Matt carried another coughing cadaver in a blanket to the damnyankee recruiter. That's when Matt figured he had damned well better start moving his legs or he would be stuck at Point Lookout until he was dead—which might not be that far off.

"I, Matthew Johnson, do solemnly swear,

in the presence of Almighty God, that I will hereafter faithfully support, protect, and defend the Constitution of the United States, and the union of the States thereunder; and that I will, in like manner, abide by, and faithfully support all laws and proclamations which have been made during the existing rebellion with reference to the emancipation of slaves. So help me God."

"Make your mark on the dotted line," the Yank said.

Matt raised his eyes from the paper. "Would it be all right, sir, if I signed my name?"

He had enlisted in the First U.S. Volunteer Infantry for three years. Later, these old boys became known as Galvanized Yankees, but back during the War, they were called traitors or turncoats. Maybe Matt was a quisling, but he was also alive. By ankle express, trains, and steamboats, Matt made his way all over the country. For twenty-one years, he had seen nothing but Tennessee and a little bit of northern Georgia, and Maryland. Now, he got to visit Virginia and North Carolina—at least the coasts, where the volunteers pulled provost duties. Next he was crammed onto a ship bound for New York City; a miserable train ride to Chicago followed.

These United States, Matt came to realize, were a hell of a lot bigger than he had ever imagined.

He saw Wisconsin and Minnesota, chased after starving Indians, the remnants of the Dakota uprising that had started in the early 'Sixties. During the summer, he slapped mosquitoes; in winter, he realized what real cold felt like. Eventually, he and those remaining Galvanized Yanks moved down to Kansas to be sun-baked and wind-burned at Pond Creek Station, and finally to be mustered out at Fort Leavenworth in November of 1865—months after all those loyal Rebs serving under Lee and other Confederate generals had been paroled.

Instead of walking back to Franklin, Matt listened to gossip. Two discharged soldiers wanted to strike out for the gold country in Colorado's Rockies, but two others argued that the diggings farther north sounded even more inviting. Seeing Matt, they asked his opinion.

Matt shrugged. "Idaho's farther," he said.

The men glanced at each other. One of the backers of Colorado asked: "So you mean you like our plan better?"

Matt's head shook. "I mean Idaho's farther from this damned country."

All four men laughed. Thus, Idaho won out, and the men invited Matt to tag along since he showed sound judgment. After waiting out the winter in Denver, in the spring of 1866, the five of them drifted up to Idaho City. Matt remembered the short letter he wrote his parents.

Dearest Mother and Father:

I take pencil in hand to hope you are both in good health, as am I. By now you likely have learned that I took an oath to the Union, and have been stationed on the frontier for quite some time. Not wanting to shame you by returning home, I want you to know that I have become taken with a bout of wanderlust.

So I am off to see more of this country. The West is filled with promise.

I send you my love, and my best wishes.

Your devoted son,
Matthew

He told himself he would write them again, let them know about the fortune in gold he had discovered. But he never sent another letter to Franklin, Tennessee.

About a year or two later, realizing how hard it was to make a fortune, or even a living, panning for gold, a man named Rex Chesser asked Matt what he knew about working cattle.

"Not one damned thing," Matt said.

"You're hired," Rex Chesser told him. "I like an honest man. I'm herding two hundred head to a settlement called Hagem."

Over the next eight years, Matt cowboyed. He forgot about Franklin, Point Lookout, all those miserable days and nights and the blisters on his feet with the U.S. Volunteers. He forgot about his freezing fingers on Elk Creek. For eight years, he knew only horses and cattle.

A long time later, he came to understand that those were the best years of his life. At least till '76, when the Payette River War broke out.

He touched his spurs to the dapple, and gave the gelding plenty of rein. For a horse bought in a railroad town, the dapple had a smooth gait, and liked the freedom of a gallop. Matt felt comfortable—though he figured his legs and backside might rebel once he reached Durango—until the trail led up a ridge lined with junipers and rocks.

Reaching the crest, he pulled the dapple to a stop. Ahead of him he could make out men, wagons, horses, and he could hear the shouts.

CHAPTER TWELVE

The Matthew Johnson from Franklin, Tennessee, and the Matthew Johnson from the First U.S. Volunteer Infantry, and the Matthew Johnson from Elk Creek or the Payette River, and even the more recent Matthew Johnson from Tucson, Arizona Territory, would have ridden on, just cut a wide arc around the troubles, all the while remembering Kim Buchman's sage advice: *Don't stick your nose into what ain't your affairs.*

This Matthew kicked the dapple's sides and rode up to the men, wagons, and animals that blocked his path.

Two freight wagons, heavily loaded, hogged the road. A man in work duds and a woolen cap held four horses behind the wagons and off the trail toward the west. As Matt approached, the man turned and called out: "Rider comin'!"

Matt nodded at the horse holder, saw no weapon on him, and looked at the wagons as he passed them. Thick canvas covered whatever these men hauled. The two drivers sat in their rigs, shotguns leaning near the brake handles, and beneath their coats might have been belted short guns. Four other men in frock coats stood in front of the four mules pulling the first wagon. One pushed back the tail of his coat, and rested his hand on a

161

revolver's butt. Matt silently greeted those men, too, and kept riding up to what had stopped the wagons and horsemen.

A plain teepee rose in the middle of the road. Just one teepee of buffalo hide—pretty old Matt figured. He hadn't seen a teepee since up in Idaho, but that had been at a village, and there had been dozens of them. Like a city. This one sure looked lonely, but it did the job.

Rocks, trees, and one massive ditch prevented the wagons from going around the teepee. The white men could take down the lodge easy enough, but they would first have to deal with four men and two women, all Southern Utes, standing in front of the structure.

"Howdy," Matt said casually, still on his horse, for no one had asked him to step down. Neither the Utes nor the white men wanted him to linger. Their faces said as much.

The three youngest Ute men, all with their hair hanging in braids, wore a mix of Indian and white clothing: moccasins, Mackinaws, battered hats, deerskin britches or decorated store-bought duck trousers. The oldest man, whose thick, unbraided silver hair fell past his shoulders, wore work boots, striped trousers, coat, vest, tie, and a bowler. A young woman wore a calico dress with a beaded belt around her waist, a shining small stone—gold maybe—hanging from sinew around her neck, her raven-dark hair in braids. The older woman wore a similar colored dress, with plain moccasins, and one permanent scowl. A plaid blanket was draped over her shoulders.

Matt glanced at the white man whose hand still rested on the butt of his revolver. "They speak English?" he asked.

"I speak English," one of the young Indians said.

Matt looked back at the Ute. "What's going on here?" he asked.

"Is it any of your business?" said the man who refused to move that hand off his revolver.

Turning again, Matt studied the six men closely. The seventh remained out of view, but he had his hands full keeping the four saddle horses from galloping for Durango or Ignacio.

"This being the reservation," Matt said, "yeah, I think this could be my business." He let the reins drop over the dapple's neck, using his right hand to pull his coattail past the holstered revolver. Since the gunman didn't want to let go of his weapon, Matt settled his right hand comfortably on the butt of his revolver.

This stalemate did not last too long.

"We're surveying," said the oldest of the men. "We work for the Denver and Rio Grande."

"They have no right to be here," the English-speaking Ute said.

"You've got no right to stop us," said the man with the gun.

Kim Buchman's voice echoed across Matt's eardrums: *Don't stick your nose into what ain't your affairs.*

"Frank, go easy," said the apparent leader of these surveyors. "We want no trouble." The man tried to smile. "We are surveying a possible route to Pagosa Springs. Northeast through Chimney Rock. We have permission from the agency and most of the Southern Ute leaders."

"They have no right," the hot-headed Ute said.

"We got every right," the fiery surveyor said. "You're just living here because the government gave you this land."

"No." Matt had his back to the six Indians. Bounce McMahon would have given him hell for that, too, but Matt wasn't about to take his eyes off that kid who wouldn't leave his revolver alone. The voice, though, had not come from the young Ute. This voice sounded old. Obviously, the young Indian wasn't the only Ute here to speak English.

"No," the old Ute repeated. "We have always lived here. Once Sinawavi, our creator, who lived with Coyote alone in the world, gave Coyote a bag of sticks. Sinawavi told Coyote to take the sticks to a place beyond the hills and valleys. Coyote, Sinawavi said, should not open the bag till he was there. But Coyote did not listen to Sinawavi for he was always curious. When he

164

had traveled but a little ways, he opened the bag, just a small opening, enough to look inside. But the sticks were people, and the people escaped, speaking all kinds of languages, and away they scattered. Coyote managed to pull the string tight, securing the bag, but only a few sticks remained. Thus Coyote did as he was told, and he brought the bag here, and let the people out. The people were us, our ancestors, and the others became the tribes of our enemies, including the white men. There is more to the story, about what Sinawavi said, about how he punished Coyote, about what he called us, but that is all I have to say for now."

"That's great," said the hot-headed white man. "Let's listen to some other big windies. Come on, Mister Holland, it's freezing cold and we got work to do."

"We do have work to do, Marshal," said Holland, the oldest of the surveyors, and obviously in charge.

Matt nodded. "What makes you think I'm a marshal?" He had not revealed his badge.

Holland grinned. "Your fame is widespread, Marshal Johnson. You are Matthew Johnson, are you not?"

The kid slowly let his hand fall away from his weapon, and the other men spread their arms farther from their sides. *Just like in some of those damned dime novels,* Matt thought, but he answered—"I'm Johnson"—and this time, he let his left hand pull away the coat just enough to show the badge.

It was flattering to be recognized, of course, but most people thought of Matthew Johnson from the illustrations in half-dime and dime novels, wearing buckskins, with hair to his shoulders, and a mustache and goatee like Buffalo Bill Cody. Matt's hair was fairly well groomed, and he had never owned buckskin pants or a shirt in all his days.

"Then you will make these Indians give us the road?" Holland said.

"First," he said, "let me see your bona-fides. A paper. Letter from the Secretary of the Interior. The D and RG. Something that tells me . . ."

The hot-head started to reach for the holstered pistol. "You takin' the words of some red- . . ."

"Frank," Holland barked, and the gunman froze. The kid turned, and that gave Matt time to find his own revolver, which he did not stop moving until it was out of the holster, the hammer was cocked, and the barrel was pointed at Holland.

The other two men on Holland's left began reaching inside their coats, but Holland managed to recover from the shock of seeing a barrel aimed at his gut. "Stop it. Everyone just stop it. There's no need for gunplay."

Seconds lasted forever. Sweat beads popped

on Holland's forehead, but after six or seven lifetimes passed, his lips started to move.

"Marshal Johnson, if you . . ." Holland's voice sounded higher.

Matt cut him off. "If you've got a letter that gives you the right to be on the Southern Ute reservation, I'd be right happy to see it."

"There's six of us," Frank said. "Seven if you count Frankenheimer."

"And there will only be five when I'm dead. Maybe four." Matt smiled. "Maybe three. You think I made it through the Payette River War and killed only one man? Hell, you should read more penny dreadfuls. Drop the belts, hands up, and let's ride up to Durango. See if we can straighten all this out. Or show me some paper that proves you have a right to be on Indian land. Federal land."

"You're siding with these . . . these . . . these . . . ?" Holland no longer sounded so pleasant.

"I liked their story," Matt barked, which stopped Holland cold. "Sort of poetic. Don't you think?" Matt softened his voice. "But all you have to do is show me a letter. Even a telegram. Here's your final chance."

"We can get you a wire at Ignacio," Holland said.

"But there's no jail in Ignacio. There is one in Durango." His eyes hardened, as did his voice. "If you don't start leaving your hardware on the ground, I'm going to lose my temper."

"I hear he ain't nothing but a drunk," one man said. Matt couldn't tell who, but it didn't really matter.

"Drunk or sober, I can still kill most of you tinhorns. And those I don't get, these Utes will chop to pieces."

This time the silence felt longer.

"You think you can get us all the way to Durango?" one of the drivers finally asked. "Alone?"

Now Matt laughed. "I'm not alone." He kept his eyes on the surveyors, but called out to the Utes behind him. "Deputy job pays two dollars a day. Any of y'all interested?"

"You can't deputize Indians," Holland said.

"I can, and I will. Even the women."

Six Southern Utes rode with him, camped with him. The two women even took turns at guard duty. At the reservation boundary the next morning, Matt paid them twelve in script and coin, thanked them, and told his prisoners, still either driving wagons or riding horses, to start moving. The quiet white men moved toward Durango, keeping silent, though brooding and mad as hell. But to a man, they feared the Matthew Johnson they had heard about for so many years. If they didn't fear him, the Colt that never left his right hand scared them.

The old Ute rode up to Matt, nodded with dignity, and told him: "We will sing songs in your honor at our camp tonight."

Which made Matt relax, even smile. "I hope it's better than the song I've been hearing for seventeen years," he said.

Revolver in hand, he rode alongside the first wagon, with a grimacing driver and a stiff-backed Holland staring ahead as they entered Durango. Matt had the lead wagon stop at the Denver and Rio Grande tracks, where he asked a man selling plucked chickens for directions to the local jail.

They turned onto Main at the massive red-bricked Strater Hotel and had traveled about a block when Matt recognized a long-haired man in denim britches. Liberty Rawlings also spotted Matt. The young deputy marshal angled away from the handsome woman in a blue dress, and stepped into the street.

"Marshal . . . Johnson?" The look on Rawlings's face left Matt grinning.

"Liberty." Matt had again recalled the young man's name. He thumbed at Holland. "I have seven men here for the jail."

The deputy stepped back, astonishment masking his face. "Christ Almighty," he said, "you . . . you . . . you . . ." His face brightened. "You got my telegram."

"Telegram?" Matt sank back into the saddle. "Did . . ." He tried to think.

"Did you get . . . my . . . telegram?"

"Yeah. But . . ."

Aware of the crowd gathering around him, and envisioning some muckraking newspaperman printing that Matthew Johnson rode into town so drunk, he couldn't remember why he even came to Durango, Matt straightened in the saddle, tried to look ramrodded into the leather, not slouched in some drunken stupor. "The charge is trespassing onto the reservation," Matt announced, "and we'll cite them all for threatening a federal officer."

"That's a damned lie," Holland said.

"Tell the judge," Matt said.

"You'll have a hell of a time getting me to that jail," Frank said.

Rawlings grinned, but Matt read in the deputy's eyes that he didn't know what the hell was going on. Matt didn't either. Rawlings backed up, turned toward a café, and yelled through the open door: "Strongo! We got business out here!"

That name Matt remembered. Strongo Stroheim . . . Rawlings had mentioned him in Denver. When Matt finally met Strongo Stroheim, Rawlings had said, Matt would know how the deputy got that name. Once Stroheim stepped out of the café and into the street, whispers and gasps came from the wagon. Matt found Stroheim's

170

face rather pleasant, chiseled out of granite perhaps, but the corn-silk hair and baby blue eyes exuded a peaceful, pleasant feeling. On the other hand, Matt had seen foothills smaller than this brute, whose arms resembled railroad ties.

"Seven men for the calaboose," Rawlings said, and he drew his revolver. "You boys will walk the rest of the way. I'll have the wagons and horses taken to the livery we use. Strongo, if one of these men resist in any way, tear his arms off."

"At the shoulders or elbows?" the big man asked, his eyes gleaming, the accent familiar. Matt remembered now. It sounded a lot like Hugo Persson's, the briber from the German National Bank of Denver.

Matt eased out of the saddle, feeling the stiffness in his legs and lower back tighten, while trying to let nobody know how long it had been since he had spent that much time horseback. Strongo Stroheim's massive right hand swallowed his, but at least the man did not test Matt's grip.

"Where's that accent from, Deputy?" Matt asked.

"Sweden," the leviathan replied, "but I come from Dayton. That's in Ohio."

"Proud to know you."

"You need help?" Rawlings said.

Strongo laughed. "Seven men? You jest with me." Strongo glowered at the prisoners, who

171

quickly climbed out of saddles and wagons. After Strongo had herded them around the corner and began marching them toward the jail, Rawlings turned to Matt.

"You look like hell, Marshal," Rawlings said.

"And you haven't even seen my raw ass," Matt said.

CHAPTER THIRTEEN

Still, Matt made himself ride to the livery stable. That he blamed on his cowboy mentality. *Don't walk when you can ride.* Strongo Stroheim arrived shortly after two city policemen brought the horses and wagons to one of Durango's livery stables, which sprawled over several lots—but had few customers. The city of Durango, Matt thought, resembled the livery. Lots of buildings. Lots of prosperity. But not a whole lot of people.

Strongo handed Matt a receipt from the jailer, which Matt shoved into a mule-ear pocket on his trousers. After the city officers left, Rawlings looked at Matt and asked: "What do you want us to do now?"

Matt pointed at the closest wagon, and raised his head to admire the mountains and mesas surrounding the city. "Doesn't look much like rain," he said, although if those gray clouds dumped a foot of snow on them this evening, he wouldn't have been surprised. "I don't see any need for those tarps. Let's see what they're hauling."

When both wagons had been uncovered, Matt climbed into the back of the first wagon.

"Ever do any surveying?" Matt called down at the two deputies.

Two heads, one big, one small, shook.

"Me, either." Matt bent to read the label on one box, then dragged out several picks and shovels that had been loaded between boxes. "Not so as you'd know it, anyway. That's why my father sold the business. He should have given it to my kid sister. June was better at it than me. Pa gave up on me when I was ten."

After finding a crowbar in the next batch of tools, Matt grabbed it and began working on an oblong crate. Stopping to rest, he smiled at the look on his deputies' faces.

"Don't look at me that way, boys. I'm not just some dime novelist's or wayfaring minstrel's imagination. And I'm not a horrible beast, either, or wasn't to begin with. Came from a fine, influential family in middle Tennessee." The box opened enough for Matt to get his hands underneath the top. He pushed it upward, hearing the popping and cracks as the nails released their holds.

Matt didn't stop until he had worked his way to the front of the wagon. His eyes and entire body focused on the chore.

Then, while walking to the second wagon, Matt explained to Rawlings and Stroheim. "Pa would be pleased," he said. "At how much I remember, I mean. If you're surveying, you need a few things. First, there's the circumferentor. That's basically a compass. Then there's a chain." He bent down, lifted a bound rope, and tossed it onto what appeared to be canvas tents. "Chain. Not rope. It's called a Gunter's chain, lengths stretching usually a bit under eight inches, totaling sixty-six feet." He moved to the side, but by now had stopped snooping through most of the boxes, mainly because these crates held food supplies. Kegs of water, and one of what smelled like Taos Lightning, butted up against the wagon's front wall.

After climbing off the wagon, Matt tried to rest his sore rump on the gate as Strongo and Rawlings walked toward him.

"Now, remember, my father was a surveyor before the War," Matt said. "Like everything else, things have changed. Or so I'd guess. But I think you still need a chain and a compass, especially to survey a railroad's route through the state of Colorado, or even the federal reserve for the Southern Utes. And a transit or a theodolite, though Pa would not trust a transit if his job, or life, depended on it. And a level to help figure out the elevations? Never seen a survey crew without one of those."

He raised his arm and jabbed his thumb toward the first wagon. "Dynamite, picks, shovels, timbers, buckets, wheelbarrows, lanterns. That's what I found in that son-of-a-bitch. A few other tools . . . hammers, saws, things like that. Those aren't what I'd say you need to survey for a possible railroad line, either. Do you?"

"Those maybe are for mining," Strongo said, his accent heavy.

Matt's head bobbed. "A particular kind of mining," he said. "I spent enough time trying to find pay dirt in the mountains of Idaho. Like hundreds of other damned fools. But we mined for placer. Panning for gold."

"All the gold mines here," Rawlings said, "played out ten years ago. Silver was king up north . . . till last year."

"That's my understanding." Matt eased himself off the tailgate. "These boys want to dig a mine."

"Not silver," Strongo said. "The market for silver is dead."

"And gold?" Matt asked.

The deputies looked at each other, and Rawlings turned back to Matt and shook his head. "I just don't see there's anything that would make it worthwhile. Even on the reservation . . . if there was gold here . . . it would've been found ages ago. I mean, there might be a little bit, but not worth all this effort."

"That is strange," Strongo said after a moment's thought.

"Or stupid." Matt shook his head. "And Holland didn't seem stupid."

"No," the big Swede said. "No. I mean . . ." He turned that granite head to Rawlings. "Missus Shelby."

Matt waited, hoping his mindless banter had led one of the deputies to something important.

"Marybeth Shelby," Rawlings said, as though translating for Strongo. "She's a widow. Has a ranch east of here, borders the reservation. That's the other telegram I wired you. Which, I guess, you didn't get, either."

That damned implication tightened most of Matt's muscles. Liberty Rawlings was thinking that Matt had been too damned drunk to realize what he had received. Which, in most cases, would have been the truth. But Matt had fooled the gods of the universe, had not swallowed a thimbleful of whiskey in days. How many years had passed since that had happened? Fourteen? Fifteen?

"What about her?" Matt asked.

A minute must have passed before Strongo spoke. "She complained that four men in a wagon came across her land, cut her fence, but her two riders stopped them, drove them off her land."

"When was that?" Rawlings asked.

"Last week," the big man said.

Matt thought a moment, shook his head, and stared up at Strongo. "Trespassing on a private ranch isn't the business of a federal marshal."

"No." Strongo's mountain-sized shoulders shrugged. "She is a nice woman. Cute daughter."

Matt's laughter echoed Rawlings's, until

Strongo said: "But if they were going to the land of the Utes?"

Well, Matt figured, that was a possibility. Could there be gold on the Ute reservation? He thought of something else, and wondered how frazzled his mind had become. "Did you get that telegram I sent you?" he shot out to Rawlings. "A man killed. Cole Stevens. Reporter for some newspaper in Pagosa Springs. Found in March on the reservation at or around Ignacio."

"I got it," Liberty said. "Sent you a reply, but I guess you were on the way to Trinidad by then. There was no reporting of a dead man named Cole Stevens on the reservation. I checked with the sheriff and the town marshal. No trace of any Cole Stevens here, dead or alive. There was a murder, and an accidental death, but both those victims were identified by family members. No Cole Stevens."

Matt wet his lips. His stomach tightened, and he realized how hungry he was getting. More than food, he really wanted to taste strong bourbon right about now.

"Well," he said before letting out a long sigh. "Shit."

With the church bells across Durango sounding noon, Matt, Rawlings, and Strongo left the livery and settled at a table inside a Mexican café near the Denver & Rio Grande depot.

After sitting, Matt looked at his two deputies.

He breathed in deeply, exhaled slowly, and made himself smile before explaining to his deputies: "That dapple and paying Ute deputies to help me get those prisoners across the reservation has tapped me out." He forced a smile. "Now if there's any chance you boys could help me out, I might be able to have something more than coffee."

Laughing, Rawlings reached inside his vest pocket and let the coins jingle.

"How will you get back to Denver?" Strongo asked.

"Railroad pass," Matt said.

"What deputies?" Rawlings asked.

Matt smiled. "Utes."

Strongo put both elbows on the table—Matt's parents would have given the big Swede hell for that—and held his head up with two thumbs as he leaned forward. "You used Ute braves as deputies?" It wasn't so much as a question from Strongo, but an accusation.

"Four braves, two women," Matt said, "though the women I'd say were just as brave as the men."

"Is that . . . legal?" Rawlings asked.

Matt shrugged.

After dinner, Matt showed his pass and asked for a ticket on the next train that could get him to Denver, only to be told it would not be leaving until seven-fifteen in the morning. That meant a hotel room. Until Strongo suggested he bunk with him.

"I don't want to put you out," Matt said.

"Then put a little more in my next check," the big man said.

Matt laughed. "Let me see what I can do."

The pleasant feeling left them when they stepped on the street. Holland, Frank, and the five other trespassers Matt had arrested walked down the boardwalk. They grinned as they approached, and Holland stopped and nodded.

"Made bail already?" Matt asked.

"Judge dismissed the charges," Holland said.

"You must have shown him your orders," Matt said.

"Something like that."

Rawlings stepped forward, and Matt could see the redness on the back of the young man's neck, so Matt put his right arm out to stop the deputy while his left thumb hooked toward the livery. "You'll find your wagons and horses in that big yard over yonder. But I'm afraid some rats got into your wagons. Made a bit of a mess of your surveying equipment."

Holland's expression did not change. "That will happen."

"I think your theodolite is busted beyond repair," Matt said.

Stepping back, Holland lost his smugness.

"My . . . ?" He swallowed down his confusion.

"My mistake," Matt said. "Must have been somebody else's theodolite." Grinning, he pointed at Frank. "Just remember, there is an ordinance against the carrying of firearms in the Durango city limits."

"We're on our way out of town." Frank sounded just as haughty as Holland.

"Well," Matt said, "don't let us keep you."

Only after they had crossed the street did Matt lower his arm. Rawlings whirled. "How in hell could they have made bail?"

"Good question," Matt said. "Since the district of Colorado has one federal courthouse, and that's in Denver." Watching those men walk away free left nothing but the taste of gall in Matt's mouth. He looked at Strongo. "You put them in the city jail?"

"Yes. We have one jail here. City, county, federal."

"There's one federal court in Colorado, as you well know," Matt said, "and I don't think enough time has passed for Holland to wire Denver and get bail set or, like he said, have Judge Perelman dismiss the charges and wire back." He looked back at the livery.

"I will follow them," Strongo said.

"No," Matt said. "You didn't see those men that woman . . ." He snapped his finger, trying to recall the name.

"Marybeth Shelby," Rawlings said.

The big head shook. "No," Strongo said. "They were gone. Mary . . . Missus Shelby's riders drove them off. Long before I got there."

"But you got a good look at these boys." His head tilted toward the stables, indicating the recently released sons-of-bitches. "So I want you to go to Missus Shelby's spread, see if Holland and his crew might be the same boys that got caught crossing her land."

Strongo grinned. "I like that job."

"Figured you would." Matt turned to Rawlings, whose face brightened now with his own wide smile.

"I like my job." Rawlings smiled, then watched Holland and his crew cross the street toward the livery. "If they cross the reservation again . . . ?"

"Arrest them again. You want help?"

"I have a Fifty-caliber Sharps with a telescopic sight," Rawlings said. "That's enough help."

Strongo laughed. "He has not lost a turkey shoot in three years."

"Good," Matt said. "Who's the jailer?"

"Daymon Rosen," Rawlings said.

"All right. I'll have a little talk with Daymon Rosen. Liberty, you follow Holland . . . at a discreet distance. Strongo, you visit with Missus Shelby and her cowboys who ran off those trespassers. Maybe we can figure out what the hell is going on down here. But first, I need to know where the federal marshal's office is, and I need to know where the jail is, and I need to know where you bunk, Strongo, in case you're not back by my bedtime."

Rawlings pitched Matt a half-eagle.

"For supper," he said. "And a bath. And feed for your horse. Don't worry, Marshal. You can put a little extra in my next paycheck, too."

Daymon Rosen was gone. The jailhouse was empty. Staring at the vacant cells, Matt started thinking. He went through the trash can and the jailer's desk but discovered no telegrams, no release orders, nothing, and the coffee pot was cold. Daymon Rosen was no Carter Bowen III. The Durango jailer saved not one damned thing. Even the ashtray held no ashes, snubbed out cigarettes, or cigar stubs. Matt looked back down the corridor at the cells, all of the doors opened, and then found the ledger. The last prisoner housed here had been released three days earlier, for drunk and disorderly conduct. No Holland, no man named Frank, no other names were listed in the jailer's booking records.

Strongo? No, Matt decided. The deputy brought the men here. Although he had just met the big man, Strongo Stroheim might be the most honest lawman Matt had ever known. The prisoners had been delivered, Matt remembered. He reached inside a mule-ear pocket and withdrew the receipt Strongo had given him. The date, time, and names were right. Seven prisoners. The signature, unlike Matt's own chicken scratches, was easy enough to make out: **Daymon Rosen**.

He returned the paper into his trousers pocket, where his fingers touched something cold. The ten-dollar piece from Liberty Rawlings. Matt took a final look at the empty cells, then left the jail.

Walking up the hill, he began thinking.

> Iron doors, cold stone
> A place like this
> So often my home.
> No grunts, curses
> No laughs or tears
> And nary a song.

He ran it through his head again, so he might remember enough to write down later, and rewrite it. Reaching the top of the hill, Matt looked up and down the main avenue. The silver panic had taken its toll on Durango, all right, so an empty jailhouse was not surprising.

Walking, Matt tried out some more words, rejecting some, accepting—for the time being—others, all the while remembering those contests with Jeff Hancock.

"Your turn, Jeff," he whispered, and thought up another one.

This just can't be.
An empty jail
Is something to see.
No jailer, no Jeff
No Bounce, no me.

Matt finally smiled, shook his head, and said: "Well, I don't think that one will be up to the standards of *Munsey's Magazine*."

The woman coming out of the mercantile with a bag of groceries stopped and stared at him.

"Ma'am." Matt tipped his hat, enjoying the expression on her face.

He stopped quickly, though, and felt tension. Someone else stepped around the corner, and removed the cigar from his lips before his grin widened with pleasure.

"Matt Johnson." Luther J. Wilson stuck out his hand. "I didn't know you were in town. How the hell are you?"

He put his arm around Matt's shoulders, and steered him inside the saloon at the Strater Hotel.

CHAPTER FOURTEEN

Someone hammered sixteen-penny nails through his temples.

"Marshal Johnson." Jean McBride's voice shamed him. "Marshal."

He rolled off the bed, breaking his fall with his hands, which slipped, and he fell onto the rug, into partially dried vomit.

His own.

Matt thought: *I dreamed I was sick.*

The door pounded. "Marshal."

It was not a dream.

"The train, Marshal. You have that train to . . ."

Swearing, Matt struggled until he finally sat up. "Coming," he said, voice hoarse, tongue awful. The voice sounded nothing like Jean McBride. It had to come from some hotel worker. Matt grabbed the sheet, wiped his face, then found the bedpost, which he used to haul himself to his feet.

He was still dressed. His hand reached inside his pocket for the watch. "What time is it?" he yelled, upon realizing that he could not make out the time the Waltham showed.

"It's after seven," the voice told him.

Swearing again, he pocketed the watch, staggered to the dresser, and found his hat, and gun belt. His coat lay on the floor. He still wore his boots and spurs. He saw the torn blanket, courtesy of his spurs, and smelled his foulness.

"I'm coming," he said again, but barely moved.

"Best hurry, sir," the voice sounded behind the door, followed by footsteps disappearing down the hall. Vaguely, Matt remembered the room. He was at the Strater Hotel. At least, he thought he was. His memories seemed to settle on that point. He had spent the night in the Strater. It was a nice room, or had been, until Luther Wilson opened the door for him, laughed, and told him to have a pleasant sleep and a safe ride back to Denver.

He found the wash basin, and the cold water snapped some reasoning back to him. Matt looked around, spotted no luggage—of course there would be no luggage. All he had was his hat, and . . . His hand sank into the inside pocket of his coat, where he felt the comfort of his wallet. Not that there was any money in that bit of leather, but he did have a railroad pass that could get him to Denver.

Moving away from the bedding, toward the door, Matt weaved, his focus inconsistent. The hat remained on his head. He had gotten far enough away from the mess he had deposited on his bedding and on the hotel room's rug so the nausea faded. He opened the door, stepped out, turned around, and came back to the coat on the floor. It took him three tries before he had pulled the coat up, draping it over his left arm. For a moment, he thought he would just drop back onto the rug, maybe unconscious, maybe dead, but, either way, in some drunken stupor. When his legs felt like they could move, he made his way to the second-story hallway.

The maid stood waiting.

Matt stared at her, wiping his lips with his sleeve, fearing he hadn't gotten everything off at the wash basin.

The whistle from a locomotive made him jump. The maid just stood there, wearing what appeared to be a uniform, hair in a neat bun—the way his mother wore hers—and with her cleaning supplies resting against the wall. The maid looked older than Matt. And meaner than Jeff Hancock, after 1875—and when in his cups.

Matt shoved one hand into his pocket, felt paper, fingered a coin, which he brought up and studied. Several seconds passed before he remembered that the half-eagle had been a gift, at least a loan, from Deputy Marshal Liberty Rawlings. A door opened down the hall, closed. When Matt swallowed, the taste almost made him retch again. He moved past the maid's cart, and dropped the ten-dollar gold piece on her cart. "I'm sorry," he told her, but could not look her in the eye.

Downstairs, he moved toward the door. If he remembered right, if he had not been that damned drunk, Luther Wilson had paid for the room in advance. Good old Luther Wilson, Matt's champion. The arrogant bastard.

Outside, the cold air left him gasping. Thoughts flashed through his mind—there was the horse in the livery, that twenty-dollar dapple with the fifteen-dollar rig. He'd have a telegram sent from the train to Rawlings and Strongo, telling them to—hell . . . something—but first he had to make it to the station, which seemed to be, if he wasn't that hung over or still drunk, only a few blocks away. He could make it—if he didn't fall flat on his face.

It took forever to get to Denver. The train moved slowly westward because travel through the passes to the east, at Alamosa, La Veta, Gunnison, and Poncha, remained treacherous. Ironically, the fastest route seemed to be north. To Dolores and Vance Junction, to Montrose and Grand Junction, where they had to wait for some snowplows to make Glenwood Springs passable. In Grand Junction, Matt found assistance at the Y.M.C.A., where he managed to bathe, shave, eat dinner at the dining room, and even replace his shirt with a clean one. That he had just two Morgan dollars and a few miscellaneous coins did not matter once someone saw his U.S. marshal's badge. He signed a copy of *Matthew Johnson on the Owlhoot Trail; or The Mormon Baron of*

Marysvale. That's all the Y.M.C.A. wanted. Matt had never been to Marysvale. Hell, he had only passed through Utah on his way to Idaho and back.

Once he finally stepped off the train at Denver, he had to glance at a newspaper, the *Rocky Mountain News*, to figure out what day it was. Saturday. The clock at the depot told him it was 6:37. The banks would be closed. So would the federal courthouse. There was nothing left for him to do but walk to Race Street.

Walk. Again he considered how Bounce, Rex, and Hancock would ride him relentlessly for that kind of thinking. But Bounce, Rex, and Hancock were all six feet under. And besides, hell, after rocking, freezing, and sweating in those passenger coaches since Durango, the thought of stretching the legs—even for a one-time cowboy—sounded like a fine idea. Even though that meant he would have to walk past several saloons. *That shouldn't be a problem,* he told himself. He had not enough change now to buy even a draught of beer, and he might be Matthew Johnson, United States marshal, the man who shot Jeff Hancock in the back, but he still had some pride left.

By the time he stood on the sidewalk in front of the open gate to Jean McBride's house, the Waltham repeater told him it was 8:15. A long walk. He couldn't remember exactly where all he had gone, but his legs and feet told him that he had been walking the whole time. The wind bit through him, making him wonder if spring or summer ever showed up in the state of Colorado. Idaho might have been farther north, but it never felt this frigid. Or maybe Matt had just been younger.

Sighing, he moved toward the statues of the dogs, up the steps, to the porch and stood at the door. He could hear voices inside, and wondered if he should ring the bell. "Hell," he whispered, and opened the door.

"Matt."

Jean McBride sprang out of the chair in the parlor, and rushed to him. He smelled her perfume, took in those beautiful eyes, and remembered to sweep off his hat.

"We've been . . . *I've* been . . . worried sick about you. No word in a week. And the *Republican* had a story in the paper two days ago with a headline asking . . . 'Where Is Marshal Johnson?' "

Matt could easily look over her head and shoulders, but he kept his eyes trained on her. Didn't want to be rude. Although he wanted to know whose brown boots stretched across the parlor rug.

"*Republican*," was all he could say.

"Yes, and I had a reporter from the *Post*

knocking on my door three straight days. And someone from the *Rocky Mountain News* called today. Where have you been? Are you all right? Were you injured? You look a mess. When's the last time . . . ?" She stopped, stepped back, laughed. "Goodness, gracious, Matt, listen to me. I must sound like an old mother."

She sounded nothing like his mother, maybe a bit like his ma's servant, though she looked like neither.

"Are you hungry? There's plenty of food left. Let me . . ." Jean must have seen his stare, because she stepped to her side, and looked into the parlor. "Oh, for heaven's sake, John. John Kimbrough. This is Matthew Johnson, my latest boarder. Or I thought so. Till this past week."

Words finally came to Matt. "I figured you'd let out my room," he said. He wasn't sure how he meant it, as a joke, or a legitimate query.

Jean's laugh relaxed him. "I thought about it. Most certainly, I surely did." Yet her arm slipped inside his, and she steered him out of the hall and into the parlor.

John Kimbrough rose from his chair. Taller than Matt, but not by much, maybe a little older, too. His hair had more silver to it, and the mustache was a thick, well-groomed white. A cleft in the chin. Solid nose. Eyes maybe darker than Matt's own. He wore duck trousers stuck inside well-worn boots. No spurs, not now at least, but Matt could see the chiseled marks left by spurs over a good many years. Kimbrough's shirt remained white, well-pressed, with a ribbon tie hanging over it. Kimbrough stuck out a big hand with long fingers, and countless, rough calluses.

"It's a pleasure," Kimbrough said in a smooth drawl, from far south of Tennessee. Probably from the Carolinas.

The grip might have matched Strongo Stroheim's, but Kimbrough kept it brief. He nodded at the chaise lounge and side table. "Jean and I were just having some coffee. Join us, won't you?"

"I can fix your supper, too," Jean said.

Matt moved toward the silver coffee pot. It seemed the safest route for him to take.

"Oh," Jean said. "I'll have to get you a cup. I'm such a dunderhead. Usually there are plenty of cups here. I'll be right back."

The rug softened her footballs, and Matt and Kimbrough stood alone. Thin but solid, John Kimbrough had the legs and face revealing a man who had been horseback a damned long time. He looked, Matt soon reasoned, like Jeff Hancock might have looked had he reached his fifties or sixties.

"Jean speaks highly of you." Kimbrough motioned at a chair. A chair, Matt realized, that was farther from where Jean was sitting and closer to Kimbrough's spot.

Matt tried to find a comfortable position on the chaise, and even though a crate would have felt wonderful after all those backbreaking benches the Denver & Rio Grande put on its coaches, he kept shifting.

"Well . . ." He stopped fidgeting once he finally understood what Kimbrough had said. *Jean speaks highly of you.* He recovered. "Well, that's her Southern manners." He glanced through the doorway, but found no sign of Jean's quick return. "You're . . ." Matt took a stab. "Renting out one of the rooms?"

"I was." Kimbrough found his coffee, sipped, settled down into his seat. "Own a ranch on the Picketwire."

"That's . . . ?"

"South. It's actually the Purgatoire. Hell if I know how folks started calling it the Picketwire. My spread's two days east of Trinidad. Brought some beeves up to the stockyards. Winter's been hard down south."

"I know."

"I think we got hit harder than the mountains."

Matt nodded. "I was just in Trinidad." He stopped.

Kimbrough filled the silence. "I know. That was the last you'd been seen or heard from. According to the *Republican.*"

No, Matt thought, but then newspapers never got his life straight. He had sent telegrams from

Trinidad, from Chama, and from Durango. But John Kimbrough did not seem interested in Matt's whereabouts.

"I like those stockyards." Matt felt like a damned fool. He didn't have a damned thing to say to this John Kimbrough, so why in hell did his lips keep spitting out idiotic banter?

"Denver had needed them for a long time," Kimbrough said. "Fort Worth's are bigger. The stockyards, I mean."

"Never been to Fort Worth," Matt said.

"Never been to Idaho." John Kimbrough sounded about as adept at making conversation as Matt. They both looked futilely for Jean McBride.

"You from Fort Worth? Or Texas? Before you settled in . . . down south?"

"Does it matter?" Kimbrough sipped more coffee.

"Rude of me to ask," Matt said. "An old pard always said you never asked a body his name, never asked where he came from, never asked where he was going. I apologize."

"No need." Kimbrough again looked hopefully for Jean McBride to ride to his rescue. When she did not emerge, Kimbrough tried to explain. "For an apology." The hard eyes softened, and Kimbrough crossed his legs. "You being a detective and all," Kimbrough said. "Guess you get in a habit of asking questions."

Matt nodded, shifted, looked down the hallway again, and sighed as he made himself look into the brown eyes of that tall, lean rancher. Hell, why was he acting like a frightened schoolboy? He was Matthew Johnson. If this son-of-a-bitch didn't like things, Matt could haul Kimbrough's arse to jail. Instead, Matt heard himself say: "I ain't much of a detective."

Kimbrough laughed. "Tell you the truth, I ain't much of a rancher."

"Cowboy?" Matt asked, and the question seemed to make both men relax.

Kimbrough's eyes now brightened. "Reckon it shows," the rancher said. "Twenty-five years. Till a couple years ago when I figured it was time to settle down." He leaned forward and, not seeing Jean anywhere nearby, sank back in the chair. "My dumb ass."

"Eight years or so for me," Matt said. "Had a hell of a ride." The face again reminded him so damned much of Jeff Hancock that Matt's shoulders finally sagged. "Well, till the end, I guess."

"Yeah," Kimbrough said. "I heard your song." He snorted. "Got sung a lot in some bunkhouses I was in."

"It's not exactly my song."

Thank God, Matt thought, figuring that John Kimbrough thought the same way too, because Jean McBride came into the parlor, carrying a

196

tray heaping with biscuits, plus slices of beef, healthy triangles of pie, and four ears of baked, buttered corn. "You must be starving, Matt," Jean said. She set the tray on a table near Matt.

"Oh, goodness, I must be walking around with my head somewhere else." Spinning around, Jean moved out of the parlor, muttering: "Went in to get you a cup of coffee, and got so caught up fixing you something to eat, I forgot the dad-gum cup."

Matt could not even focus on the delightful aromas rising off the tray. In horror, he saw Jean vanish again, which meant he had to find enough courage to turn back to John Kimbrough.

The rancher appeared out of sorts himself, but at least he had a coffee cup to hide his discomfort.

CHAPTER FIFTEEN

He woke that morning feeling . . . alive. No shaking hands, no headaches, no worries. Matt shaved and dressed quickly, motivated by the smell of pancakes and coffee that wafted through the keyhole of his door. Ready for work, he slipped into the hallway, and moved quietly down the rug toward the dining room. His Waltham told him it was 6:30, and he didn't want to wake any of Jean's boarders who didn't have to be at work so early. John Kimbrough's voice from the dining room stopped Matt, though.

"You don't read the newspapers, Jean."

A coffee cup settled onto a saucer. "I read all newspapers. I just don't believe all the news I read."

"He's a drunk. He's a cold-blooded murderer."

"Not according to the *Cattlemen's Clarion*."

"Which spits out lies for the cattle barons."

"You're a cattle baron, aren't you, John?"

"I'm a rancher. There's a big difference."

Matt backed down the rug carefully, to his door, which he had not yet locked. He opened it softly, and closed it hard. Clearing his throat, he headed again down the hall, but this time he made his boots thud loudly. He smiled when he peered into the room.

Jean's eyes told Matt that her smile was forced,

and he cursed himself as a damned fool. He should have just walked out the front door and headed to the courthouse. Now, he stared into two uncomfortable faces. "Good morning," he said. He longed for a drink.

" 'Morning, Matt." Jean tried to be cheerful, while Kimbrough nodded and stirred sugar into his coffee cup. "We have pancakes and ham for breakfast," Jean went on. "Coffee?"

"Sounds delightful." Matt found the chair next to Kimbrough, who had been sitting across from Jean.

Jean filled his cup with coffee and went to the kitchen to bring his breakfast. "How many pancakes?" she asked. "They are big."

"Two," he said.

"Maple syrup, butter, or both?"

"Nothing. Just the cakes." She tilted her head with curiosity.

"Got my fill of syrup and honey growing up. Then after that Yankee prison camp, I could hardly touch anything sweet. Except for pies. Especially yours."

She disappeared through the door, and Matt turned to Kimbrough.

"Isn't there sugar in bourbon?" the rancher asked.

Mr. Childs of the Denver Telephone Dispatch Company and the apothecary soon joined the table, followed by the clerk, and the conversation switched to the news in the morning papers, and the weather in the higher elevations. Matt finished his meal quickly, thanked Jean for another fine meal, and rose.

Kimbrough also stood. "I'm leaving, too," the rancher said. "Mind if I join you?"

Matt and Jean studied Kimbrough hard, but Matt shrugged. "You got business in the federal courthouse?"

"It's on the way to the depot."

That made Matt smile. "Leaving town?"

"I'll be back." Kimbrough turned to Jean. "Might as well book my room before I leave."

Matt nodded at the two other boarders, both focused on newspapers and pancakes, and mumbled something about getting his things from his room. He met Kimbrough by the front door. By then, the schoolteachers had emerged, so Jean was busy being a scullery maid, leaving Matt and Kimbrough to their own devices.

"Little chilly," Matt said as they stood on the porch.

"Winter just won't end this year." Kimbrough adjusted the two grips he carried.

They stared at the steps, the pathway, and the sidewalk.

"You want to walk?" Matt asked.

"Hell, no," Kimbrough said. "I want to ride. I'm a cowboy."

"So am I."

"You mean you used to be."

Matt let that slide. Having a U.S. marshal arrested for a go at fisticuffs with a visiting rancher would be blasted across the front page of every Denver newspaper, then spread to hundreds of papers north, south, east and west. He said: "Best we can do in this town is find a hack."

Kimbrough said: "One thing I hate about this city."

Moving down the steps, Matt called back to the rancher. "We won't find a hack standing here." He did not offer to help Kimbrough with his luggage.

They found a closed rig—a blessing since the wind began blowing again—a few blocks from the boarding house, and Matt told the driver to head to the Denver & Rio Grande depot first, then go to the federal courthouse.

"You running me out of town?" Kimbrough said when he settled into the seat. Matt rode across from him, his back next to the front of the rig.

"I don't think I have the jurisdiction to do that," Matt answered.

The rancher found a cigar. As he lighted it, he said: "I'm not sure you know what your jurisdiction is, Marshal." Matt knew what would come next, so he waited until the cigar glowed red and the match was shook out and tossed out the window.

When the smoke came out and slowly drifted toward the ceiling, Kimbrough said: "Jean's a married woman."

"I've met her husband," Matt said, "and you are out of line."

"Am I?"

"Your herd is straying, Kimbrough. Don't go there."

"Or what? You murder me like you killed Jeff Hancock? She's married. You're married, too, from what I read in the newspapers. You gonna abandon her like you did your wife and kids?"

Maybe it came from being sober, but Matt did not feel the urge or the need to slap Kimbrough's face. He found a newspaper a previous passenger had left, two days' old, but Matt didn't care. He lifted the *Rocky Mountain News*, glanced at the cover, saw the words **US MARSHAL**, **TRINIDAD**, and **STRIKE** in a headline, and quickly turned the page and stared at the advertisement for a grocery store.

"I just don't want to see Jean hurt," Kimbrough said.

That cut it. Matt laid the paper on his lap. "You don't have a damned thing to be jealous about," he said.

The cigar slipped from Kimbrough's grasp, fell on the floor. His lips trembled as he struggled for words, so Matt crushed out the cigar with his boot.

"You're preaching to me about fidelity when any damned fool can see you're in love with her." Matt's statement served like a punch to the jaw.

Kimbrough blinked rapidly. His mouth moved, but seconds passed before he actually spoke. "Listen."

Matt didn't listen. He started talking fast. "Jean and I come from the same area of Tennessee. That's what we talk about. I know I'm married. I mail money to Boise every month. She walked out on me . . . though for damned good reasons. But if you're going to question Jean's honor, I'll have the driver stop this rig, and we can settle our affairs on the street."

Seeming to remember that he had been smoking a cigar, Kimbrough searched for it, but must have decided he had tossed it out the window. He didn't bother looking at the surrey's flooring. "You challenging me to a duel?" Kimbrough said, though his voice had lost much of its frankness.

"Dueling fell out of favor a long time ago." The calmness in Matt's voice surprised him. "You seem to know all about me, so you know how I operate."

"You'd shoot me in the back." Kimbrough snorted and shook his head.

"Maybe." Matt kept his voice level. "If you keep talking about Jean this way."

"Well." Kimbrough's façade crumbled. "I'm not in love with her. I'm just . . ."

"Horseshit."

The rancher found his resolve again as the carriage began to slow. Leaning forward, he whispered: "Well maybe I am. But I can bide my time till that walking whiskey vat of hers drinks himself to death, blows his brains out, or gets his head shot off by a better gambler or a jealous husband while he's peddling whatever he's selling this month."

"Then you have nothing to worry about from me," Matt said.

Now Kimbrough smiled with understanding. "Horseshit."

The hack stopped, and Kimbrough opened the door, taking his luggage with him. "Driver," Kimbrough said, dropping one of his grips to the sidewalk. "Here's payment for bringing me here and that should be enough for you to take the marshal to hell."

"I'll pay my own . . ."

Kimbrough used the grip in his left hand to slam the door shut. Matt muttered an oath, but decided against continuing the brawl. He picked up the *Rocky Mountain News*, again skipped the article on the front page, and looked inside, glancing at the train schedules, international news, advertisements, but stopping at a story.

BODY FOUND

Denver city police reported the discovery last night of a young man found bludgeoned to death behind a chapel on Clarkson Street.

The man, appearing to be in his early 20s, had no identification, or money, thus police suspect robbery as the motive. He had black hair, no identifying features, no facial hair, and was dressed in a common suit of navy wool, winter boots, a muffler. His hat might have been taken by the thieves and killers, too, or blown away with the wind. Eyeglasses were found crushed nearby, along with a copy of *Munsey's Magazine*.

There was another paragraph, but Matt threw the paper aside as the carriage began turning around. Pushing himself out of the seat, he opened the door, keeping a firm grip on the handle, and leaned slightly outside.

"Driver!" Matt called out.

The old man turned around.

"Instead of the courthouse, take me to the city morgue."

"Did you know him, Marshal?"

Hat in hand, Matt stood in the cold, windowless

room, staring down at what was left of Lawrence Tarleton's head and face. Whoever wanted the young poet dead had certainly made sure. Matt wondered how the police figured out that Tarleton had black hair, but Matt saw enough in the small, pale face, and the open eyes. He looked at the blackened indentations in the forehead, and one on the cheek.

The mortician said something again, but Matt did not hear the gray-headed man in Denver's morgue. He was back in Idaho, eighteen years ago.

• • • • •

"The dead always look small, don't they?"

Matt's head whips around, his eyes and mouth open wide. He had been about to vomit, but the words from Jeff Hancock turn sickness into disgust.

"Jesus Christ, Jeff," Matt snaps. "Don't you feel anything anymore?"

Hancock's smile vanishes, and he holds up his old revolver, the handle dripping with blood and maybe the sheriff's brains. "This murdering bastard would have done the same to me."

"You didn't even give him a chance," Matt barks back.

"Did he or any of them lawdogs give Sawtooth Stan a chance when they shot him from ambush? Did any of those jackleg ranchers on the Payette give you or me or anybody who once rode for the

brand a chance? The hand they dealt us came from the bottom of the deck just like they've been dealing men like us for years. Just like they did to you in the war, in the gold fields, and now because you ride with me." Jeff laughs, wipes gore off his revolver before shoving the old Spiller & Burr into the holster.

"Here's one for you, Matt," Hancock says. "It has been said of Walter Raines/Noble sheriff from Snake River Plain/That the son-of-a-bitch had no brains/But such lies I hereby now dispel/For I was handy when the lawman fell/As I saw his brains flow from his head to hell."

Hancock laughs again. "Your turn, pard. Top that one."

• • • • •

"Marshal?"

Blinking rapidly, Matt shoved both hands inside his trousers pockets to steady himself. He looked at the mortician, sighed, and spoke evenly. "His name was Lawrence Tarleton. At least that's what he told me."

"Federal business?" The old man pulled pad and pencil from the pocket and began writing.

Matt shook his head. "No. He wanted me to look into a death he thought happened near Durango. But there was no death, at least . . ." He stopped.

Tarleton had never returned for another meeting with Matt. That boy must have been scared of everything and everyone, just like he had said.

"Was he from Denver or visiting?"

"I don't know." *Some detective I am. No wonder the Pinkertons cut me loose.*

"Well, I shall look in the city directory before I telephone the police. Now that I have a name." The mortician looked at Matt for more information.

Matt looked back at the body. "His clothes?" he asked.

Nodding, the cadaver of a man walked to a filing cabinet, opened a drawer, and removed a white sack, which he brought to a white-covered table near the board upon which lay the remains of Lawrence Tarleton. He tugged open the drawstring, and stepped away.

"Help yourself, Marshal," the man said.

Tentatively, Matt moved to the table, reached in, and pulled out a pair of pants, pockets turned inside out. Looking at the mortician, Matt let his eyes ask the question.

"The investigating officers said the trousers were found like that," the old man said without emotion. "Another reason they suspect robbery." The old man's smile resembled a corpse. "Of course, with our city police . . . ?" He left the rest of the question to Matt's imagination.

The shirt was ripped, stained with dried blood. The shoes were heavy, scuffed. There was no hat, just as the newspaper had reported. The coat torn, also bloodstained. Matt saw no need in checking Tarleton's underdrawers, so he stuffed the clothing back in the sack, and held it out for the old man.

"You may keep those," the undertaker said.

Matt looked at the bag, then at the mortician.

"They aren't worth selling, and we have more than enough . . . garbage."

He felt like a damned fool standing in this cold room holding a bag of worthless clothes that had once belonged to a young poet. But Matt was at a loss as to the proper action. So he just kept holding the bag of dead man's clothes.

"What else can you tell me about the deceased?" the mortician asked. "So I might inform the police."

"There's not much I can say, really. Other than, well, he could write a damned fine poem." Shaking his head, Matt sighed before studying the corpse again. He remembered something he had blocked out for years: carrying body after body to the Death House at that prison camp in Maryland all those years ago. "He said his brother-in-law worked for a newspaper in Pagosa Springs," Matt added, remembering more. "Cole Stevens. That was the brother-in-law's name."

"Do you know which newspaper?"

Again, Matt shook his head. "It might be written down in my office." He straightened, tried to sound like he was a federal peace officer and knew exactly what he was doing. "Have the policeman looking into this murder drop by my office today," he said, "or use that damned telephone."

"Oh," the mortician said. "I'm not sure how much effort the police will put into this. They're still fearful that the railroad strike will break loose again. It could be disastrous for our city, the state, and our country."

Matt tilted his head toward the pale corpse. "Something was disastrous to that kid's head."

The old man didn't get what Matt was suggesting, but he nodded and stared at the body. "He was beaten cruelly, that's a fact. I suspect the killer used a hammer." Now his head shook and the man's mouth made a *tsk-tsk*ing sound. "Poor lad."

"It was a revolver," Matt said flatly.

The mortician looked up in surprise. "A revolver?" He started to point a gray, bony finger at Tarleton's forehead. "But . . ."

"Those were made with a lanyard ring," Matt said. "Remington came out with a revolver a few years back. With a ring on the bottom of the grips. The ring swivels, so that explains how the wounds look different."

Now the old man's Adam's apple bobbed before he said: "But if he had a revolver, he could have . . ."

"Gunshots make a lot of noise. At least more

than crushing a man's face and skull," Matt told him. The undertaker didn't seem to be moving, so Matt put on his hat, and pulled the sheet over Tarleton's face. He waited until the old man looked away from the covered corpse and back into Matt's hard eyes. "It's the Eighteen-Ninety model. Remington. Not as popular maybe as the Colts, but you can find one in town to test my theory. Maybe even on the police force. Even the U.S. marshal's office."

"How . . . ?" the undertaker said.

"Jeff Hancock had a lanyard ring on the butt of his revolver," Matt said.

The old man's smile revealed teeth stained by tobacco. He must have thought Matt was joking. "Well, surely Jeff Hancock did not kill this poor soul."

"Surely not." Matt was already making a beeline for the door. Damn, could he use a bourbon just now.

CHAPTER SIXTEEN

He made himself drink coffee again. Five cups, black, at a café on the street corner until he felt the chill from the morgue leave him, as well as those haunting memories that made him want to drink himself into oblivion.

When he entered the office, Carter Bowen III rose quickly from the desk and glanced nervously at four seated men in woolen suits with winter coats folded over their laps. They had the look of men who had been waiting a damned long time. Matt turned toward the Seth Thomas on the wall. It was 10:20.

"These men are here to see you." The way Carter Bowen III sounded, the four men rode for Lucifer or St. Peter, though none looked like Death.

Matt removed his greatcoat and hat, hanging them on the stand in the corner. "I didn't know I had any meetings scheduled this morning, Carter," he said as he turned around.

By then, a tall, red-mustached man had stood. "We just dropped in, Matt," he said in a familiar twang. "Come in town for the Cattlemen's Association annual meetin'." He shook his head and relieved his mouth by spitting tobacco juice into the spittoon. Matt found the tall man's aim quite impressive. "Don't care much for meetin's, Matt," he said. "Like I reckon you prefer the range to bein' cooped up behind a desk."

Matt opened his office door, and held it for the four men, two probably older than Matt, one a few years younger. Matt couldn't read the last man's age, but he knew that fellow had rarely, if ever, been horseback. That gent wore city shoes, not boots, and his face had never felt too much wind or too much sun. Matt recalled that face from his first meeting with the newspapermen after being sworn in. The *Cattlemen's Clarion of Colorado* editor carried a notebook in his left hand.

After Matt closed the door and walked to his desk, where he stuffed the bag of Tarleton's things in the bottom drawer, the leader of the group made the introductions. Matt remembered one name, J.S.G. Early, who was identified as a rancher on Adobe Creek, but Matt recalled him as being the chairman of the Citizens Alliance Committee—from one of the letters of introduction Luther Wilson had given him. The fourth man was the *Clarion* editor; this had to be the first time Matt actually met him.

"You reporting news from the cattlemen's meeting, Mister Richmond?" Matt asked.

The smile that appeared on the pale, chubby face of Stanley Richmond did not seem genuine. "Do you read our newspaper?" he asked.

Matt nodded. "I don't read newspapers often. Read too many some years back, but you have been pretty kind to me. I'll give you that."

"Better than them lying bastards at the *Evening Post*," said one of the ranchers whose name Matt had forgotten.

"We'd like to keep things that way, Matt," the leading rancher said.

Matt moved behind his desk, sat down, and studied the four men. "Go on," he said.

"We're havin' some trouble down south, Matt," the leader said. "On the Picketwire River."

Matt remembered the leader's name now. Russell Winthrop. But the Picketwire was not where Matt expected the trouble to be. He had Durango in mind.

"That's the Purgatoire," J.S.G. Early explained. "They just . . ."

Matt raised his hand. "I know." He took another stab. "There's a rancher on the Picketwire I met. John Kimbrough."

The men looked at each other and shrugged. Matt said: "He said he had a small spread east of Trinidad."

"Oh," Winthrop said. "Well, we're closer to Las Animas. Near Fort Lyon. Trinidad's way south of our ranges. Charley here might as well cast his votes in Kansas as far east as his spread is."

Charley chuckled and said: "This Kimbrough.

214

He's probably a small outfit. Feeds those coal-mining bastards."

"Or them damned anarchists working to ruin the railroads," Early said.

Winthrop cleared his throat to put the focus on himself. "What did this Kimbrough fellow want with the U.S. marshal?" It came out as a question, but the rancher's eyes told Matt it was anything but an inquiry.

"Not a thing," Matt said. "He was just boarding in the house where I'm staying."

"Oh." Winthrop relaxed. "Well, Luther Wilson said you'd be a good man to talk to."

Matt nodded.

"We figured as much," Winthrop continued. "Knowin' what you done in Idaho all those years ago."

Which led Charley to break out in song.

> **Payette Valley**
> **Became filled with badmen.**
> **Rustlers and thieves.**
> **The country did bleed.**
> **Matthew Johnson**
> **Donned a gun and a star.**
> **He rode for justice**
> **To help those in need.**

"Now I know why you never sung in choir," Early said.

Charley said: "Go to hell."

"Shut the hell up!" Russell Winthrop barked.

Matt looked at the desk drawer. In Idaho, he had always kept a bottle in the bottom drawer, but this wasn't Idaho. Although right now, it sure as hell felt like it. He lowered his hands and sat on them, wondering if he had started sweating as much as he imagined he was.

"Well, Luther suggested that we see you," Winthrop continued.

"I didn't know Luther was a cattleman," Matt managed to say.

"That bastard puts money in anything if he thinks he can make a profit," Charley said.

Early laughed. "Which he didn't in that silver mine."

Which was news to Matt.

"You two sons-of-bitches speak more than a couple of ol' biddies at a mercantile," Winthrop said. Those men fell silent, and Matt noticed that the *Clarion* editor had not taken one note.

"Matt." Winthrop spoke sharply, again to get the proper attention. "Let's stop beatin' 'round the bush. You know what nesters do to the small ranges. Especially when they're stealin' our water and rustlin' our stock."

Matt pulled his hands from underneath his thighs, glanced at them, relieved to see they were not shaking. "If they are taking advantage of your water rights," Matt said, "and if they are rustling

216

your cattle or horses, then you should be talking to the sheriff."

That was not what Winthrop wanted to hear. The man's stone face looked at the newspaperman, giving the journalist a silent command.

"Marshal," the editor said, "the *Cattlemen's Clarion* has been quite supportive of you. Even while the other newspapers in Denver, and, indeed, the entire state, have been damning you from here to Kingdom Come."

Matt waited.

"We'd like to continue to offer our support," Stanley Richmond said.

Russell Winthrop found the spittoon near Matt's desk and proved his aim remained that of a marksman.

"The governor's been burnin' up the telegraph wires all the way to Washington City," Winthrop said. "Demandin' that the President unpin your badge. You've seen what the *Mornin' Herald* and 'em other papers print 'bout you. You mishandled that damned mess with those strikers in Trinidad, they all say. You disappeared on what the *Mornin' Herald* called a drunken ride across the Utes' land. For days. You rode down to Durango for no reason, at least not that anyone has been able to figure out." He shook his head and sighed. "To be frank with you, Matt, most folks I talk to say they don't know how in hell you still got a job. But you do. And here's why."

He leaned forward as though to let Matt in on the state's biggest secret.

"It's because the Cattlemen's Association has a lot of bark and a lot of bite behind that bark."

"As does the Citizens Alliance Committee." Early smiled broadly.

Winthrop sat back in the chair. "You help us," he said plain enough. "We help you."

"What do you want me to do?" Matt said. "My authority has its limits."

The chaw in Winthrop's mouth switched cheeks. He nodded. "You familiar with what happened up north of here, in Wyomin', a couple years back?"

"Johnson County," Matt said.

"That's the one."

Matt leaned back in his chair. Charley shook his head and muttered: "Damned fool sons-of-bitches."

"Those ranchers had the right idea, of course," Winthrop said. "And a legal right to do what they done, but they were all fools." He snorted, almost spit again, but decided to keep the sermon going. "Try to gun down a bunch of thicvin' vermin, and find that whole part of the territory ag'in' 'em. It taken the damned Army to keep ever' last one of 'em from gettin' lynched."

Which, Matt figured from what he had read and heard, seemed to be a fairly accurate description of Wyoming's Johnson County War.

"Well, we ain't plannin' on doin' a damned thing till spring gets here, and it'll be gettin' here soon. These storms is just God's way of lettin' us know that He's in charge. But you rode enough ranges before you become a famous lawdog. You know that as well as all of us in this office knows that after a wet winter, the grass is green and the water's good, so we think we can make up for a few dry years. And ain't no two-bit nesters and rustlers gonna ruin that for us."

Winthrop spit again, hit again, and wiped his mouth. "That railroad trouble won't be done no time soon. When we send word to you, all you got to do is not be around. There ain't no soldier boys at Fort Lyon. You can't find soldiers hardly nowhere since the Indians got themselves wiped out or plantin' taters. Have your deputies in Trinidad, fightin' those anarchists. Or in Durango, in case there's some land rush into that desert those Utes call home. You savvy what I'm askin' of you, Matt?" He smiled before Matt could answer. "And we clean up our country, Matt. Just the way y'all done in Idaho all those years ago."

"I see," Matt said.

"Good."

Matt cleared his throat. "But I wore a badge when the Payette River War ended."

Winthrop turned to the newspaper editor, waiting.

Stanley Richmond could not look Matt in the eye. He focused on his gaiters, wet his lips, and bent his head even lower. "We have a report . . . one we have not committed to running . . . that you took some hundred and fifty dollars from the German National Bank of Denver. A . . . a . . ."

"Bribe," Winthrop said.

"A . . . cashier . . . from that bank," Richmond said, still not looking up, "confirmed the veracity of the report and said you threatened him for more money. While . . . you . . ."

"Were intoxicated." Again Winthrop finished the sentence.

"The cashier's landlord . . ."—Richmond paused to inhale and exhale—"he . . . witnessed the . . . altercation."

Looking at their faces, Matt remembered the cattlemen of Idaho who had talked him into taking the sheriff's badge all those years ago, the same faces that had smiled and applauded when he was sworn in as U.S. marshal. Those cattle barons in Idaho had been strong enough not to need newspapers to do their fighting. Damn it all to hell, why did this world have to change?

"That story," Matt said, "isn't accurate. That's not what happened."

"You could say that," Winthrop said. "Shout it from the courthouse steps, write letters to every newspaper in Colorado, and send telegrams to Washington City. But, with your reputation the past ten years, do you think anyone in Colorado or this whole damned country would believe your version?"

"Hell," Charley said, "I reckon Matthew could deputize us and make it all legal."

"We don't need no badges to make what we plan on doin' right." When Russell Winthrop stood, the other men rose in unison.

"That story don't get reported, Matt," Winthrop said. "If you do what's right. So . . . when I tell you it's time, you get the Army out of my sight. And don't forget that while the *Cattlemen's Clarion* ain't been around as long as the soppin' *Post* or that gentrified *Rocky Mountain News*, it can have the bite of the *Mornin' Herald*. More importantly, it's got the money. The money that the governor, and our United States senators, and even the attorney general in Washington City tend to listen to."

But Matt was remembering something else Winthrop had just said. *We don't need no badges to make what we plan on doin' right.* And he was thinking: *Yet they pinned a badge on me in Idaho to do something that was wrong.*

"What do you say?" Early asked.

Matt felt sick, but he had to say something. "What if the *Post* or the *Herald* runs a story about me allegedly taking a bribe?"

"They won't," Winthrop said. "Because they don't have the . . . the operatives that Mister

Richmond has workin' for his paper." He pulled out his well-chiseled plug and pitched it into the spittoon. "But if they was to report it, somehow, and you done what I'm askin', we'd make those editors eat their words. But if you don't help us . . . hell, every newspaper in the state and most of the West and a lot of the East'll be printin' 'bout your latest and final scandal."

Before leaving, Charley and Early had the audacity to thank Matt, tell him how proud they were to have met a living legend. Of course, none offered to shake Matt's hand, before they filed into a line and followed Russell Winthrop out of Matt's office like twin calves trailing their mama.

It took a moment before Matt realized the newspaper editor remained seated. Matt let his eyes burn through Stanley Richmond before he said: "You going to tell me you'd like an interview with me now, Mister Richmond?" His tone lacked any trace of friendliness.

"No." The editor had trouble swallowing. "We are the *Cattlemen's Clarion*," he said, and tried to smile. "Voice of the cattlemen."

"The big cattlemen," Matt corrected.

Richmond began returning paper and pencil to the inside pocket of his coat. After rising, he spoke to Matt, although his eyes looked at the painting of Grover Cleveland on the wall behind the big desk.

"We support cattlemen, Marshal," he said. "We support the businessmen of the state, the visionaries. Like Luther Wilson. He told me to tell you that. He also told me to let you know something else. Luther Wilson is the biggest investor in my . . . our . . . newspaper."

"He told me that a while back."

"Well," Richmond said, "he has been your friend, your advocate."

"Meaning I support him, too," Matt said without changing expressions. "Or I'm ridden out of Colorado on a rail."

"I am just . . ."

"Get out," Matt told him.

When the door shut, Matt planted his elbows on the desk and buried his head in his hands. Jeff Hancock's laughter bounced off the walls of the big office, and Matt wondered how everything in his life always turned to hell. He cursed himself for being so damned stupid, for thinking he could pin on the badge of a U.S. marshal again and this time make everything right. "You're a stupid son-of-a-bitch," Matt whispered. Only now he heard Darlene's laugh. He could see her shaking her head, telling him how once again he had failed her as a husband, failed her daughters as a father, failed at everything he ever set out to do. He had taken the offer to become marshal of Colorado for the money. Money to send to his wife and daughters, who wanted not one damned thing from him but money . . . if Darlene ever let the girls see a dime.

Jeff Hancock kept laughing.

Hancock could be charming sometimes, like when he had laughed when one of Matt's poems truly amused him. But things had changed. He remembered the laugh after Hancock had bashed in the head of the county sheriff in southern Idaho. Alien. Haunting. Frightening. Sometimes, Matt imagined that was the laugh he heard at Rattlesnake Station. But Jeff Hancock had not laughed that evening. Though he had smiled. Matt never had forgotten that smile.

His head lifted off his hands. Matt leaned back, realizing how badly those hands shook, and the only thing that could save him would be a drink. He had a bottle. There was always a bottle.

Matt shoved the chair away from the desk, reached down, jerked open the bottom drawer.

CHAPTER SEVENTEEN

Jerking the door open, Matt stepped into the cavernous room. From the look on Carter Bowen III's face, Matt had almost made the secretary wet his pants. Matt walked out, looking at the empty chairs, then at Carter.

"Do you have a city directory?" Matt asked.

Carter blinked. He must have thought Matt was drunk.

Not today, Matt thought. *Not yet. I'm sober as I've ever been. But damned close to getting roostered. Good thing this isn't Boise.*

He hadn't found bourbon in his bottom drawer, but the bag of Lawrence Tarleton's belongings from the city morgue, and, near it, a crumpled note he must have dropped there. Now, he wet his lips and waited for Carter Bowen III to snap out of this hypnosis.

Matt urged him a little. "Well?" he said.

"A . . . city directory?" Bowen seemed puzzled.

"You do know about city directories," Matt said.

That did the job. Bowen turned his chair around. "Yes. Of course." He sprang out of the chair, and hurried across the room to the shelves of books on the far wall. "For Denver, I presume," he said as the fingers on his right hand began brushing past leather volumes on the third shelf.

"That's where we are," Matt said.

Carter Bowen III's hand stopped. He turned suddenly. "For the current year?" he asked.

Matt nodded, but added. "Last two years."

He did not think about offering to help until Bowen laid two volumes on his desk. Matt turned the first book around, and opened it, but before he started flipping through the pages, he looked at Bowen, studied him closely, and said: "Would you like some coffee?"

"No, but thank you."

He tried a different approach. "Maybe you could find that café and bring me back a cup."

"Oh." The man looked flummoxed. "Certainly. Of course." Matt found a coin and slid it toward him. "And if you happen to get thirsty on the journey, buy one for yourself."

He had not needed to send the little man away. There was no Lawrence Tarleton, no L. Tarleton, not even one damned Tarleton, listed in either city directory. Cursing, Matt returned the two directories to their place on the third shelf, and went back through directories to 1898. Discouraged, Matt walked back and sat in the secretary's chair. He reached inside his pocket and withdrew the paper he had found in the bottom drawer next to the bag of the dead man's clothes.

Cole Stephens Stevens
Pagosa Springs Wkly Item, reporter
Found dead S of Durango
Ignacio
Ute reserve

Turning the page over, he tried to make out more of his scratches. Stevens had been murdered. A Ute woman had told Tarleton that. Robbery. Matt shook his head. *Who would rob a newspaperman? They made less money than peace officers.*

Then he studied that last line, something Lawrence Tarleton had told him. He heard the young poet's voice. *Cole was up to something. I just don't know what it was.*

If Tarleton didn't live in Denver, he had to be staying somewhere. Matt thought back, and recalled that part of the conversation. Twice Matt had asked him where he was staying, and Tarleton said he kept moving around. The boy had been nervous, Matt understood now. He must have thought somebody was after him, just as they had apparently been after his brother-in-law.

"A brother-in-law means a wife," Matt said aloud, but almost instantly he pictured the bloodied, battered corpse he had seen at the city morgue.

Unless his wife is dead.

If Tarleton were staying in town, hotel,

boarding house, wagon yard, what would have happened to the room? The owner or someone would have taken any valuables left behind and let out the room as quickly as possible. He didn't think any landlord would place an ad or a query in the local newspapers. But Matt looked through the pile on the table between two of the chairs in the waiting area anyway. Nothing.

He made his way back inside his office, sat at his desk, and opened the bottom drawer again to stare at the sack containing the clothes of Lawrence Tarleton.

That's what he was doing when Carter Bowen III returned with the coffee. Closing the drawer, Matt left his office and crossed the anteroom to Bowen's desk. He drank most of the coffee down hurriedly, wiped his mouth, and remembered to thank the secretary. He remembered something else, too.

"Wait a damned minute." Bowen looked aghast.

"No," Matt said. "I just remembered something. You remember that young guy? I had a meeting with him. Said he worked for a magazine."

"Oh, yes, the man who claimed to be an editor at *Munsey's*."

"That's right. He said he left all his information, where he was staying, how I could reach him."

"I don't recall that," Bowen said, but added with prompt efficiency, "but let me check my files and the calendar."

Bowen sat at his desk, unlocked the bottom drawer, pulled it open, withdrew a file, and laid it in front of him. As Matt finished his coffee, he walked over and glanced in the drawer. Feeling better from the coffee, Matt shook his head and let out a quick laugh. "You do save everything, don't you, Carter?"

Confused, Bowen looked up. "I . . . well . . . I try to be . . . efficient."

"You are." Matt set the empty cup on a newspaper on the secretary's desk. "Thank you again for the coffee."

Bowen's face beamed with delight.

The little man thumbed through a book, found a page, read through it, and held it up for Matt's inspection.

"You see," Bowen said, "there is just no other information on Mister Tarleton except, *Munsey's Magazine*, New York City." Matt handed the book back, feeling that he thought he had been close.

"I am sorry, Marshal," Bowen said. "I let you down. I am usually much more . . ."

"Efficient." Matt smiled. He held out his hand. "Thanks anyway, Carter."

He had almost reached the door to his office when he whirled. "Where's Caleb Dawson?"

Bowen almost toppled out of his chair. "Caleb . . . ?"

"Dawson." Matt crossed the anteroom in great strides.

"Oh." To prove his efficiency, Bowen opened another drawer, retrieved another ledger, found the appropriate line, and reported: "He left Denver in pursuit of the counterfeiter. He said he was on his way to Glenwood Springs."

Matt glanced at the map between two windows overlooking Denver.

"Western part of the state," Bowen informed him.

"Yes," Matt said. "The train stopped there when I was coming back from Durango." He left the desk and studied the map, tracing a line from Colorado Springs to Greeley. "That counterfeiter seems to get around."

Bowen made a rare joke. "Well, Marshal, he has the money to spend."

Matt grinned. "Telegraph Dawson. Tell him to report to my office. Forget about the counterfeiter, at least for the time being, and get back to Denver."

"Well." Bowen fidgeted. "He might have trouble. Another spring snowstorm hit that part of the state last night."

Matt cursed. "Send the telegram."

"It might take some time to even get a telegram over the passes."

"Just send it, Carter. It'll get there when it gets there."

"He might not be there by then."

Matt stopped looking at the map and let his eyes bore through Carter Bowen III.

"I am sorry, Marshal," the little man said as he lowered his head. "I'm . . ."

"Efficient." Matt smiled. "He knows to report in, right?"

"Those are the orders you gave. Upon changing locations and at least once a week."

Matt turned back to his office. "When's my next meeting?"

"Deputy marshals M.J. Hannah and Noah Harvey are here to report on their investigations in the McClave case in . . ."—he glanced at the wall clock—"thirty-five minutes." His eyes fell to the schedule on his desk. "And at one sharp, you are to see Judge Perelman in his chambers."

"Very good, Carter. Thank you again." He moved toward his office, opened the door, and looked back. "One more chore for you, Carter."

"Yes, sir. Of course, sir."

"Find out the name of the editor at the Pagosa Springs newspaper."

"Which newspaper?" Bowen quickly explained. "It is big enough to have more than one these days."

Matt had to fish the paper from his trousers pocket. "The *Item. Weekly Item.*"

"The *Weekly Item.* Yes, sir. Very good, sir."

Matt stepped into his office, and looked back

again. "Just send Hannah and Harvey inside when they arrive. Is there a file?"

"I put it on your desk this morning."

"You're damned efficient, Carter."

"I try, sir."

"It's Matt. Remember."

"Yes, sir. I remember."

When deputies Hannah and Harvey pointed at the big state map hanging on the office wall, Matt walked up for a closer look. "Can a man like . . ."—Matt looked at the name on the report Deputy Hannah had given him—"Choctaw Black find a place to hide in this country?" He turned to the two young deputies. "Looks pretty flat."

"It's rough country," Hannah said. "And a man like Black has plenty of friends."

Choctaw Black was neither Indian nor Negro, and according to the report Matt had, the man's real name was unknown. What was known was that he had been convicted of murdering a federal deputy in Wyoming two years back, had been sentenced to hang, and had busted out of the prison. Before that, he had robbed a federal paymaster in Montana.

"Why would a man facing the gallows head south?" Matt asked. "He . . ." Matt stopped, remembering all those newspaper reporters, walking whiskey vats, and everyone else always asking him why Jeff Hancock had stayed in southern Idaho when the noose kept tightening. With as many friends as Hancock had, he could have easily made his way to Canada, disappeared, and lived to a ripe old age.

"He was one of those gunmen the big ranchers brought in from Paris, Texas, during those troubles in Johnson County, Wyoming," Harvey said. "You know the type."

"Yeah." Matt sure knew the type. And someone else had brought up Johnson County earlier this morning in this very office. "I know the type."

He ran his finger south and west until he found the Purgatoire River.

"Could he be hiding out on a ranch?" Matt asked.

Hannah laughed. "Choctaw Black . . . work?"

Matt made himself grin. "Maybe not work cattle," Matt said, and when he turned, he saw the smiles fade off the two deputies' faces. "He wasn't hired to ride up to Johnson County to brand the calf crop or break horses." Quickly, Matt changed the subject. "Do you know a rancher named Winthrop? Russell Winthrop?"

Harvey nodded. "I know of him. Big spread on the Picketwire."

"Show me."

Harvey faltered. "Well, I couldn't place it. . . ."

Matt said: "General area is all I need."

Stepping closer to the map, Harvey raised his right hand, found the Purgatoire River, and let his finger fall south a bit. "Somewhere around here," the lawman said. "Between Rule Creek and the Picketwire."

Matt traced his finger up between the two blue lines until the Purgatoire—alias Picketwire— River moved eastward, and then up north to the barren, sparsely populated section on the map where the deputies had been searching for a cold-blooded killer named Choctaw Black. The distance, by Western standards, wasn't far. Hell, Jeff Hancock and Matt could have crossed that country on a good cow pony in a day, if they knew that a couple of fresh mounts would be waiting for them at the end of trail.

"What are you getting at?" Hannah asked.

Instead of answering, Matt checked his watch, slipped it back inside a vest pocket, and said: "You two have a train to catch after dinner. I've taken enough of your time and I appreciate your dedication. . . ." Hell, here he went again, speaking like the damned politician he needed to be. "Report in whenever you change locations with the nearest county sheriff or town marshal. You're both still working primarily out of Fort Lyon?"

"Yes, sir," came the simultaneous answer.

Harvey explained: "I mean, there are no soldiers there anymore. The Army shut it down."

"Like it has closed a lot of posts." Matt shook his head.

"They say the frontier's closed," Hannah said.

"Hell of a thing." Matt shook his head. He walked back to the map and pointed at that spot between the crooked blue lines, and asked: "Do you need any help?"

"We'd rather not." Hannah bristled at such a suggestion.

"Good." Matt slapped Hannah's shoulder. "I like that in a lawman. But I'm going to send a couple of deputies up from Trinidad to help you." He recognized the ire in both lawmen's eyes, but he held up his right hand. "You boys have to trust me on this one. There's something bigger here than Choctaw Black. And believe me, Black is one son-of-a-bitch I'd like to hang myself."

The deputies smiled again, and Matt tapped on the same spot. "I'm not at liberty to say much more, until our own investigation is finished." That gave things a ring of authenticity, as though Matt knew what he was talking about. "But there's a chance I might need you two down here." His eyes focused, trying to read the country, and at length he stepped away and extended his hand. "Keep your eyes open. And watch your backs."

"Marshal?" Hannah asked.

"Yeah?"

"You think it's wise bringing deputies out of Trinidad? I mean, no disrespect, sir, but Trinidad's a railroad town and . . ."

"I know. But I've met the local marshal in Trinidad. He's a cut above the rest. Just like you two."

Yet once the newspaper in Trinidad reported that Matt had dispatched two deputy marshals, every other paper in Colorado—and especially those in Denver—would demand that U.S. Marshal Matthew Johnson be put in, like the song went, that *big pine box.*

He rushed through his dinner at a coffee shop, reading through every newspaper for the first time, although he just ran a finger down column after column, looking for other reports of a dead body found bludgeoned to death behind a chapel at Clarkson Street.

Unless Matt was mistaken, the *Rocky Mountain News* had no other articles about Lawrence Tarleton's murder. The *Evening Post* had an even smaller notice about the body's discovery the following afternoon. The *Morning Herald* added what some editor must have found colorful in that: *Since the dead man was found near a church, the* Morning Herald *wishes that the deceased found peace with God before finding death in the dark.* The *Republican* gave the death even fewer words than the *Post*, and Matt did not bother looking at Denver's *Svensk Amerikanska Western* since he didn't read or speak whatever language this newspaper used.

After dinner, he received the name of the Pagosa Springs *Weekly Item*'s editor, gathered the papers Carter Bowen III had prepared for him, and moved down the hall to Judge Perelman's chambers.

He tried to remember these kinds of meetings over the six months when he had been federal marshal in Idaho, but those were different times. The frontier remained wild, lawless, not so civilized, and Matt doubted if Idaho back then had as many people as Denver had today. Yet then he started to think that his deputies weren't just after an elusive counterfeiter. A range war might leave the Picketwire running red with blood once winter finally loosened its grip, more striking railroaders could lead to more dead bodies, and, although Matt couldn't put his finger on it, something was brewing down along the federal reserve south of Durango. And a young man and possibly his brother-in-law had been murdered. Matt just didn't know why.

"You'll have your deputies ready to testify?" Perelman said.

Matt had scarcely heard a dozen words the jurist had said. But he nodded, nonetheless.

"There's a reason these laws are made, Marshal," the judge said as he removed his spectacles and let those cold eyes lock on Matt. "Even the laws I disagree with, I must follow. The same as you must."

"Yes, Your Honor."

The judge let the glasses rest on a Bible. "You seem to follow your own laws."

Matt leaned back in the uncomfortable chair. "Sir?"

Perelman waved at a stack of telegrams and stationery on the other side of the Bible. "Governor Waite is not happy. Attorney General Olney is dissatisfied. President Cleveland is wondering if his selection of you for this job will be a blight on his record he will never be able to erase." He leaned forward. "I must concede that while I will not convict a man from the printings in a prejudicial newspaper, or newspapers, your conduct in . . . what . . . weeks?" His big head shook. "Well, you trouble me, Marshal."

"I don't mean to, Your Honor."

"Honestly, I do not know why President Cleveland made the appointment."

"Maybe he thought I deserved a second chance."

Matt was hearing something else.

They pulled me out
From under a horse,
Said run him for sheriff
Hell, what could be worse?
To get Hancock
They gave me a star,
Said bring him in dead, Matt

And you will go far.
U.S. marshal,
That's what I could be.
Jeff Hancock's a killer
As we all could see.
Ride for the brand
Was always my creed.
At Rattlesnake Station
I did that foul deed.

"It's your turn, pard." Matt must have said it, although the words appeared to come from out of nowhere, spoken by Jeff Hancock.

"What?"

Matt jerked his head. Judge Perelman had removed his eyeglasses, letting his gray eyes bore through Matt.

"Sorry, Your Honor," Matt said.

Perelman laid his spectacles on a volume of Blackstone. "As I was saying, Marshal, politics usually provides such an opportunity."

Matt managed to put the poem, and Hancock's voice, behind him. "Ask anyone who knows me, Your Honor, and they'll tell you I don't know one thing about politics."

"I would not overrule that statement in a court." At least Perelman smiled, but that did not last. "I will say this of you, Marshal. When your name started being bandied about as a replacement for our last federal marshal, I read up on you . . . not in dime novels, but only the newspapers I trusted. You killed a friend, perhaps your best friend, but from the reports I read and believed in, I'd say that killing was justifiable. Then, it appears, that quick fame seemed to . . ." He searched for the word.

Closing his eyes, Matt spoke softly. "When I peruse the conquer'd fame of heroes, and the victories/of mighty generals, I do not envy the generals,/Nor the President in his Presidency, nor the rich in/his great house."

To his surprise, Judge Perelman continued the quotation. "But when I read of the brotherhood of lovers, how it was/with them,/How through life, through dangers, odium, unchanging, long and long,/Through youth, and through middle and old age, how unfaltering, how affectionate and faithful they were,/Then I am pensive—I hastily put down the book, and walk away, fill'd with the bitterest envy."

They stared at each other the longest while, until Matt broke the silence. "I was unaware that you were acquainted with Walt Whitman."

Perelman laughed and patted the thick book that held his glasses. "Blackstone might own my soul, Marshal, but my heart belongs to Whitman." He shook his head again. "We should have supper one night, Marshal. Recite poetry."

"That would be . . ." But he thought again of Jeff Hancock.

Perelman must have seen something in Matt's eyes. The pain, perhaps. The memories. He cleared his throat and made himself look at the Regulator on the wall. "Well, I did not mean to keep you from your duties, Marshal," the judge said, his voice formal again.

Matt rose, shook hands, and turned to the door.

"Marshal."

Matt looked back.

"I pride myself on honesty. And on duty. These are troublesome times for our state and, I fear, our own country. There is a lawless element running wild from east to west and north to south. We cannot let lawlessness ruin Colorado."

"I know, Your Honor." Matt opened the door. "It's my job to stop that lawlessness."

"Our job!" Perelman called to Matt's back. "I am here to help you. If I can."

CHAPTER EIGHTEEN

Leaving the courthouse that afternoon, Matt decided to walk back to Jean's boarding house rather than find some hack. He made it past at least a half dozen saloons before stopping in at a place called Modory's. One bourbon, that's all, he told himself, and, by thunder, he left after that drink. Four blocks later, he tested himself inside another establishment, sipped his second bourbon, and walked out. The rest of the walk tested his will, plus his nerves, until he saw Jean McBride standing in front of a shop's window.

"Y'all ain't drunkards," Rex Chesser once said while trying to sober up Matt and Jeff Hancock. "But you boys do binge. That can get a man into trouble."

Two bourbons, he thought. *Not bad. I made it. I'm not drunk, not even light-headed.* Yet frowning, he kept walking, thinking that if Jean did not spot him, he could walk past her. If she did notice him, called out his name, he might be able to pretend that he hadn't recognized her.

People filled the sidewalks, going home to supper, to saloons, or to finish their shopping. That played in Matt's favor, as Jean McBride kept looking through the window. Matt moved past her, but instead of walking, he stopped, turned around, removed his hat, and slid closer to the window.

Her eyes turned. She smiled.

"Ma'am," Matt said. He could hear Jeff Hancock's voice: *You're one cocky bastard. You think you can get away with anything.*

She stared for what seemed like minutes, shocked, but not upset. Finally, she relaxed, even smiled before reminding him: "Jean."

Oblivious to the people rushing past them on the sidewalk, Matt realized he was staring at her far too long, so he turned to the window. **Chandler's Automatic Phonograph Parlour**.

Still facing the sign, he said: "I don't think I'm familiar with this sort of business." He stared through the window. Inside this long rectangle, dozens of people, young and old, leaned against some types of cabinets, holding what appeared to be stethoscopes in their ears. Of these men and women, his father would have said: *They look like damned fools.*

"They're fairly new to Denver." Jean's voice rose above the bustle of pedestrians, the barks of whistles, the clopping of hoofs, and the squeaking of wagon wheels. "You listen to music on these cylinders. I guess the phonographs are expensive, so this is how . . . other people . . . hear . . . music."

"I've heard of phonographs," Matt said. "Seen one or two."

"I asked Reg- . . ." She stopped, swallowed, and turned back to gaze through the window.

Hell, Matt thought, he had heard music in saloons, at camp meeting, at churches, at socials, and in opry houses. He wondered if someone had recorded a cylinder of "Matthew Johnson, United States Marshal." If he found one, he'd stomp that cylinder to pieces.

Inside the parlor, a middle-aged man tapped his right foot. A woman in a flat-brimmed hat trimmed with ribbon and lace closed her eyes. Two younger men lowered their earpieces, and quickly swapped machines. A minute later, a young couple did the same thing.

People, Matt observed, moved from one machine to another. He started to say—"This is the damnedest thing I've ever seen"—but stopped, remembering Jean stood next to him. He could smell her over the scents of sweat and horses and smoke.

"Do you like music?" Jean asked.

Looking back at Jean, Matt chuckled. "As long as I'm not singing."

When a man in a business suit and fedora removed his ear devices and walked outside, and nobody seemed to be waiting for the vacant phonograph, Matt turned to Jean. "You want to give it a whirl?" He extended his hand, nodding at the shopping bag she held, which she let him take. Remembering his manners, he held the door open. She wore high boots, a gray skirt and matching jacket with puffy shoulders, and a navy blouse. Matt's mother would have called something like this her "going-to-town outfit."

His heart fluttered. Maybe he imagined that. Like maybe he was dreaming that Jean McBride actually entered Chandler's music store with him.

The woman in the trimmed hat had moved to that vacated station, so Matt led Jean to the big box the lady had left. Jean stood next to him. No one spoke, but even with dozens of men and women standing quietly, dim chords and faraway voices mingled in the stale air of Chandler's Automatic Phonograph Parlour. For a full minute, Matt focused on the tall wooden box before turning to Jean only to remember that this type of business remained equally foreign to her. He understood one thing from the directions posted on the box.

It cost a nickel a song.

When Jean brought up her purse, Matt said: "I have a pocket full of nickels." Change from his two bourbons.

She lifted the stethoscope, but he knew she felt uncomfortable. So did Matt. These phonographs were meant for one listener, although across the room, a couple shared ear pieces. It brought them close together. Very close. "Maybe." Jean stopped, watching another couple come inside and hurry to the station vacated by an older woman. "Maybe we should . . ." She sighed. A mustached man stepped inside, frowned, and then leaned against the window, waiting for a unit to open.

"You can listen," Matt told her.

"No." She hesitated, but finally pointed at the young couple. "They seem to be doing it . . . this way." She moved closer.

Still holding her bag, he breathed in the scent of her perfume. It smelled like lavender. After withdrawing a nickel and dropping it into a slot, he gently took one side of the stethoscope and held it next to his ear.

The scratchy voice of a man made him gasp. He figured he would hear someone talking, singing, or playing a fiddle, but the sound still shocked him. "Edison Recording Number Eight Hundred and Sixty-Four." The voice sounded human, though diluted by strange noises. Human, yet mechanical, unreal. "The song is entitled 'Down on the Farm'. Sung by Mister Edward Clarance."

When the song ended, Matt noticed a young man in a straw hat next to them, staring. The boy held out the ear piece, and Matt understood. The youngster wanted to make a trade, and Matt figured that whatever song played on their device had to be better than Edward Clarance.

It wasn't.

"I Wish They'd Do It Now", sung by Mr. Len

Spencer, came out garbled, hard to understand. Apparently, this brown cylinder had been played too many times, or perhaps Mr. Len Spencer carried a tune as well as Matt.

Every couple of minutes, after another nickel had played another one of those brown phonographic cylinders, Matt and Jean moved to a new machine. The piano accompaniment on George Gaskin's "After the Ball", Matt and Jean agreed, sounded remarkably better than J.W. Myers's rendition of "Bell Buoy". By the time Edward M. Favor sang "Daisy Bell", Matt had gotten used to the scraping sounds, sometimes louder than the songs, but as Baldwin's Cadet Band of Boston performed "The Beau Ideal March", Matt smiled at the sight of Jean's right foot tapping along with the melody. Having one nickel left, Matt quickly pulled Jean to the nearest machine. By this time, people began forming lines at the automated phonographs.

"One more," he told her.

"Yes," Jean said, smiling. "Because if I don't get home shortly, you won't be eating supper tonight."

He slipped the coin into the phonograph, and put his side of the stethoscope into his ear. Breathing in Jean's perfume, he heard a similar crackly voice tell him that he was about to hear Jules Levy play "The Last Rose of Summer". Matt waited to hear Thomas Moore's poem sung or recited, but the only noises that came were a cornet's mournful notes.

When the second verse began, however, words, sung softly, sweetly, came from outside the irritating piece stuck in his ear. He lowered his listening apparatus and stared at Jean McBride.

She sang:

> **I'll not leave thee, thou lone one**
> **To pine on the stem;**
> **Since the lovely are sleeping,**
> **Go, sleep thou with them;**
> **Thus kindly I scatter**
> **Thy leaves o'er the bed,**
> **Where thy mates of the garden**
> **Lie scentless and dead.**

The last verse began. Slowly, Matt looked away from Jean. Ear pieces had been lowered at other automated phonographs. Jean sang. Her voice lacked the rawness of the brown wax cylinders. She didn't sing loudly, though Matt figured she could have had she felt like it. Her eyes closed, head bowed, still holding her end of the stethoscope in her ear, she sang with honesty, with sensitivity.

> **So soon may I follow,**
> **When friendships decay,**
> **And from love's shining circle**
> **The gems drop away!**

**When true hearts lie wither'd,
And fond ones are flown,
Oh! who would inhabit
This bleak world alone?**

As soon as the song ended, Jean's eyes opened, and quickly teared at the sight of people staring at her. The ear piece and tube slipped from her hand. Her face reddened.

"I'm sorry," she said. "I'm . . ."

The patrons inside Chandler's Automatic Phonograph Parlour applauded.

"Oh." She turned to Matt, confused, uncertain. Smiling, Matt took her arm, and led her toward the door. As they passed, an old man removed his hat.

"Ma'am." The voice sounded sincere. "That's the best nickel I ever spent in this place."

Outside, after walking a few yards away from Chandler's Automatic Phonograph Parlour, Matt let Jean recompose herself. He still had her bag. He fought back the urge to hold her.

"I'm such a fool," she said. "I . . ."

She breathed in and out, too fast. Matt wet his lips. He tried to think of something to say.

"I've never felt so . . . ashamed," Jean said.

"Don't be," he said, and smiled when she looked into his eyes. Matt's resolve faltered, and he put his arm around her, pulled her closer, and smiled. "Those folks know what it's like to be

249

sung to, now, Jean. You should sing all the time."

Her face softened. "You . . . really think so?" She didn't fight his embrace.

"Mama had a pretty good voice," Matt said. "I wound up sounding like Pa. Or Aunt Lois. Even my kid sister sang better than me." He waited, praying the words took effect. Hell, he had said nothing but the truth.

Her head shook, and she spun around, and Matt let his arm fall to his side. "Oh, my. What time is it?" Without waiting for an answer, she said: "We'd best hurry back to the house. You must be starving." Jean started walking, and though she was much shorter than Matt, he had to stretch his legs to catch up with her.

"What are we having tonight?" he asked, walking alongside her now, relieved when she slackened her pace.

"What would you like?" They covered another block, before stopping to let a fire engine roll past. "You're the only one eating tonight," she said. "The others . . . they're dining elsewhere."

The fire engine turned east. Matt helped Jean across the street. "Well," he said, "I don't want to be bothersome." He nodded at a café at the end of the block. "I could treat you to supper."

She stopped short, and he had to spin around.

Oh, hell, he thought, *what am I doing? Inviting her to dine with me. Putting my arm around her. This must be the bourbon talking.*

250

"I . . ." He tried to think of a way to retreat. "I meant no improprieties. I just . . ."

"I can't," Jean blurted out, and resumed walking. He followed her to the intersection, and waited for her to cross. Instead, she turned and stared at the café. It wasn't crowded inside.

He tried to read the menu, but could not shake Thomas Moore's words from his mind, nor could he forget Jean's angelic voice singing them.

A man in a black suit opened the door, smiling, letting the aroma of fresh baked bread mingle with that of roasting beef and potatoes. "Will *mademoiselle* and *monsieur* be dining with us this evening?" he said. Not one word sounded French.

"No," Matt said.

"Yes," Jean said as she moved toward the door.

Matt swallowed, found a way to smile at the man in the black suit. A glance at the menu's price list on a sign next to the window sobered him. *Shit,* he thought. He had enough money to pay for the meal, but those German National Bank of Denver federal notes he had refused a while back sure would have come in handy this evening.

"I feel like I've been playing hooky all day," Jean said when they walked through the open gate of her house.

Matt laughed. "It has been a very pleasant

evening." He slipped his arm inside hers, leading her down the path, up the steps, past the statues of the dogs, and to the front door, where he let her go. She opened the door, stepped inside, and waited for him by the parlor entrance.

The house sounded empty.

Remembering the bag, he held it toward her. She shifted the purse to her left hand, accepted the bag, stared at the rug, her boots, before finally lifting her gaze. "It's Walt Whitman," she said.

"Oh." He had to fill the silence with something.

"I've always read Lord Byron." She found the nearest table in the foyer and laid her purse on that. Reaching inside the bag, she pulled out a copy of *Leaves of Grass*. "I saw it in your room all those times when I was cleaning. I just figured . . ." She looked at him again.

"You could have borrowed mine," Matt said. "I've read it so much the cover's coming off."

When she said nothing, he again felt the urge to fill the silence.

"Byron is a fine poet. So is Thomas Moore, but I doubt if his words ever sounded so good to him as they did tonight." *Jesus Christ,* he thought, *what are you doing?*

"I've tried to write a poem," she said.

He smiled. "I'd admire to hear it." Quickly, he remembered to add: "Jean."

She looked at the book, at Matt, down the hall, inside the foyer, back at the front door, again at

252

Matt. "It's stuffy in here," she said. "Maybe the . . . porch?"

It wasn't stuffy on the porch. It was turning cold, again, but he made himself walk to the door. Once he held it open, he looked at Jean. "After you?" he said.

Instead of to the left, where the rockers sat, Jean went to the swing, sat, and nodded at the seat next to her. Matt glanced at the street, dark now, empty, quiet, and followed her. If he sat on the swing with her, nobody from the street would see them because of the latticework and shrubs. She could have gone to the rocking chairs on the other side of the porch.

He walked to the swing, sat beside her, pushed forward, and the swing moved. Although it had to be dropping into the forties by now, he felt flushed with heat.

Jean said softly: "I have never seen the ocean." She stared across the porch at the empty rocking chairs. "Just the mountains/Here and home/And while I love those towering pillars at dusk/The sound of the sea I believe/Would make me feel small/But strong."

Matt moved his right arm to the back of the swing.

"That's very nice," he said.

"It's your turn," Jean told him.

Briefly Matt tensed, but swallowed, tried to

relax, and said: "Sounds a bit like Byron." Turning to her, he saw that she had slid closer to him. "Have you really never seen the ocean?" he asked.

Her smile brightened, and he saw a new look in her eyes. Eyes that seemed so inviting, while also scaring him. "There was no sea in Gallatin, Matt," he heard her say.

When he found his voice, he thought he told her: "I remember that much." He tried to forget the ocean he had seen at Point Lookout, thought about the Great Salt Lake in Utah, back when he and his pals kept trying to earn enough money for passage to Idaho's gold fields.

"It's your turn," she said again.

He closed his eyes. "It's my turn," he whispered. His arm moved around her shoulder. His heartbeat accelerated, or maybe he had started shaking. When he opened his eyes, he felt her close to him, and he turned, saw those blue eyes beaming. He bent his head, and kissed her, knowing that the next thing he would hear would be Jean McBride's scream. The next thing he would undoubtedly feel was her hand slapping his face.

"It's your turn." This time, Jean whispered those words.

He opened his eyes, saw her in his arms. *God,* he thought, *what is going on? What have I done? What the Sam Hill am I thinking?* The swing had stopped moving. Matt had no idea how long they had been here.

"It's my turn," he said. And he kissed her again.

"It's still your turn," she murmured.

"Yeah." He wished he could see through the latticework and those shrubs, because that apothecary, or that son-of-a-bitch from the Denver Telephone Dispatch Company, or those school-marms or clerk, perhaps even John Kimbrough, would certainly be coming back from supper soon. Or maybe . . . Jean's husband. Yet he did not want to leave. Ever.

"Your turn," she said once more.

He tried to laugh, and eventually found enough strength to remove his arm from her shoulder. She blinked, smiled, looked like the most gentle, most precious, most beautiful angel in the world. He said the only thing he could remember:

The smell, the noise, the heat, the dust,
I sweat, I swear, I clinch, I curse.
The iron is hot, I feel the heat.
Slap the brand, hard yet neat.
The calf, he rises, runs off to Mother.
His pain subsides, but not mine, brother.
The days are long come branding time.
Burn fifty a day, not one of them mine.

"That's funny." Jean's eyes sparkled, reflecting the flames from the porch's lamps. She straightened, sighed, and looked toward the street. "It's getting cold," she said. "We should go inside."

"I know." He felt a lot of things at that moment, but not cold. After pushing himself out of the swing, he helped her up.

Inside, they reached Matt's room. He stopped, looked at her.

"It was a lovely evening, Matt," she said. "I haven't had one of those in a long time."

"I . . . Yes . . . It was . . . nice." His hand touched the cold doorknob.

"I need to get everything set for breakfast tomorrow."

"All right."

They stood there, like the dogs that guarded the steps to the front porch, unable to move. He waited for some signal, confused but comforted at the same time. He wanted to sweep her into his arms, but the front door opened, bringing in the ear-splitting voices of two schoolteachers, though the staircase blocked his view of the women.

Jean stepped back quickly, her face changing instantly, and one of the teachers said: "Howdy, Jeanie Gal."

That one sounded tipsy.

"Good evening," Jean said, and turned to Matt. "Good night, Marshal."

"Good night, ma'am." Matt stepped away from the door, remembering everything he had learned as a politician. He smiled at the teachers, as though they didn't hate his guts. "Ladies," he said, bowed slightly, and found his key, his heart racing again, and tried to keep his hand steady enough to unlock his door.

When he had undressed, he glanced at *Leaves of Grass* on the bedside table. The schoolteachers' voices rang loudly in the parlor, and a moment later a gruff laugh announced the return of Mr. Childs, the telephone man. Sitting on the bed, staring at the door, Matt said to himself: "It's your turn."

CHAPTER NINETEEN

"It's your turn," Matt says. He sits on his saddle, on the floor in a line shack, having just finished reciting his branding poem.

Sitting in a chair near the fireplace, Jeff Hancock takes a swig from the bottle of rye, passes it to Matt.

"Well," Jeff says. "Try this one on, pard."

I've had two very scary dreams.
I'm now afraid to sleep.
They deal with the pit of Hell,
That lies below so deep.
Of men knocking on Heaven's door,
Then singing a sad, sad song,
And being forced to turn away,
For their religion was wrong.
Of the moon exploding in a
Fiery shower of sparks.
People cry, kneel, and pray.
The world turns cold and dark.
Now I, my brothers, have no fear,
For I know my Maker well.
But please my brothers, find your God
And escape the jaws of Hell.
The world may not end tonight,
Just go on as before.

But the day will come, soon enough,
And man will be no more.
And so I make one final plea
Before the skies do redden.
Take upon you the Holy Ghost
For coming is Armageddon.

Matt takes another swig, pitches the bottle to Bounce McMahon. After wiping his mouth, Matt stares at the smiling Hancock, and tells him: "We seem to be drifting in different directions. I'm having fun. You're preaching hell and damnation."

"Hell and damnation is all I see these days, pard," Hancock fires back. "And it's all you'd see, too, if you'd lay off that rotgut. It's all we can see since those bastards started calling us rustlers. And . . . anarchists." He laughs, takes the bottle thrown by Bounce, and stares at what's left of the amber spirits. "Anarchists," he says, kills the rye, and smashes the bottle against the fireplace in the cabin. "I still ain't exactly sure what the hell it means."

Bounce McMahon speaks quietly: "An anarchist is one who incites revolt. Or promotes disorder."

Both men stare at the old cowhand, who isn't looking at either man, his eyes reflecting the flames. He sits on the old chopping block they've brought inside. His head tilts back, and he smiles.

259

"Father taught at the university," he says. He turns back to Matt and Hancock. "Grammar in the fall session, and analysis in the winter. But I tended to like Professor Quackenbos's natural philosophy." He sighs. "Then the war started, and my education came to an end. To be replaced by an education under Colonel Smith. And other learned professors . . . Buell . . . Rosecrans . . . Grant."

"I never knew you were a Yankee," Matt says.

"You never knew I was a poet, either," he says, looks back at the fire, and says:

> *There is a Reaper, whose name is Death,*
> *And, with his sickle keen,*
> *He reaps the bearded grain at a breath,*
> *And the flowers that grow between.*

"You wrote that, Bounce?" Hancock asks.
Bounce sniggers.
Matt says: "That's Emerson, I think."
"Longfellow," Bounce corrects.

• • • • •

Matt frowned as another image replaced that scene of old Bounce McMahon, remembering Henry Wadsworth Longfellow. He could never forget the sight of Bounce as a bullet-riddled corpse left on the prairie. Of Jeff Hancock galloping into the woods. And of himself, leg pinned underneath the body of his dead horse, staring up at more than a dozen rifles pointed at him, figuring this is where it all would end.

The tapping on the door awakened him, and he rolled over, sending *Leaves of Grass* sliding off his chest and thudding on the floor.

"Matt." Jean's voice brought him out of the haziness. The lamp still burned, and he threw off the covers.

"Yes," he said, sliding out of the bed, next wiping his eyes, and finally moving toward the dresser to find the repeater. It was 5:18.

"I'm sorry to wake you up so early." Jean kept her voice low so as not to waken any other boarders. "There's something I thought you might need to see. In the papers."

The papers. Great. He pulled a shirt over his head. *What has Matthew Johnson done now?* He started moving toward the door when he remembered he had yet to find his britches.

"I'm coming," he said, grabbed the trousers off the floor, and managed to get them on without falling onto his face.

A moment later, he looked into Jean's blue eyes.

"Good morning." She smiled.

That's a relief. Last night he thought she would probably slap his head off, evict him, drag his hide down the steps, down the pathway, and all the way to the Picketwire River.

261

The smile faded as she brought up one of the morning newspapers. "I don't know if this is important, but . . ." She handed him the *Cattlemen's Clarion of Colorado*. When he unfolded the paper, he failed to find prose damning Matthew Johnson, United States marshal. But what he saw snapped him fully awake.

**IS THERE GOLD ON
THE UTE RESERVATION?
Hundreds Swarm to Durango!
GOLD! Gold! GOLD!
The Clarion is the First
TO BREAK THIS
EXTRAORDINARY NEWS
Details of the strike
Which remain hidden
GOLD Turns the Silver Panic
INTO A MOTHER LODE**

"None of the other newspapers have anything about this," Jean said. "At least, not that I could find."

Matt nodded, still trying to wake up.

"I'll get the coffee ready," she told him. But she did not move.

"Yeah." Raising his gaze, he found hesitation and doubt in her face. "Last night," he whispered, "I had two bourbons before I saw you at that phonograph parlor."

She tensed.

"But I knew what I was doing," he said.

Her eyes sparkled. "I knew what I was doing, too," she whispered.

"Let me shave, get dressed." He stepped back inside his room.

"I'll make your breakfast," she said.

He realized that he still held the *Clarion*.

"Keep that," she said. "Read it. It could be wonderful news for our state."

"If it's true," he said. He closed the door, and stared at the newspaper as he walked to his dresser. *Great news for the state,* he thought. *But not the Utes.*

She set a plate before him piled with a biscuit, two thick slices of bacon, scrambled eggs, and a sea of grits.

Matt smiled and waited for Jean to sit next to him. "You think the schoolteachers know what grits are?"

"Yes, indeed, Marshal Johnson," she said lightly. "If you stay at this boarding house long enough, you know what grits are." She laughed. "Mister Childs learned that grits are nothing like biscuits."

He put a spoonful in his mouth, swallowed, and smiled. "They taste fine. Like home." He lowered the spoon to the plate, and found her hand.

The squeeze warmed his body. When she let go, he heard her sigh.

"This could be complicated," she whispered.

He said: "It is complicated."

"There are other people to consider."

He thought: *Like John Kimbrough.*

"You might just want to run away from me, harlot that I must be."

"I've been running too damned long," he said. "And you're no harlot."

The telephone rang. Sighing, Jean rose and hurried to the hallway to stop the racket from waking up the other boarders. He heard her voice, thought about eating grits or at least sipping coffee, but felt paralyzed. She came back into the dining room.

"It's the governor," she told him.

A janitor let him inside the courthouse.

Matt's boots echoed across the marble floor, sounding even louder when he climbed the stairs to his office. After turning the switch, he let the electric lights flicker to life, before moving to the desk of Carter Bowen III. The wall clock said it was 6:45. Sitting in the secretary's chair, he began writing telegrams to be sent. To Liberty Rawlings in Durango: **HIRE AS MANY EXTRA DEPUTIES AS NEEDED STOP I WILL BE THERE IN 1 OR 2 DAYS STOP KEEP PROSPECTORS OFF UTE**

LAND STOP. To Caleb Dawson: **ABANDON COUNTERFEITER AND REPORT TO DURANGO IMMEDIATELY.** He also wrote one to Deputies Hannah and Harvey asking for updates on the search for Choctaw Black.

The telegraphers wouldn't be at work yet, so Matt left the messages with a note to Bowen to send them as soon as he arrived. After rereading the *Clarion*'s long article on Durango and the gold strike, he tossed the newspaper aside, set his elbow on the desk top, and rubbed his chin, thinking, plotting, considering, and coming up with nothing but a sore elbow.

The governor had asked Matt what he intended to do, and Matt had said to protect the Utes. That, the governor had said, was not in the best interest of the state of Colorado, and Matt had responded: "Then you should take that up with the U.S. attorney general." "Which I shall do, Marshal," the governor had said, and ended the telephone call.

Sighing, Matt let his arm lie on the desk. The note from Carter Bowen III caught his attention, and he picked it up, remembering he had asked his secretary for the Pagosa Springs *Weekly Item* editor's name. He slid back the chair and opened the bottom drawer, withdrew the notes he had written when Lawrence Tarleton had visited, tossed it next to the editor's name, and withdrew the white bag he had taken from the city morgue.

Standing now, he emptied the contents, and let the bag fall to the floor.

Lawrence Tarleton said Cole Stevens had been killed at Ignacio. Over gold. Those surveyors with mining equipment had been found northwest of Ignacio, on the Ute reservation. Cole Stevens was, according to his brother-in-law, dead. Tarleton's head had been brutally smashed with the butt of a revolver with a lanyard ring in the butt. This whole damned situation stank, and it all came down to Cole Stevens and Lawrence Tarleton. Somehow.

He sifted through the pile of Tarleton's clothing. The shirt had no pockets, and the pockets in the pants remained turned inside out. Matt fingered the socks, dropped them back into the drawer, and sat down to examine the shoes: laces undone, tan leather satin-oiled, scuffed from wear, probably two sizes smaller than Matt's boots. He picked one up, turned it over, even checked the heel, and pounded the shoe on the desk. No clue, no note, nothing fell out. Yet whoever had beaten Tarleton to death had likely found whatever he was looking for—if he had been looking for anything—or the Denver coppers had stolen it. And, well, maybe Tarleton had been the random victim of a ruffian. The panic after the silver market had collapsed left hundreds, thousands of people out of work.

Tossing the shoe aside, Matt grabbed the pants,

and stuck his finger inside the watch pocket. But that was empty, too, and he cursed as he rubbed the grit off his fingertip with his thumb. Next he looked at his thumb.

He found the lamp on his desk, turned it on, and held forefinger and thumb under the light that flickered and hummed before becoming steady.

Whispering a curse, he grabbed a handkerchief and wiped off the flecks.

Gold. Or maybe fool's gold. Perhaps just his imagination. He wanted to laugh, tell himself that what now stained his handkerchief held more gold than he had ever found in Idaho Territory. He found his notes about Cole Stevens and looked once more at his secretary's handwriting.

Two minutes later, sitting at Carter Bowen III's desk, Matt jerked the handle on one of the side drawers. He cursed that efficient secretary for locking his drawers.

When he heard footsteps entering the waiting area, Matt rose from the chair in his office and walked to the open door in time to see Carter Bowen III drop his satchel on the floor.

Matt stepped out of his own office, and the little secretary spun around and gasped. "Marshal," Bowen said softly. He pointed a shaking finger at his desk. Matt kept walking. "Someone . . ."

The backhand sent Bowen sailing against his

now-cluttered desk, spilling papers, pencils, and a ledger to the floor.

Bowen raised a trembling hand to his cheek. His lips quavered.

"The problem with you, Carter," Matt said, "is your efficiency. You save everything. Even things that could put Luther Wilson, Stanley Richmond, and Russell Winthrop in prison. And you, too." When the little man's mouth opened as though to speak, Matt punched him in the jaw, sending Bowen to the floor and a trash can rolling toward a bookcase.

"And I imagine Caleb Dawson would bash your head in the same way he did Lawrence Tarleton's."

Matt bent down, lifted Bowen by the lapels of his coat, and shoved him into the chair. He clamped his right hand firmly on Bowen's shoulder, but kept his thumb pressed hard against Bowen's throat, and made himself laugh as footsteps sounded on the marble floor in the outer hallway. When those died away, Matt glanced at the clock. Lawyers, judges, and clerks would be filing into the courthouse now. Maybe even some deputy marshals.

Letting go of the secretary, Matt fingered the note he had taken from Bowen's meticulous folders.

"You save everything," Matt said. "Except all the information on Lawrence Tarleton. Including where he was staying when he scheduled that interview with me. You showed me the entry for our second meeting. The meeting he never showed up for. I went back, Carter, to the day of our original meeting. Information is filed for every other person that met with me, even those who canceled. But not for Lawrence Tarleton."

He dropped that paper into Bowen's lap. "You even saved receipts for the telegrams you sent. Like when you were letting the whole damned world know where I was going, what I was doing. So here's what happened, Carter . . . After I met Tarleton, you told Dawson. Efficient as you are, you were listening through the keyhole during every damned meeting I had. That's why you said he *claimed* to work for *Munsey's*. You didn't know that before that first meeting. And your efficiency at spying on me like some chicken-shit Pinkerton, listening through a keyhole, explains the receipt for the telegram to that rancher, Russell Winthrop, after my meeting with deputies Harvey and Hannah." Matt let out a long sigh. "How much were Wilson and Winthrop paying you?"

Bowen started to speak, but Matt silenced him. "Tell me I'm wrong, Carter. But you damned well better make it convincing."

More footsteps in the hallway made Matt step back. This time the sound stopped, and the door opened.

He drew a breath, exhaled, and looked down at Carter. "We'll have to do something about this mess, Carter," he said, hoping his voice sounded natural. Out of the corner of his eye, he watched the jailer walking into the anteroom. "Marshal," the big man drawled. "Mister Bowen. I got a message here for Deputy Marshal Day."

Matt had to look up. Recognition came slowly, but when Matt remembered, he shouted: "Fletcher!"

The black man stopped, glanced at the paper in his left hand, then at the disaster that was Carter Bowen III's desk.

"What brings you out of the dungeons this early, Fletcher?"

The old jailer tried to smile. "One of the prisoners wanted me to give this to Deputy Day, Marshal." His dark eyes again scanned the papers, pencils, pens, calendars, receipts, and ledgers scattered about Bowen's work area.

Matt held out his hand, took the slip from the jailer, and said: "I'll see that Deputy Day gets this, Fletcher. Thank you for bringing it up here."

The big man nodded, turned, but got only three steps toward the door before Matt called out his name. When Fletcher turned back, Matt said: "I have a job for you."

"Yes, sir," replied the jailer.

Then Matt looked down at Bowen. "Am I

wrong?" he asked the pale, sniveling secretary.

Bowen weakened under Matt's glare. "You up to doing me a favor?" Matt asked the jailer without lifting his stare from Bowen.

"Yes, sir," Fletcher said.

Matt looked up. "It could get you into a bit of trouble."

"That's all right, Marshal, sir. Like I told you once before, my children been singing that song about you since I first taken the job of locking folks up."

Matt smiled. "This could get you locked up."

Fletcher laughed. "Wouldn't be the first time, Marshal."

Stepping back from the desk, Matt pointed at Bowen. "I need him locked up in the cellar. No visitors. But give him plenty of writing paper and pencils. A proper confession to being an accessory to murder might keep him from a long term in Cañon City. And hiding him in jail might keep him alive in case this doesn't go the way I'm hoping."

More color left Bowen's pale face. Fletcher seemed skeptical.

"Him?" Fletcher nodded his big head at Bowen.

"Him," Matt said.

"Is that what I'm supposed to say he's locked up for?" Fletcher asked. "Accessory to murder?"

Matt shook his head. "That's not a federal crime," Matt said. "Let's call it . . . treason. But only if someone asks. And if they press you, just tell them that I ordered it."

"You want me to do this right now, Marshal?"

"Just as fast as you can, Fletcher." He shook the jailer's hand, then whispered to Bowen. "While you're in that cell, you best do some honest writing. That's your only hope to keep from staying in prison a long, long time. Providing they don't hang you. You know Judge Perelman's record when it comes to such things, don't you, Carter?"

CHAPTER TWENTY

When Deputy Day arrived, Matt handed him the message Fletcher had delivered, then dispatched the young deputy to send the telegrams to Rawlings and Hannah. After tearing up the telegram he had planned to wire Caleb Dawson, he dropped by Perelman's office three times, only to be told that the judge was tied up in court, but that, yes, Matt's messages would be delivered.

Yet Matt had a pretty good idea what Perelman would tell him if he ever got out of the courtroom. That all of this evidence wouldn't get a conviction, or even an indictment, except for maybe—if the grand jury felt so inclined—a few penny-ante charges. Matt needed something stronger.

No newspapermen came to the office, probably because every one of them had likely started making dust for Durango. Which, Matt decided, is where he needed to be, too. The governor had been right about that. After walking to the D & RG depot, Matt waited in line two hours only to be told the next train south, with room for more people, would be in three days.

"I don't think you understand." Matt showed the agent his badge and railroad pass.

"That's good when we have a seat, Marshal,"

the agent said. "Which we don't have till Tuesday. Everybody in this city is bound and determined to get to Durango, damned fools."

Matt sighed. "But I want to go to Pagosa Springs."

"That's a spur line, Marshal, which runs out of Gato. But the thing is, any train taking you to Gato is on its way to or from Durango. And there ain't no seats available on any of our trains leaving from here till Tuesday."

Someone shoved him from behind. "If you ain't buyin' a ticket, mister, get the hell out so the rest of us can."

The blow-hard fell silent when Matt showed him the badge and gun, but the line behind the man left Matt speechless. Men, women—even a handful of children—stretched to the street corner.

"Hurry up!" a woman called out.

Matt faced the ticket agent, and tried something else. "I can ride in the locomotive."

"Not on this railroad. Company policy."

"Livestock car?"

"You ain't a horse, though you are mule-headed."

He felt another shove, somewhat harder this time, followed by curses, one whispered, two others shouted.

"Marshal, for the love of God," the agent whispered with urgency.

"Let us through!" a woman yelled.

A baby cried. *Who would bring a child to a gold camp?*

The teller, now sweating and paling, pointed over Matt's shoulder. "There'll be stagecoaches hiring out. Probably folks already galloping south. Please, Marshal, I'd like to sell tickets. And make it out of here alive."

He bought an *Evening Post* as he walked back to the office. The governor said the whole affair had to be a hoax, though he also prayed it was true, because a gold strike could lift Colorado out of this recession. The *Post* noted that the *Cattlemen's Clarion* article did not say exactly where the strike had been discovered and that the federal reserve for the Utes covered a thousand square miles. It did, however, report that a line of wagons and horses could be seen leaving Denver before noon. Southbound roads were congested. So were the pikes from Greeley and Cheyenne, according to "one Capt'n Stotz, returning from an assignment at Fort Washakie in Wyoming," because gold-seekers from northern cities filled all lanes.

Matt stopped at the Colorado Midland Railway's depot, surprised to find a long line at the ticket office there, too. A man wearing a bowler stood in line reading the *Morning Herald*'s special afternoon edition, but this crowd did not seem rushed. Matt cleared his throat and waited for the man's eyes to rise from the newspaper.

"This train doesn't go to Durango, does it?" Matt asked.

The man must have figured Matt to be another man driven mad by the promise of gold.

"It goes no farther than Pueblo," the man said. "Which is where I live. But I guess that's close enough to Durango for this rabble."

Matt found something soothing about the statement, even as the older gent's eyes fell back to the newspaper. At least someone remained sane in Denver.

Behind the depot he found the telegraph office, stepped inside, and showed the operator his badge. "I want to send a wire to Colonel Schmidt, commanding officer at Fort Logan," he said.

"Why don't you ride over there?"

Matt's glare persuaded the telegrapher to nod at the pad.

"Can I just dictate?" Matt asked. "Save us some time."

"We charge per . . ."

Matt slapped down a five-dollar note, which quickly disappeared.

"Request four cavalry troops sent to Durango to protect reservation boundary," Matt said. "Stop. Sign it, Matthew Johnson, U.S. marshal. Have him reply here. I'll grab a bite at that café." He pointed. "And be back directly."

The man began singing as he tapped out the message. "Strong as an ox, sly as a fox. Matthew Johnson, United States marshal."

Matt closed the door before the man finished the verse.

When he returned, Colonel Schmidt had replied: **DISPATCHED ONE SQUAD WITH FOUR WEEKS RATIONS YESTERDAY STOP PER GENERAL'S ORDERS STOP.**

"Send a reply," Matt ordered. "Tell Colonel Schmidt to go to hell."

The telegrapher looked uncomfortably at Matt. "I can't use profanity, Marshal."

"It's not profanity," Matt said. "It's a place." He tossed the dollar coin on the counter. "Send it."

Seeing the telephone box on the wall, Matt asked: "Is it all right if I use that?"

The telegrapher sighed. "I reckon. That son-of-a-bitch, though, will eventually end my job."

Matt had the operator connect him with General McCook at the Department of Colorado headquarters. When no one answered, Matt returned to the telegrapher. "You won't be losing your job anytime soon." So he wired McCook, requesting that he change his orders and have Colonel Schmidt send four troops of cavalry by express train, and not horseback, to protect the

Ute boundary, because a squad could not even begin to cover a thousand square miles.

He cursed, fought the urge to find a saloon and get roostered, and remembered that mention of a Captain Stotz in Denver's *Evening Post*. "Stotz," he whispered, and walked back to the telephone. This time, a voice other than the operator, came over the line.

Still, it took ten minutes before the sergeant who answered the call brought Captain Karl Stotz to Fort Logan's telephone.

"Karl," Matt said. "It's Matt Johnson."

"You little bastard," the voice sang out. "I had hoped you had forgotten all about me."

"Been a long time," Matt said.

"Twenty-four years," Stotz said. "I never figured you to be a lawman."

"Never figured you would stay in that man's army," Matt said. "After we got our walking papers at Leavenworth."

"It's a living," Stotz said.

"So's marshaling."

"Well, I'm not as famous as you."

"But you've got more power than I do right now, Karl. I need a favor."

"You gonna tell the newspapers that I was a Reb in the Rebellion, Matt? Ruin my career?"

"I'm going to give you the chance to be the hero of Colorado and the nation, Karl. Your colonel didn't send enough troops to Durango. And he sent them south on horseback. And I can't reach General McCook."

"Colonel Schmidt's a martinet. For all I know, the general went to dig up a fortune in nuggets."

"I might get some soldiers coming up from Fort Marcy, but, hell . . . you're my last hope, Karl."

"That's progress for you. There's just not much use for soldiers today."

Matt said: "There's a lot of use for them on the Ute reservation."

"Matt, I don't have authority."

"I don't either. But I'm asking. I don't have enough deputies to cover all that country."

He heard static, thought Stotz might have disconnected, but what sounded like a sigh came over the line, and then Stotz said: "Matt, you're a civilian peace officer. The governor hasn't declared martial law. And . . ."

"You remember Minnesota, Karl," Matt said. "And, more recently, Wounded Knee. And you weren't far from the Little Big Horn."

"I am not the commanding officer, Matt. I've already told you that I just don't have the authority. I'm just a captain."

"You're a captain, Karl. I'm a lawman. But we can, maybe, just maybe, prevent a bloodbath."

"Matt, this is just crazy."

"Is it as crazy as when I caught those rats for you at Point Lookout? And kept you alive?"

• • •

He heard Jean humming and the swing's squeaking chains as he moved to the steps. Both stopped as Matt's boots climbed the steps. On the porch, he leaned against a column and smiled.

Jean wore a tulip bell skirt of dark blue, with a top of lighter blue trimmed with diagonal scallops of yellow lace.

"This is the first day that actually felt like spring," she said.

Matt swallowed, tried to find something to say. He hadn't even noticed the weather.

"Busy today?" she asked.

His head bobbed.

She patted the place next to her. "Want to sit down for a while?" When Matt looked at the front door, she laughed. "Everybody's gone," she said.

"To Durango?" Matt hoped the question didn't sound sarcastic.

Her head shook. "Only Childs caught the gold fever. But he said he'd still pay rent on his room." Her eyes rolled. "He must think he'll find the mother lode. And it being Saturday, everybody else had plans."

"I guess it is at that." He laid his hat, crown down, on the porch, took the chain in his left hand, and sat next to Jean.

The swing moved. He looked across the porch at the empty rocking chairs.

"Rough day?" she asked.

His head moved slightly.

The chains squeaked. He smelled Jean's perfume.

"Hungry?" she asked.

"No."

"Thirsty?"

His head shook. His Adam's apple bobbed.

"Are you all right?"

Turning to her, seeing those eyes, he smiled. "Horses I can handle. Stagecoaches, not so much. Trains, barely. And swings . . ." He let out a long breath.

"You did pretty well last night," she said, and slid closer. The next thing he felt was her head on his shoulder, and his arm around her back.

"What are you thinking?" she asked.

"That I don't know what I'm doing." Her head lifted and her eyes locked on him. "But," he added, "here I am."

The head returned to his shoulder, and he tilted his toward her, breathing in the scent. He felt his pounding heart.

"Where were you fifteen years ago?" she asked.

He said: "You wouldn't have liked me fifteen years ago."

"I'm not so sure about that." He wasn't aware he had answered.

She lowered her feet to the floor, letting her shoes drag on the wood until the swing slowly stopped. He couldn't look away from her. She smiled, murmured: "Feel better now that we're not moving?"

"I feel . . . different."

"Are you all right?"

He turned, brought his left hand to her face, touched her cheek. "My life has been one mistake after another," he said.

Her body tensed, he could see the hurt in her eyes, and he realized how what he said might have been interpreted. "Is this . . . a mistake?" Jean asked.

"No." He kissed her, softly at first, a little harder, before pulling back. His heart wouldn't stop hammering now. He swallowed. A dog barked down the street. He brushed hair off her forehead with his fingers. "I have to leave early in the morning," he told her.

"Durango?" she whispered.

He nodded. "Eventually."

"How long will you be there?"

He shook his head. "I have no idea." Then he let out a mirthless laugh. "Till I'm fired, probably. Which won't be long."

"And then what?"

He kissed her again. "Oh, Jean," he whispered. "I wish I'd known you twenty years ago."

"You might not have liked me then, either," she said.

"I don't see how I couldn't have."

Her fingers traced his lips, smoothed the mustache, found the scar on his chin, came up the stubble already appearing on his cheek, and moved through his hair. Traces jingled and hoofs clopped down the street, and they pulled away from each other, forgetting that the latticework and shrubs kept them hidden. After a surrey rolled down the street through the gloaming, Jean and Matt laughed at their nervousness.

"I don't know what you see in me," Matt said.

She cocked her head. "Well, there was a while when I didn't think very much of you."

"With good reason." He tapped the swing's arm rest. "I slept here my first night as a boarder."

"I don't smell whiskey on your breath tonight."

He shrugged. "No time to even shoot down one shot tonight."

"Then you brought Reggie in after he . . ." She looked away, but only briefly, and turned back to him. "You want to know when I really fell for you, truly?"

He couldn't answer. Couldn't look away from her gorgeous eyes.

"It was at the automatic phonograph store." She rubbed his cheek, settled back down on his shoulder. "I've been stopping at the window there once or twice a week for two, three months. Never had the courage to go inside. I hinted at Reg . . . at . . . Oh, how I wanted a phonograph. Wanted music to be played . . . and not from my piddling attempts on a piano. He said we couldn't afford one, and that was when he was big in silver. And he never would take me inside that parlor." She raised her head, found his eyes. "But you did, Matt. You did."

They both exhaled.

"You also did something else, Matt," Jean whispered, then giggled. "I've lost count of how many cups have up and walked away to parts unknown."

Crickets sounded. Crickets. Maybe spring had arrived at last. "Listen, Matthew Johnson," Jean said, smiling at first. "You should know this about me. After the War, things were hard in Gallatin. So when Beau Halstead came over and asked for my hand in marriage, I took it, and damned Pa to say anything different."

By then, Jean's smile had disappeared.

"Because Beau was bound for Colorado, and Colorado seemed a far place from Tennessee," she said. "That's how I got here. The first time."

Matt nodded. Jean laughed. "Pa had better sense than I had. I don't know what exactly became of Beau Halstead. One morning he was gone, I had a baby girl, a bunch of bills being waved in my face, and folks letting me know just how much I owed them. Next six years were hard. Real hard. I did everything I could to . . . everything proper . . . to keep my baby girl and me fed. And then here came along Reginald McBride, a mining

284

engineer, and he must have seen something in this scrappy girl with a baby of her own, and he didn't offer me love, but he did offer me . . . a foundation. And, eventually, I gave him a baby girl of his own." Her head tilted back and she sighed. "I did bring up two lovely women. Mothers themselves now, though Judith's only eighteen. She's the rambunctious one, like her mama. She's in San Dimas, California. Diana, my oldest, the scrappy one, also like her mother, she married a soldier. They're at Fort Sill in the Indian Territory." Jean paused, studied Matt long and hard, and smiled. "I'm forty-nine years old, and I don't tell everyone that."

"I'm fifty-two," he said. "And I don't believe that you're forty-nine."

She reached forward, put her hands on his shoulders and pulled him close, kissed him, and pushed back just enough to look into his eyes.

He smiled like he had never smiled before.

"I followed Reggie to Tombstone, then back to Colorado," Jean said, to continue her story, to fill the spaces with words, to keep from shaking. "He was a good . . . provider, just not . . . a good husband. Back then he wasn't drinking himself to death. Well . . . when he finally found pay dirt, I mean, real silver, in Silverton, he . . ." She sighed. "The crash came hard, you know, Matt, but I've always been a scrapper."

"You're a fine woman, Jean," Matt whispered. "And you're . . . beautiful."

"Want to go inside?" Jean rose from the swing.

He picked up his hat, stood, and followed her to the front door.

A couple pushed a baby carriage down the sidewalk, husband and wife, waving at Jean and Matt. Jean returned the wave, and opened the door. Aromas of coffee and cake wafted from the parlor. He discovered her hand again, led her down the hall toward the dining room, but stopped underneath the staircase. They looked at the door to Matt's room.

"Well," he said, and looked at the key he had withdrawn from his pocket. Moments later he tossed his hat toward the dresser, but missed, and looked back at Jean.

"Ummm."

She stepped inside, put her arms around him, kissed him.

"Jean," he whispered.

"Matt," she said.

He pulled away, saw the bed, looked back at her, then went to his hat, picked it up, hung it on the rack, spotted the copy of Whitman, the wash basin, his clothes, the items he had never gotten around to putting up. He pulled out the Waltham, unfastened it from the vest, laid it on the dresser. Then he turned back at Jean.

His trembling fingers reminded him of the time

286

Rex Chesser asked him to ride his first bronc.

"Ummm. This . . . this is my room," he said, as though she had never seen it before.

She smiled again, and nudged the door closed with her foot.

"It's my house," she told him.

He woke to the sound of church bells in the distance, rolled over, and felt the warm body next to his. Jean whispered his name, and Matt mumbled something intelligible. Her face turned, and she stroked his hair. "I have to go," she said. "Get breakfast ready. It's Sunday. Big day here." Her lips came back to his, and when their mouths parted, she asked: "What time do you have to leave?"

He sighed. "Soon."

He wanted to remember every detail of her face—the blue eyes, the smile, the freckles, the curve of her nose, the blonde bangs. He would never forget this moment. When she rolled out of the bed, he grabbed the pillow she had used, breathing in deeply while she dressed. Parts of Lawrence Tarleton's poem came back.

> If I were a chemist
> I could uncork a bottle
> of
> Her stories
> More laughter

The boats to build
and the scent of her perfume
on my pillow

"What would you like for breakfast?" The bed squeaked as she sat beside him, reached over, and took his hand in hers.

"I won't have time to eat," he whispered.

"Coffee?"

"No."

She bent over and kissed him. "Will I see you again?"

"I'll never leave," he said, and she laughed, sadly, and kissed him once again. "Well, thank you."

The door opened, she blew him a kiss, and said: "I love you."

The door closed before he could tell her the same thing.

For a while he lay there, hugging the pillow, only knowing the repeater would start chiming shortly. He knew where he had to go, but it certainly wasn't where he wanted to be.

First, though, he stepped into the kitchen, a coat over his arm, the grip in his left hand.

Jean turned, pushed the bangs from her eyes, and wiped her hands on the apron. Her lips moved, but she found no words.

"I . . ." That's as far as he got.

"Will you be back?" she asked.

"I hope so."

She looked right, then left, and at last back at Matt. "You sure you don't want any coffee?"

His head shook. "I've a train to catch."

"Well . . ." Tears formed in her eyes, but refused to fall.

"Jean," he said. "You told me about you. Well . . . this is what you ought to know about me."

CHAPTER TWENTY-ONE

He sits in the darkness, the long-barreled Colt in his right hand, hearing the wind bang a shutter in the abandoned station's lone window. A horse whinnies, and his big dun, in the small corral out back, answers. Matt ears back the hammer on the .45. Hoofs clop on the road, stopping at the corral. Saddle leather creaks. He doesn't hear the spurs, but figures Jeff Hancock took those off. Finally, boots crunch gravel on the side of the cabin, and Matt follows the noise with his head to the corner, past where the porch used to hang before wayfarers chopped it up for firewood. At the front door, the first long silence begins.

At last, the warped door drags against the dirt floor, bathing a path of light that stops near the cold hearth.

"Kim?" Jeff Hancock calls out.

Kim Buchman is dead, too. Hell, Matt thinks, everybody's dead now.

"It's me," Matt says.

Silence. It won't end. But Matt knows that Hancock has not moved, and after the wind dies down, Hancock says: "Let me see you, Matt."

So Matt stands, the rocker creaks, and he steps past the curtain that still separates the bedchambers from the main room of Rattlesnake

Station. Matt stays in the shadows, but the light from the doorway is enough so that Jeff Hancock can see the .45 in Matt's right hand, and the badge on his vest.

"Never figured you'd want that two hundred and fifty dollars so bad," Hancock said.

"I never figured you'd shoot Bounce's horse from under him so the posse would catch him . . . and me . . . and you'd just ride away."

"Bounce was better off dead."

"I think the same of you."

Hancock laughs. "Do you?" He points with his left hand at the badge. "Or is that what you want? Authority. Power. They made you a county sheriff before anyone even cast a vote, and word is they'll have you made U.S. marshal once you bring me in." He spits on the floor. "You're like them ranchers who call us rustlers. They say . . . 'We can't afford to pay you regular wages . . . take a yearling here and there.' Then when they see how many we've burned, they call us rustlers. That's how this whole damned thing started."

Matt says: "Burn fifty a day, not one of them mine."

Hancock chuckles. "That was funny back then. It ain't no more."

An even longer silence fills the room.

"Where's Kim?" Hancock says at last.

"Dead."

"You kill him?"

Matt shakes his head. "You did. Even if he pulled the trigger and blew his head off."

"Well," Hancock says. "Try this one, Matt." He steps fully inside, and Matt sees the revolver hanging by his legs, barrel aimed at the floor, finger inside the trigger guard, hammer cocked. He can also see Hancock's smiling face as he begins:

> *I rode for justice once,*
> *A long, long time ago,*
> *How many friends I buried?*
> *Well, boys, I just don't know.*
> *There was Bounce and Matthew,*
> *And prob'ly twenty-three,*
> *All driven off our homesteads,*
> *And all following me.*
> *Branded as an outlaw,*
> *You see how I was wronged.*
> *But once I die with glory,*
> *They'll always sing this song.*

"It's your turn," Jeff says, and jerks the revolver up.

• • • • •

He didn't remember dropping his hat, coat, and luggage, and he wasn't sure when he sat on the stool he'd pulled up to the kitchen counter. Yet he recognized that he held his head in his hands and could not stop sobbing.

Jean pulled him to her bosom, whispering, though he hardly heard her: "It's all right, sweetheart," she said. "You did what you had to do. He would have killed you."

His head shook violently. "No," he said, raising his head away from her. "No. When Jeff drew, he turned around so . . ." He struggled to finish the sentence. "So . . . those stories were all right. I did shoot him in the back."

"But . . ."

He sniffed. At least those sobs had stopped, for now.

"But," Jean said again, "you didn't know he would turn. He must have . . ."

"Wanted to die?" Matt laughed. "Or wanted me to live with that fact? Which I have. Matthew Johnson. The back-shooter. Jeff's final joke. On me."

"From what you've told me," Jean whispered, "he had turned into some mad dog. Remember what he did to Bounce?"

"I know." He leaned his head against the counter, and felt Jean kiss his forehead, then use the hem of her apron to wipe his face. She stepped back, then out of his view. He bent over, picked up his hat, swallowed. Something warm came into his right hand, and somehow he smelled the coffee. Jean dragged over another stool and settled in beside him.

"Drink," she ordered. "It'll make you feel better."

He stares at the steaming coffee.

"They sang songs about me," he said. "Not him." He shook his head, coughed out a mirthless laugh. "The damned range war had been going on for over a year by then." He sighed. "I mean, when Chesser's 'stock detectives' and a party of marshals waylaid us, Bounce got cut to pieces. Rex Chesser pulled me from underneath my dead horse. Those boys with him wanted to string me up. But Rex, old Rex, he had a better idea. Thirty pieces of silver. Pin that badge on me. Have the governor appoint me county sheriff to replace the one whose head Jeff caved in. Run me in the election. Backed by the cattlemen's association, I couldn't lose. And after Jeff was dead, I become United States marshal. 'Strong as an ox, sly . . .' "

"Drink," Jean whispered.

The cup rose, and he tested it. "Jeff did go crazy," Matt whispered. "I know that. But what we started . . ." He shook his head. "When we started . . . God, I thought we were in the right."

"Maybe you were," she said.

He tasted more coffee. "Maybe. But that's the story of my life." He turned to her, shook his head, and offered a sad grin. "I've never made the right decision. Joined the Confederacy. Well, we all know how that played out. Then become a Galvanized Yankee, chasing after starving Indians. Lot of justice in that, right?" He sighed. "And rather than go back home, see my folks, the parents who gave me a pretty good education, taught me right from wrong, my baby sister, I write them one letter and take off for the gold fields. Only I never found much of anything. But then came those cowboy years." His smile flashed, faded. "And those were fun times. If I'd drifted into Washington, Oregon, Montana maybe, or south to Texas . . . I might still be doing that."

He sipped from the cup.

"So a war breaks out. Small outfits against the cattlemen's association. I ride with Jeff Hancock, and, yeah, maybe we were right at first." He shook his head. "But not after a while. All I had to do was leave Jeff. But I didn't. You stick with your pards. That's what Bounce always said. Kim Buchman, too. And they stuck. They stuck and died. But not me."

He stared at the floor, before finally looking up at Jean. "Hell, I voted for myself in the election, even though I'd already been appointed . . . that being temporary, you understand. Till the people cast their vote, and the people were the wealthy cattlemen like Rex Chesser. And those who rode for him. And others just like him."

The rest came roaring back through memories. The appointment as United States marshal. And Darlene, who wanted to be married to the United States marshal people sang songs about, first in Idaho, Montana, and eventually across the territories and states. Till other stories started being told. That Matthew Johnson had shot an unarmed man in the back. That Matthew Johnson had murdered his best friend for a federal appointment. After that, God, how the bourbon went down his throat without pause. And Darlene? Well, that was another one of those wrong decisions. He loved the two daughters, but he had never been a father. Or, he had to admit, a husband. She wouldn't divorce him. Nor would she let him have anything to do with Linda, named for Darlene's grandmother, or Anna Marie. Whiskey got much of the blame, but Matt knew all those fingers rightfully pointed at him.

The U.S. marshal's job didn't last long. Presidents and attorneys general don't like being embarrassed in newspaper and magazine stories across the nation. There was that bit of theater Matt tried, telling folks in the East how he had killed the notorious outlaw Jeff Hancock. The band would play that song, and people from the orchestra to the balconies would sing. Before long, though, the songs in the audience would not be the songs sung by school-children.

Matthew Johnson,
United States marshal,
Drunk as a skunk,

Bullyragging punk.
Matthew Johnson,
When his pistol sounds CRACK,
Bet you all he sees
Is an old pard's back.

Now he couldn't stop telling Jean everything. About drifting. Jobs here and there. That disaster as a Pinkerton man. Bank guard in Omaha. Messenger on a stage line from Cheyenne to Deadwood. Why had he never gone back to cowboying? He could have changed his name, become somebody else. Instead, he filled beer mugs in Prescott, Arizona Territory, and finally became a stock detective in Tucson.

The coffee cup, he realized, was empty.

Jean took it from his hand, said she would refill it.

"No." Matt gathered his clothes, pulled his hat on. A door opened upstairs, and he knew someone would be coming down for breakfast before the rush for Jean's Sunday brunch.

"I have to catch that train." He stared into those soulful, soothing eyes. Footsteps came down the stairs.

Their lips moved, but no words came out until Jean asked: "Was last night a wrong decision?"

"No. That was easily the best decision I ever made," he said, and turned, only to see the list of guests pinned on a board. Arriving tomorrow would be John Kimbrough. He would be staying for a whole week.

There was nothing to do about that. After moving into the hallway, Matt nodded at the apothecary, and walked to the front door.

CHAPTER TWENTY-TWO

He stood close to the rails, holding the grip in his left hand, watching the train as it poked along, smoke pouring from the stack, the bell ringing. People crowded the sidewalks, and Matt had to admit this was something to see. Every seat must have been filled on each car, and he wondered how an engine with this heavy a load could manage the Rocky Mountain passes.

As the ten-wheeled Baldwin hissed, creaked, groaned, and eased past Matt, he pitched the grip into the engine, grabbed a handle with his left hand, and pulled himself into the cab.

The engineer cursed, and the fireman with silver side-burns reached for a shovel, but left it leaning against the cab wall upon seeing the Colt in Matt's right hand.

"Is this a damned hold-up?" the engineer asked.

"No," Matt said.

"Well, you can't ride in here. It's . . ."

"I know," Matt said. "Company policy. But this is my policy." He aimed the barrel at the engineer's face, and used his left hand to pull back that damned coat one more time to show his badge. "And so is this."

The fireman leaned closer, sniffed, tugged

on his beard, and stared at Matt. "Are you *the* Matthew Johnson?" he asked.

After Matt's nod, the fireman and engineer exchanged glances, the former shrugged, and both men went back to their work. Shaking his head, the engineer muttered: "The things some fools'll do these days just to see Durango."

"Mister." Matt looked for a comfortable place to pass the time and watch the country. "Right now, I'm just going to Gato."

By the time No. 463 stopped at Gato twenty-six hours later, Matt had determined that the best place to ride a train was in the engine's cab. Sure, it was hot and dirty. Smoke irritated the eyes. A person couldn't avoid soot. The furnace blasted heat that made a man sweat no matter how high the train climbed or how cold the wind blew. But not once did Matt feel sick.

At the depot, Matt sent telegrams to Deputy Hannah in Las Animas, Deputy Rawlings in Durango, and Judge Perelman in Denver, helped himself to coffee on the stove, and waited for the train to take him to Pagosa Springs.

This time, Matt rode in a San Juan Lumber Railway passenger car, which swayed like a ship in a gale, barely kept a grip on the narrow rails as it wound around curves, over cañons, through gorges, before finally stopping in the bustling lumber town of Pagosa Springs. The only reason

Matt did not head to the nearest grog shop was that he doubted if his stomach could hold anything, solid or liquid, until his body stopped shaking.

Dick Meyers, editor of the Pagosa Springs *Weekly Item*, smoothed his thick black mustache, shook his head, and sighed behind the mountain of newspapers that rose from his desk. "I can't say I'm surprised that a federal marshal would be asking about Cole Stevens," the little but solid man in spectacles and sleeve garters said.

"He did work for you then," Matt said.

Meyers shook his head. "He was what we in the business call a correspondent. If he filed a story that I thought was worth running, I'd pay him half-a-cent for every five words that I put in the paper. He could be a long-winded bastard."

"When did you last see or hear from him?" Matt asked.

"February," Meyers replied. "That's when he quit. Said he knew how to make enough money to buy the *Inter-Ocean* in Chicago and not write for dimes." The journalist shrugged. "Not that I blame him. This business isn't for those out to make a fortune. It's for those who seek the truth."

"No word at all?"

"No," Meyers said, shaking his head.

"How about his wife?" Matt asked. "Does she still live here?"

"If you'd call that living." The man found a pencil in his top drawer, tore off a corner of one of the newspapers, and scribbled down a name and address and slid the slip across the desk to Matt. When Matt picked it up, Meyers pulled a notebook from underneath a stack of rolled newspapers, and placed the lead tip on the first page.

"Now that you've interviewed me, Marshal, you won't object if I interview you? Would you?" The man's eyes shined like a rattlesnake's.

Matt stood, and stared.

"What do you think of salubrious Pagosa Springs?" Meyers asked.

"I'm not healthy enough to answer that," Matt said, "not having enough time to recover from the train trip from Gato."

Meyers laughed. "Your wit is as sharp as your aim was at Rattlesnake Station."

Matt set his hat on his head.

"This gold strike near Durango," Meyers said. "If . . ."

"I haven't seen dust or nugget yet," Matt said.

The journalist scribbled, nodding and smiling as he wrote, and looked up when his pencil stopped moving. "Will this be another Black Hills rush?"

"No."

"Why not?" Meyers chuckled. "Another Wounded Knee could be good for Colorado's economy."

Matt's eyes burned, he turned, and had reached the front door before Meyers called out a final question. "How long do you think you can hold onto *this* job, Marshal?"

Without looking back or answering, Matt opened the door.

"Marshal," Meyers called out in a jovial voice, "don't see Missus Stevens empty-handed. Old Forrester. But since you'll be there, too, maybe you should fill both hands." Meyers was still laughing when the door slammed.

"You don't look so strong as no ox," Janice Stevens said in the hovel behind the Lacy J's Eating House. "Not sly as no fox, neither." But her lips smacked when Matt uncorked the bottle and filled her dirty tumbler to the rim.

"You might be lookin' better, though." Leaning low and forward, she sipped about a quarter inch of bourbon from the glass, smiled, and picked up the glass with both hands, trying not to spill a drop as her shaking hands lifted the bourbon higher.

How close did I come to becoming just like this? Matt thought as she sucked down the liquor.

When the glass slammed onto the dusty table, she nodded, pointed, then shoved the glass toward the bottle.

"I need some answers first," Matt said.

She frowned, then stuck out her tongue,

giggled, and leaned back with a sigh. "Name your pleasure, sweetheart."

"When was the last time you saw Cole?"

"Yesterday."

"The constable says you were in jail all day yesterday. And the night and day before."

"What does he know?"

"When was the last time you saw your husband?"

"Which husband?" She slammed her palm on the table, her boisterous laugh detailing the rotten teeth still in her mouth.

"Cole Stevens," Matt said patiently.

"Cole Stevens." Janice's head bobbed. "What a *pendejo*." She giggled. "Know what that means?"

"And the last time you saw him?"

"I don't remember." She slid the empty glass next to the bottle.

Which is how it went for the next forty-five minutes. Matt could hear Kim Buchman saying: *You gotta have patience when you're breaking a horse, Matt. Don't rush the job. Just see it through.* Or maybe Jean McBride snapping at him: *Don't you dare compare a poor woman defeated by John Barleycorn to a mustang, Matthew Johnson.*

But he poured two fingers of bourbon into the glass.

Smiling, she leaned in toward Matt. "You got a girl, honey?"

"Your husband?" Matt tried to prime her.

This time, it might have worked. "My husband was a cardsharp, the low-down bastard." She found the glass, guzzled Old Forrester, slammed the empty container hard on the table. "Son-of-a-bitch." She let a few other profanities fill the dark, stinking hovel, obscenities that would have made young deputy marshals blush.

"So why did he go to Ignacio?"

"For salt, you dumbass peckerwood," she snapped, and grabbed for the bottle only to have Matt jerk it away.

"Salt?" Matt asked.

"Yes, you mule-headed bastard. He was minin' salt. Gonna bring me back a fortune. That's what he told me. From his salt." Tears welled in those bloodshot eyes, and Matt slid the bottle back to her.

"When did you last see Cole?" Matt asked.

"March." Not bothering to pour whiskey into the glass, she lifted the bottle to her lips. "I think. March." She drank some, and set the bottle down. "Yes, March. He'd been goin' down to Ig-, Ig-, Ig-."

"Ignacio," Matt said.

"For 'bout a month." She sighed. "One day he went, never come back. The jackass. Prob'ly run off with some redskin whore."

"What about the salt?" Matt tried again.

She laughed. "Or pepper." She slapped the

table, sucked down more bourbon, laughed a final time, and said: "Salt." She cried briefly, shook her head, and stared pitifully at Matt. "Would you bring me back . . . more?" She waved the bottle before Matt, who sighed, feeling like a procurer or the biggest bastard ever to ride a train into Pagosa Springs. "I'll pay you."

She stood, stumbled to her knees, but by the time Matt rose from the rickety chair, she had knee-walked to the dresser. She reached not inside a drawer, but underneath, fumbling, finally grinning, and pulled out a leather pouch.

"It's 'bout gone," she said, knee-walking again to the table. "Cole had better come home soon. Or he'll be sorry." She tossed the bag onto the table, tried to find a way to get into the chair, and Matt had to move around the table, and help her to bed, instead of the chair.

She patted his hand. "You're a good boy, Peckerwood. Good, good boy. Take some of me salt. Bring me . . . back . . . some . . . Ol' . . ." A second later, she lay snoring, and Matt settled into the chair. He picked up the pouch, surprised by the heft, and tugged on the drawstring. Then he tipped the edge of the smelly piece of rawhide over his cupped palm.

Staring at his hand, Matt whispered: "Salt. Of course. *Salt*."

CHAPTER TWENTY-THREE

"You have any wires for me?" Matt asked the Pagosa Springs telegrapher.

When the bald man wearing eyeglasses glanced up, Matt showed his badge. "You Johnson?" the telegrapher asked.

Matt nodded, and the little man flipped through some papers before pulling out a yellow sheet and handing it to Matt.

Colonel Schmidt's response from Fort Logan did not surprise Matt, who pitched the yellow paper into the wastebasket. The small man slid Matt another telegram. This time, though, Matt smiled.

"Well, maybe my luck's changing." He reread the telegram.

CHOCTAW BLACK ARRESTED AT WINTHROP RANCH STOP ARSENAL IN BARN STOP INCLUDING STOLEN MILITARY WEAPONS STOP ARRESTED WINTHROP, TEN OTHERS STOP NO CASUALTIES STOP SIGNED HANNAH, HARVEY, DEP US MARSHALS

Matt looked back at the bald man. "You up to sending a few more telegrams?"

"If you've got the money, Marshal, I'm at your service. Where are we sending these?"

The first wire went to Liberty Rawlings in Durango, reminding him to hire as many good men as deputies as he could, that he might get Army troops from Fort Marcy or Fort Logan but could not count on it, that Matt would be coming in from Pagosa Springs, and that he would like Rawlings and Strongo Stroheim to meet him at the Ute agency at Ignacio in two days.

The second went to deputies Hannah and Harvey, congratulating them and thanking them for their dedication to duty. The last went to Colonel Schmidt.

NOW THAT DEPUTY MARSHALS FOUND YOUR STOLEN GUNS ETC SEND AS MANY TROOPS AS YOU WANT TO UTE RESERVATION STOP

The telegrapher laughed, tapped out the message, and looked up at Matt. "That colonel, he'll bust a boiler, won't he?"

"I certainly hope so. But I doubt if he'll send any troops here unless he's ordered to by a general, or the President, or our governor asks for martial law."

The machine began ticking, and Matt wrote out telegrams, one for the Secretary of War, the Secretary of the Interior, and the attorney general, all in Washington, D.C. The last wire was sent to the Indian agent at Ignacio. After the telegrapher tallied up the words and gave Matt the price, he paid the fee, got his receipt, and asked: "Is there a livery stable here?"

"Sam McDowell rents out some horses." The bald man pointed at a cabin and barn on the other side of the tracks. "But I can't tell you if he's got anything left for let or sale. Folks are going crazy to get to Durango."

"That's where I'm going."

"Well, the next train's due here in three hours," the telegrapher said. "You could ride it to Durango."

"I'd rather stay off trains for a while, my friend," Matt said, and shook the small man's hand. "But if McDowell doesn't have any horses, I'll be back."

McDowell had one horse, a piebald mare, but he wasn't renting anything these days, fearing people just wouldn't bring those horses back once they hit Durango. Matt paid twenty dollars for a ten-dollar nag, and forty more for saddle and tack. But on this trip, he had brought plenty of money with him, recalling how pricy things were in Denver back during the winter of '65-'66 and in Idaho's gold camps over the years.

He rode the trail that led southwest out of Pagosa Springs to the northern boundary of the Southern Ute reservation, and followed the Río

Nutria a ways before turning west over what he thought to be the reservation boundary. He didn't find a deputy marshal until he reached a small settlement on the Piedra River. The deputy called himself Jonas Hammerstein, and he couldn't have been older than nineteen. Despite the sun and the wind, Jonas Hammerstein was pale as a ghost.

"You scared?" Matt asked.

"There ain't nobody here to help me," Hammerstein said. "Nobody here between the San Juan and the Pine excepting me, Marshal, and I ain't the gun hand you are."

Matt stared south. "You're right. This ought to be a job for soldiers." He kept staring south down the Piedra, which had started to flow with snow melt from the mountains. It was the first time Matt felt the warmth of spring since he had arrived in Colorado. With all the snow in the high country, it would be a wet year. Cattle and sheep would have plenty to eat.

"Have you seen Liberty Rawlings?" Now Matt faced Hammerstein.

"Not since he brung me here and told me what to do." Matt grinned. He hadn't needed to send Rawlings a reminder to hire more deputies.

"What's the quickest way to get to Ignacio?" Matt asked.

The boy shook his head and shrugged. "I don't know how quick it is," he said, and pointed west.

"But the next big river . . . and it ain't real big . . . you'll run into is the Pine. You follow that south and you'll find yourself in Ignacio."

"Say 'I do,' " Matt ordered, and the kid cocked his head in confusion but whispered the words as a question. "You're duly sworn in," Matt said, stepped into the saddle, tugged the reins, and started west.

"What am I supposed to do, Marshal?" Hammerstein called out.

"Like the sergeant told us a long, long time ago . . . 'Just hold your ground, just hold your ground.' "

"What does that mean?" the kid cried out.

"Don't know," Matt said. "I never got into battle." He rode a few yards, twisted in the saddle, and yelled at the shaking Hammerstein: "I'll send you some deputies, Jonas! Quick as I can!"

But he wondered if Hammerstein would still be at Piedra when help finally arrived.

Dusk came quickly, so Matt made camp, watering and graining the pinto, building a small campfire but making only coffee for supper. Lying on his bedroll, listening to the owls and coyotes, he thought of Jean McBride, all the while turning a small stone over between thumb and forefinger, watching the flames reflect off this gold nugget he had taken from Cole Stevens's widow.

• • •

When he reached the Pine River, he found the trail easier, and made good time, trotting into Ignacio station before noon. The depot was empty, and the agency looked abandoned, but Matt rode up anyway, and felt something close to relief when Mr. Gottselig, the Southern Ute agent, stepped outside.

"You get my telegram?" Matt asked, looping the reins around the hitching rail.

"Yeah," the agent said, "but it doesn't make a lick of sense."

"Have Rawlings or Stroheim shown up?"

"I wouldn't know them from Wild Bill Hickok."

"Sure you would," Matt said. "Hickok's been dead for sixteen, eighteen years or so." He pointed at the depot. "Where's the stationmaster?"

"Quit." Gottselig stopped moving. "Out somewhere in this godforsaken piece of misery looking to make his pile."

"And all those workers?"

"Probably the same."

"And why aren't there any Utes here?"

The agent wet his lips. "I don't like being the only white man here, Marshal. Nobody told me . . ."

Matt's face hardened, and he rested his hand on the Colt's grips. "Cole Stevens. Remember?"

"Like I told you the first time you come here, Marshal, I don't know any Cole Stevens."

"Because he wasn't using that name. And he didn't take the train. He rode from Pagosa Springs. But he was a white man. And he had a Ute woman helping him out. I telegraphed you for a translator and asked for a meeting with the Ute leaders. And my patience is running short."

By four that afternoon, Utes filled the grounds, but Liberty Rawlings and Strongo Stroheim had not shown up. Gottselig kept pacing, and sweating.

The Indians here did not speak English—or they pretended they didn't—and Matt wondered if those Utes he had deputized would ever show up. Thirty minutes later, he spotted dust on the trail that led to the fork at the hill. Borrowing the agent's binoculars, Matt looked and felt the joy of relief.

Four Ute men rode ponies. Three women walked beside them. Matt recognized the lead rider, that old man who had told the story of how the Utes came to be here. Once again, he had dressed in his white-man-go-to-meetings, the store-bought trousers and coat, the bowler topping his long, silver hair. Matt focused the binoculars, however, on the women.

When they arrived and dismounted, and a young boy ran forward to take the horses and lead them to the corral, Matt walked to the old man. He saw the younger Ute, the one who had translated for Matt back when he had stopped those miners pretending to be surveyors.

"I thank you all for coming," Matt said, and hoped the young Ute would translate.

Instead, his eyes angry, he asked: "Why do you come here? Why . . ."—he pointed at the badge on Matt's vest—"when white men flood our land? Do you come to take away our land, the land my father told you about?" He gestured at the silver-haired man. "Do you want to find the gold, too?"

"There is no gold," Matt said. "I want to know where the body is buried."

The Ute's eyes narrowed. "What body?"

Matt pointed at the young Ute woman. The calico dress had been replaced by a deerskin one, and she wore a garnet sash instead of the beaded belt, but the gold nugget still hung around her neck from sinew.

"She knows." Matt reached inside his vest pocket, withdrew the thumb-sized nugget from Cole Stevens's widow's room, let the old man, the young woman, and the Ute see it. He let all of the Indians, and even Gottselig, see the stone.

The Ute girl remained unreadable. The old man looked at her, the translator, at Matt, and spoke with authority. Other women hurried forward and began rolling blankets onto the ground, while another walked forward with a quill-decorated bundle that, when rolled out, revealed a pipe.

Two other men escorted Matt to the blankets, where he sat in front of the silver-haired leader.

Silently, Matt prayed that the tobacco in the pipe would not make him sick.

The woman's name was Juniper Berry. The man who gave her the stone wanted her to show him a good place. A place to dig a hole. Closer to the land of the white men. Far enough from the Ute villages.

Matt asked the young Ute to ask Juniper Berry if she would show him this place.

Her head shook violently, and Matt guessed why.

"Did you see them kill Cole Stevens?" He waited for the translator to ask the question.

Her head dropped, but the old chief barked something to her, and she looked at him. Eventually, she nodded.

"Some of us will go with you," the young Ute said.

By the time their horses were out of the corral, Liberty Rawlings had arrived.

"When I saw all those Indians," Rawlings told Matt as they left the agency, "I thought you were going to deputize the whole damned tribe. Like you did before."

They rode abreast, following the Utes, with a few more Indians riding behind them.

Matt laughed. "I'm not that stupid. Deputizing Indians to drive white gold miners off their land would be the best way to start a war." He hooked his thumb back toward Ignacio. "Though I thought I might be able to deputize the railroad workers." He changed the subject. "Where's Strongo?"

Rawlings sighed. "He quit."

Matt muttered an oath and shook his head. "I can't believe he'd get greedy. . . ."

"Oh, no." Rawlings cut him off. "He hired on to work for Marybeth Shelby. Keep those damned fools from ruining her grazing land, trying to find the Seven Cities of Cibola." This time Rawlings swore underneath his breath. "You wouldn't believe the people crowding Durango."

"Oh, I believe it. I was part of that crowd in Idaho in my younger days. Any troops arrived yet?"

"No."

"No help from the governor? Anybody?"

"The governor's calling for your scalp, Matt." He tensed, realizing what he had just said, but if the closest Indians understood, they kept it to themselves. "And according to this morning's paper, the *Cattlemen's Clarion* is demanding your removal."

"That figures."

"That's Luther Wilson's paper. Well, he owns a good chunk of it."

"I know."

"And the commanding officer at Logan and some general in Denver have accused you of overstepping your authority."

"The only reason I still have a job," Matt said, "is because President Cleveland is trying to find a way to save what little clout he still has. It's politics, Liberty."

"I don't understand politics at all."

"Nobody does."

He remembered the trail, the place where the Utes had pitched the teepee to stop the fraudulent surveyors. They rode past that, and continued north, followed a dry wash, climbed higher, and stopped. Matt pointed at the shaft someone had dug inside the hill.

Rawlings straightened in the saddle. "If there's a body in there," he said, "and it's been in there since March . . . wolves, coyotes . . ." He shook his head. "Even if there's anything left . . ."

"I'm not looking for a corpse," Matt said. "I just wanted to know where it was."

The Ute translator spoke to the woman, then to Old Silver Hair, and at last let his horse walk him to Matt and Rawlings.

"This is the place you wanted to see," the Ute said. "This is the place all those white men come to find, the white men that you cannot stop, that we cannot stop."

"We can stop them," Matt said. "Now." He

shook his head. "What a damned waste. All for nothing."

He frowned, and remembered.

• • • • •

Squatting behind the well at the line shack, Matt levers the Winchester, catches his breath, looks back at the tree line where the rest of his posse waits. The air stinks of sulphur. Matt wipes his mouth with the back of his hand.

"Kim!" he calls out. His heart races. "Kim Buchman! It's Matt!"

"I know."

His throat burns, but he does not realize the irony until minutes later. Here he sat, dying of thirst, behind a well with some of the sweetest water in the Payette range. And he couldn't get a bucketful without getting his head blown off.

"It's all for nothing, ain't it, Matt?"

He can't think of a proper reply.

A few minutes later, Buchman calls out: "Hey, Matt?"

Matt's breathing has returned to almost normal. "Yeah?"

"How about a poem?" A long pause. "For old time's sake."

"Whitman?" Matt tries to smile. "Longfellow? Byron?"

"How about your own? Those always sounded more real to me. Not fancy, I mean. But real."

"Not poetry is what you mean." Matt laughs.

318

"I wouldn't know about poetry, Matt. I wasn't educated like you. Or Bounce."

Matt dams the tears that start to flow.

"I always," Buchman starts, pauses, continues, "liked that one about . . . the skies."

Wetting his lips, Matt lowers the Winchester, looks back at the trees, sees the movement of men, horses, and rifles, and then raises his gaze above the forest. After drawing in a deep breath, and exhaling, Matt begins.

> *When I see the sky*
> *Azure*
> *So pure*
> *So vast*
> *I remember her eyes*
> *When I see the clouds*
> *Fluffy*
> *Lovely*
> *So white*
> *I can forget the shrouds*
> *When I look above*
> *At stars*
> *And Mars*
> *At night*
> *I am touched by God's love*

It hurts to swallow. He wonders if Kim Buchman could hear him. When a gunshot from the line shack ends the quietness.

Using the Winchester, he pushes himself to his feet, and he turns, staring at the rotting old building. He screams Buchman's name.

But hears only the echoes of a gunshot that he fears will never stop ringing.

CHAPTER TWENTY-FOUR

The Utes were gone that evening, leaving Matt and Rawlings at the mine shaft, looking at bones scattered with bits of clothing, and a shattered skull butted up against some timbers used to brace the mine.

Rawlings brought a torch closer to the skull. "I don't think a wolf did that," he said, his words just audible.

"No," Matt said. "It wasn't a wolf. Revolver. With a lanyard ring."

Outside, Rawlings sat on a rock, face paling, chest rising and falling.

"Was that . . . that . . . the Stevens fellow you were looking for?" the deputy finally asked.

"That's my guess." He headed to the horses. "All I have is coffee."

Rawlings raised his head. "We're camping here?"

"Might as well."

Though neither man slept much that night.

When they topped the ridge that morning, Matt pointed north. "Recognize this country?" he asked.

Rawlings nodded.

"Where's the Shelby spread from here?"

Standing in his stirrups and leaning over the bay's head, Rawlings finally nodded. Then he sank into his saddle and turned to Matt. "I think I understand," he said softly.

Matt pointed to an arroyo down the hill. "If you had a gold mine, on Indian land, you'd want to keep it a secret. No road. No trail. And the best way to get to it is . . ."

"From Marybeth Shelby's place," Rawlings said. "But . . ." He twisted in the saddle to look back down the hill to the Cole Stevens mine. Turning back to Matt, he continued. "But it was the *Clarion* that first reported there might be gold on the reservation."

Matt nodded. "Wilson dabbles in real estate. He told me that. With Durango dying, he'd be able to make a good bit of profit, renting and selling homes to eager young gold seekers. Mind you, I'm still guessing, but word was bound to get out about that gold mine. You said Durango was like Bedlam. So deputies . . . soldiers, too, if they ever decide to do what they're supposed to be doing . . . will be patrolling the boundaries, and the main roads and trails. People would still be renting property or buying homes. While Luther Wilson and his crowd milked that mine for all it's worth. Marybeth Shelby's place is deeded land, right?"

Rawlings seemed to understand.

Matt kicked his pinto down the slope. "With

an easy path, it would be hard to spot anyone traveling from her land to Cole Stevens's final resting place."

"They couldn't keep this a secret forever," Rawlings said as he caught up alongside Matt.

"No. But who knows what all would happen? I bet you've never been to Deadwood. I have. Pretty country. You're probably a little too young to remember that the miners that founded Deadwood did it illegally. The Black Hills belonged to the Indians, and that led to Custer getting cut down at the Little Big Horn. And even I wasn't born when the Cherokees got driven out of Georgia and Tennessee.

"And if you've worked in gold camps, like I did when I was young and stupid, you'll learn that the men who make the most money most of the time are those who are selling things, not working pickaxe or pan. Luther Wilson figured to make his fortune that way, and get a little bit from this mine, which isn't worth spit."

"You keep saying that." Rawlings had to steer around a cactus and pile of rocks. When he came back alongside Matt, he pointed behind them. "But you saw the gold back there. And that wasn't fool's gold on that Ute squaw's neck." He paused. "Was it?"

"It was gold," Matt said. "Hanging from her neck. And a few nuggets in that hole Cole Stevens dug in the hillside."

He reined up, as did Rawlings, both men seeing the dust at the same time.

When the first wagon rounded the bend, Matt, standing in the middle of the arroyo, had his badge in full view, the Winchester braced against his shoulder, his finger on the trigger.

The driver pulled hard on the lines, and the man in the back of the wagon stood, dropping his hand for a belted revolver.

"If your man Frank touches that pistol," Matt bellowed at Holland, "my posse kills every one of you sons-of-bitches! And you're first, Holland!"

Matt had not forgotten the trespassers he had arrested on his first trip through the Ute reservation, almost immediately recognizing that "surveyor", Holland, and Frank, the loud-mouthed squirt with a six-shooter. Sitting next to the driver, Holland kept screaming at Frank to stop before he got everyone here killed.

Slowly, Frank moved his hands wide from his body.

Matt did not lower his rifle, but heard Liberty Rawlings barking orders behind the second and last wagon.

"Left hand," Matt said. "Unbuckle the belt, fling it into that cactus. And you two, keep your hands up."

When the holster and revolver had landed ten yards from the lead wagon, Matt lowered the rifle slightly, and walked to Holland, Frank, and the red-headed driver.

"Second time you've been caught trespassing on the reservation." Matt kept walking to the end of the wagon, noticed the driver and three men in the second wagon, hands raised, and looked in the back of Holland's vehicle. This time, no canvas was needed to cover the wheelbarrows, dynamite, and hard-rock mining tools. The only thing covered lay closer to the rear, a canvas sheet, that, warm as the weather had turned, attracted flies. Frowning, Matt pulled himself into the bed, called out Rawlings's name, and moved to the sheet. He recognized the smell, and saw Frank lunge.

The rifle barrel smashed the gunman's jaw, sent him sailing against a wheelbarrow. Rawlings yelled—"Hold it"—but Matt didn't know who he was talking to. Frank whimpered, and Matt jerked his carbine toward Holland and the redhead. He read the fear in their eyes, realized neither posed a threat, so he slid back to the canvas, held the rifle with his right hand, the stock braced against his left hip. His left hand reached under his right arm, grabbed the slick canvas, and jerked it back.

The next thing he could recall seeing was the face of Liberty Rawlings, his mouth moving, but all Matt really noticed was how bright the sun was this time of day. Then words found his ears.

"Stop it!" Rawlings was shouting. "Stop it! You'll kill him!"

And Matt understood that was exactly what he wanted to do. Sanity must have returned, and he looked down at the bleeding face, the busted nose, the split lips of Holland. He saw the rifle in his hands, the blood dripping off the barrel, looked away from Rawlings, and found fear etched in the wagon driver's face.

Then he turned back toward the bed, where Frank cowered, and Strongo Stroheim lay dead.

Rage almost returned, but Matt fought it down, though he thumbed back the Winchester's hammer and pressed the barrel against Holland's groin.

"You don't answer promptly, you don't answer truthfully, I pull the trigger. And that's just the first time."

He waited, let Holland spit out blood and part of a tooth. "How many are at Missus Shelby's spread?" Matt asked.

"Six. Ten." Tears welled in Holland's eyes. "I . . ." He spit out more blood. "Ten. No more."

"Is Wilson there?"

"Yes."

"Missus Shelby? The little girl?"

"They're . . ."

"Alive?" Matt roared.

"Yes, yes, for God's sake, yes."

"How about the men riding for her brand?"

This time Liberty Rawlings answered. "They all quit her, Matt. That's why Strongo went to work for her."

Matt waited, almost turned toward Strongo's corpse, but couldn't make himself do that. The body reminded him too much of the bludgeoned county sheriff in Idaho, and, more recently, Lawrence Tarleton. Most likely, shortly before Tarleton was murdered, Cole Stevens had met a similar end by the same son-of-a-bitch.

"Caleb Dawson?" Matt whispered dryly. "Is he there?"

"I don't know that name."

Matt made a vague gesture to the dead body. "Did he do that?"

"Who?"

"Dawson. A pal of Wilson. You know who I mean."

"Honestly . . . ," Holland began, but the driver of the second wagon cried out: "It's Dawson, all right. It's Dawson."

Matt let the Winchester's barrel slide off Holland's groin. He looked at Rawlings. "How many manacles do you have?"

They locked Holland and Frank together with the pair of leg irons, running the chain between the rear wheel of the first wagon. Holland got the shady spot, underneath the wagon, but that also put him closest to the ant mound. Frank would bake in the sun till it started to dip later that evening.

The handcuffs were used on the two men who weren't driving the second wagon, with the shorter one on the outside, and the man in the checkered pants leaning against the arroyo's wall.

While the four prisoners were being shackled, the two drivers buried Strongo Stroheim. Not deep. Under Matt's instructions, they placed his covered body next to the arroyo wall, caved it in so that sand and gravel covered the body, and then scoured the area for heavy rocks to keep the carrion from finding his corpse. Like the wolves and badgers had found Cole Stevens's body some miles back.

"That's just temporary," Matt whispered to Rawlings. "We can't bring him with us."

Rawlings nodded. "What about those two?" He pointed at the two drivers.

Matt had been thinking about that. He didn't trust tying them with lariat, or rawhide, and he damned sure wasn't bringing them with him. So he waved the Winchester at both men. "Walk," he said. "Just keep walking till you reach Ignacio. If you get there, if the Utes don't catch you and cut off your balls, tell the agent about these four. Then you damned well better find a way out of this territory, because if I ever see your two faces again, I'll remember that good man you were hauling away to bury without a trace. And I'll kill you on sight. And you best remember who I am. I'm Matthew Johnson."

The two never looked back, never slowed their pace.

Matt and Liberty sat in the back of the second wagon, cleaning their weapons, sipping water, reloading rifles and revolvers, and considering the firearms confiscated from these trespassers. Matt hefted the nickel-plated pocket pistol he had pulled out of Holland's boot top.

Rawlings glanced at it, then laid the Sharps across his legs. "That's only good for short distances."

"That's what I'm thinking." It was a .41-caliber Colt Cloverleaf, four shots, barrel less than three inches. He checked the cylinder, figuring Holland was too careful to keep all chambers filled. Yes. The chamber underneath the hammer remained empty, but that was all right. He opened his coat and slipped the revolver into the inside pocket.

"You got a plan?" Rawlings asked after Matt slid off the wagon.

"To get Missus Shelby and her daughter out of their house," Matt said. "Alive."

Rawlings dropped to the ground, and followed Matt up the arroyo wall, where they walked to their horses they had hobbled in a shady spot.

CHAPTER TWENTY-FIVE

Riding toward the Shelby ranch house, Matt smiled as Jeff Hancock's words sang out in his memories. *There's not a cowboy with any sand who'd ride a pinto.*

Well, Matt thought in reply, *this little mare has about as smooth a gait there is. Maybe the Indians had the right idea all along. Hell, they are better horsemen than we are.*

Matt rode in from the north, on the main road, and he liked the layout of the Shelby place. A good cañon to block the wind, with a fine view of the pastures. Looked to be an orchard off toward the cañon wall. He found the windmill, the bunkhouse, the round pens, and the cook shed. There was the dinner bell, just as Liberty Rawlings had described. Four men stepped out of the bunkhouse. The front door to the main house opened, and Matt kept riding to the hitching post.

"Luther!" Matt called out as he reined up.

"Marshal Matthew Johnson." Wilson shook his head, and laughed. "Where have you been the past few days, hoss? Other than robbing trains." He laughed. "Demanding passage to Durango. The *Morning Herald* said you must have fled your job for the promise of a fortune in gold."

Matt kicked free of the stirrups, but just leaned closer. "And what does the *Clarion* say?"

"I fear you have lost our support." Wilson placed his right hand against the frame wall. "I warned you, Matt. You could have been set, made a pile. But you just turned everybody against you." He laughed again. "How about a drink?"

"I heard Missus Shelby was a follower of Carrie Nation."

"We brought our own." Wilson moved to the door, pulled it open, and waved his hand. "Come on in, Matt. Let's chew the fat."

Matt swung from the mare, loosened the cinch, rubbed her neck, and tethered her to the post. Slapping dust off his clothes, he walked to the steps.

"You must be thirsty." Wilson held the door open, grinning.

In the library, Marybeth Shelby sat in a plush, silk-trimmed sofa with colorful fringe hanging from the arms and bottom. Matching armchairs surrounded a cherry-wood table, but Matt felt drawn to the bookcases. He had taken off his hat when he entered the house, but he bowed at the widow and pretended not to notice how red her eyes remained.

Wilson stood beside the bar while Matt looked at the spines on the shelves, finding not one collection of poetry.

"Bourbon, Matt?" Wilson called out.

Matt turned, shook his head, and asked Mrs. Shelby: "Where's your daughter, ma'am?"

"Sleeping."

Matt nodded. *Good.*

"I've never heard of Matthew Johnson turning down a bourbon." Wilson raised two tumblers.

"Well, I'm here on official business."

Wilson sipped from one glass, set the other down. "I never heard of Matthew Johnson turning down a bourbon even when he was on official business."

"I'm looking for Strongo Stroheim," Matt said. He saw Maryanne Shelby stiffen, and the glass freeze in Wilson's hand.

"Stroheim?" Wilson looked at another door. "I thought he quit marshaling."

"He did."

Wilson killed his drink, and reached for the one he had poured for Matt. "Well, he's not here, Matt." The glass shook. "Is he, Marybeth?"

"I know that, too," Matt said as the second door opened. Caleb Dawson held a cocked Remington revolver in his right hand. He wasn't smiling.

"You're fired," Matt told him.

Dawson laughed. "I quit. I found a better way to make a living."

Matt did not move.

"I'm gonna make you real pretty, Matt." Dawson lowered the hammer, and showed Matt the revolver's walnut handles, and the lanyard ring on the bottom of the grips.

Matt moved to one of the chairs, settled in the seat, and looked back at Wilson. "You're under arrest." Glanced over at Dawson. "You, too."

Wilson finished the second bourbon and rushed over, sitting on the edge of the table. "Matt, don't be a damned fool," he said, hands shaking. "There's enough gold in this to make us all wealthy. It's the mother lode. Between this mine and the fortune I'll make in . . ."

Raising his left hand slightly, Matt grabbed his coat at the lapel, but he looked at Dawson for permission. "You mind?"

The Remington wasn't cocked, but Dawson turned the barrel toward Matt. "Just be careful, Marshal."

Matt pulled the coat open, and used his left hand to reach inside the pocket. After withdrawing the pouch, he let the coat fall back in place, and tugged on the drawstrings with his teeth, turned the leather pouch over, and shook out a couple of small gold nuggets.

Fingering one, he tossed it to Wilson, who fumbled it, but quickly knelt, and rose, staring at the stone.

"It's gold." Wilson grinned, while Matt closed the pouch, tossed it up, caught it, and his face hardened.

"You got hoodwinked, Luther," he said. "You,

too, Caleb. Cole Stevens was a grafter. He just didn't count on getting killed after showing you that mine he wanted to sell you."

"What the hell are you talking about?" Dawson said.

"I worked in gold country in Idaho." Matt focused on Wilson. "It's called salting. You salt the mine you want to sell. Make it look like a fortune." He tossed the bag up, caught it. "Like I said, hoodwinked."

Matt kept tossing the pouch up, catching it, watching Dawson's face turn burgundy.

"He's lying." Wilson's voice cracked.

"Am I?" Matt pitched the pouch up again. "And you figured once I got the U.S. marshal's job that I could help y'all with everything. Or you'd just keep me too drunk to get in your way. But here I am, sober, and you'll swing for murder."

"Murdering a chiseling thief?" Dawson laughed. "Where's your proof? Besides, it ain't a federal offense, either."

"It is if it happens on a federal reserve."

"You still can't prove anything. Not even who stoved in that big Swede deputy's head."

Now, Matt laughed. "How did you know Strongo's head was bashed in?" He flipped the pouch again. "Like Cole Stevens's. And Lawrence Tarleton's."

"And soon yours," Dawson said.

"Maybe." Matt opened the coat, shifted the

pouch, and dropped it inside his pocket. "Maybe not." The Cloverleaf came out, Dawson staggered back, tried to bring up the Remington. The hideaway gun was small, but the .41 sounded like a Sharps in the room.

Dawson slammed against the wallpaper, eyes crossed, a small dark hole in his forehead, bladder and bowels emptying, the Remington bouncing off the tile floor while Dawson, already dead, slid to the floor.

Marybeth Shelby, a rancher's widow, did not flinch. She leaped from the seat, screamed her daughter's name, and rushed out of the room.

"Meet me at the front door." Turning, Matt slammed the little Colt against Wilson's side. "Move." Matt shoved Wilson toward the foyer.

From outside came shouts, footsteps, and through the windows he saw armed men taking positions. One man was charging up the steps. Matt kicked open the door and let the small Colt bark.

The man twisted, clutching his stomach, and fell into a heap.

Matt shoved the hot barrel against Wilson's head. "Tell them," Matt hissed. "Tell them if they fire one shot, make one move toward this house, you're dead. Tell them." He tried to drill the small barrel through Wilson's temple.

Wilson screamed nonsensical words, tried again, not calmer, but clearer.

Marybeth Shelby came to the entrance with her daughter. Matt hoped she had not taken the little girl through the library.

"Howdy," Matt said with a smile to the girl, and tried to think of which of his own daughters the six-year-old reminded him of. "My name's Matt. What's yours?"

She didn't answer, but buried her head into her mother's shoulder.

Matt looked back through the doorway and ordered: "You're going to tighten that pinto's cinch, and you're going to bring out three other horses." He turned to Marybeth Shelby, lowered his voice. "Does she have her own pony?"

The woman's head bobbed slightly. "A buckskin."

"The buckskin!" Matt called out. "With the girl's saddle. Wilson's horse." He waited to hear the woman's voice. "Mine's a bay. Last stall on the south side." Matt told them that.

"If those horses and tack aren't to my liking, there will be hell to pay," he informed them.

"Just who in the hell are you?" a Texas accent twanged.

"Matthew Johnson," he answered. "United States marshal."

Now came the waiting, the sweating. Even beside the front door, he could hear the ticking of the kitchen clock, and smell the gun smoke from the library. He handed the Cloverleaf butt

336

forward toward Marybeth Shelby. "There's only one round in it," he said. She took it, and shoved it in the pocket of her skirt.

"Is that a gun, Mama?" the girl muttered.

Matt knelt and smiled. "You still haven't told me your name," he whispered. "My name's Matthew. But you can call me Matt."

She looked at her mother, then back at Matt. "Eunice," she said softly, and Matt grinned, tousled her hair. "That's a lovely name."

"The horses are ready!" the Texan barked.

"Leave them on this side of the dinner bell," Matt ordered, and he stood, grabbed the shivering Luther Wilson, and palmed the Colt. He thumbed the hammer back, pressed the barrel against Wilson's back, and whispered: "Remember Caleb Dawson. Because I won't forget Strongo Stroheim."

Two pigeon-toed, lanky men walked up to Matt's pinto, grabbed the reins, and led the mare away.

Matt breathed in, let it out, and said: "Let's go."

Wilson walked first, trembling but keeping the pace Matt wanted. Matt came behind him, down the steps, the Colt now pressing against Wilson's skull. Past the hitching post, Matt counted eight men spread out across the yard, not blocking the way out, just close enough to make a stand.

Ten men, Holland had said. That might have included Caleb Dawson, or even Luther Wilson, but Matt didn't think so. He figured two men hid somewhere. Where? It didn't matter.

After Matt told Wilson to stop, the Texan stepped forward, resting his right hand on a revolver's ivory handle.

"Matthew Johnson," he said with a smile. "From what I hear, you're a worthless drunk. So just how the hell do you plan to get out of here . . . alive?"

Matt moved the Colt over Wilson's shoulder. The gun barked. Wilson jumped, but Matt grabbed Wilson's shoulder with his left hand, and thumbed back the Colt's hammer, not knowing if he had hit the bell or not. Wilson kept sucking in breaths. Matt waited.

"So you hit a . . ."

The bell rang again, loudly, dust flying off one side, but moving farther this time, ringing again and again as Wilson's gunmen—even the Texan—spun around while a rifle's report accompanied the ringing dinner bell.

"That's Liberty Rawlings." Matt shoved the barrel against Wilson's spine. "You local boys know how my deputy never loses a turkey shoot. That's a Sharps rifle, with a telescopic sight. And every one of you sons-of-bitches make a real neat target. The four of us are riding out of here. You cough, you scratch, you die."

The Texan licked his lips. "You can't get us all."

"Yeah." Matt smiled. "But how many can we get? The first man to move . . . he's dead. And then I'm killing as many of the rest of you as I can. Drop all your hardware, put your hands atop your hats, and remember, you move and Liberty blows your guts out."

Those twenty yards felt like a hundred miles, but they reached the horses. "Ladies first," Matt whispered, and watched Marybeth Shelby help little Eunice onto the pony before climbing onto her bay. Both side-saddles. Well, those would have to do. He followed Wilson to the buckskin, kept his Colt trained on the man's body. "You don't ride," Matt said, "till I'm in the saddle and I say ride. And remember . . . you flinch, you die."

When he had the pinto turned around, he did not look back at the gunmen.

"Ride," he said, and watched the mother and daughter kick their mounts into hard lopes, Luther Wilson behind them. Matt urged the pinto. They rounded the corner. Twenty yards. Thirty. Then Wilson's saddle slipped, the horse kept running, and Wilson pitched into the dust.

Matt couldn't stop. Didn't want to rush a shot. Glimpsed Wilson rolling over, stunned, not dead. A shot echoed—Rawlings's Sharps—and then the girl, Mrs. Shelby, and Matt galloped toward the Durango pike.

CHAPTER TWENTY-SIX

Dust rose from the slope as Liberty Rawlings raced downhill, fearless, trusting the horse to get him down safely. They met at the main road, none slowing down, beating a path for the hills beyond.

Reaching the first hill, they thundered up the ridge. A glance back told Matt Wilson's riders were coming. But Marybeth Shelby's mare began faltering before they crested the hill, and Matt swore. *That Texan has a few tricks of his own.*

Rawlings reined up first, swung out of the saddle, and raised the mare's left front foot.

"They must have loosened the shoe," Rawlings said.

"Yeah." Matt dismounted, looked downhill, then at the rocky terrain ahead. Pulling the reins, he led his pinto to the woman. "Take my horse," he said, then pulled the Winchester from the scabbard.

"No." Rawlings still held his Sharps. "That's my job."

"No arguing, Liberty," Matt said. "I'll hold them off as long as I can here. You get Missus Shelby and the little girl to Durango, but don't stop there. Get on the train. Get to Denver. Have them make a statement to Judge Perelman.

That'll end it. That'll end everything." He shoved the reins into Marybeth's hands.

"You can't hold them off . . . ," Rawlings started to say, but Matt cut him off.

"I can give you enough time."

"The cavalry," Missus Shelby said.

Matt laid the Winchester on the ground, and lifted the widow into the pinto's saddle, spun toward Liberty. "Time's wasting. Hand me that Sharps."

"But the Army should be here," Mrs. Shelby said. "That's what brought Wilson to my house. The Army's coming."

Matt blinked.

"Troops from Fort Logan," she said. "They . . . they're in Durango already."

Good old Captain Karl Stotz.

But it wouldn't matter. Matt faced downhill. "Go," Matt said. He spun back to Rawlings, held out his hands. "You have to get these two out of here." Reluctantly, Rawlings let Matt take the heavy rifle from him. "Liberty." Matt smiled. "Is that your real name?"

"July Fourth's my birthday," he whispered.

"Get out of here," Matt said.

Rawlings pulled three giant cartridges from his back pocket, placed them in Matt's left hand. "All I got. Plus one in the breech."

"It'll do. Ride."

He did not watch them go. He shoved the long

shells into his coat pocket, heard the pounding of hoofs, and swatted the rump of Marybeth Shelby's lame horse, watching it limp down the hill after the trio. Below, the dust cloud drew closer as Matt found a place in the rocks. He leaned the Winchester against a boulder, brought up the Sharps, saw the double triggers, and pulled back the hammer.

Finding a target proved impossible at this range, and he was shooting downhill. He touched the set trigger, did not even hear the click, and pulled the second trigger. The Sharps slammed his shoulder hard, but he must have hit something, because the dust thickened, and now he spotted a riderless horse down below. A man limped to the rocks. Another man rolled into the ditch carved by run-off water.

Matt ejected the smoking cartridge, fished out another shell, shoved it in. A horse lay dead in the road, but two riders made a wide loop down around the hills. He brought up the rifle, aimed, stopped.

No. He'd never hit them. Besides, it would take them two hours before they could work their way around him. More time than Liberty needed. A gunshot popped from the bottom of the hill, but Matt heard no whine of a bullet, saw no dust, heard neither ricochet nor thud.

Matt braced the Sharps against the sandstone rock, and looked through the telescopic sight.

The dust had settled now, and he saw Wilson, obviously recovered from his fall, barking orders, trying to prove that he was no coward. The sight settled on Wilson's chest, and Matt breathed in, out, touched the set trigger. Before he moved his finger to the second trigger, he remembered what the Yankee captain had told him in Minnesota. *Aim low. Even when shooting downhill. Aim low.*

He brought the barrel down. A rifle popped, but Matt made sure Wilson had not moved. The Sharps was deafening, and his shoulder already ached. Out of the corner of his eye, he saw men running up on the other side of the hill. Knowing he needed to save his ammunition, he let them run, brought his eye back to the scope, saw someone dragging Wilson through sage and cactus, then dropping him. The man rolled, back and forth, his face apparently a bloody mess. Not dead, but wishing he could just die.

Matt put the next-to-last bullet in the Sharps. He brought up the Colt from his holster, cocked it, laid it on the side. A bullet spanged off the rock over his head, the shot coming from Matt's left. He let the Sharps slip, moved back, and found the Winchester. The carbine barked repeatedly. He laid it on the ground, crawled forward, picked up the Sharps again, and found his position. A man ran toward a pile of rocks. The Texan, Matt thought, recognizing the hat. Matt aimed, lowered the barrel, touched both triggers almost simultaneously, and fell hard to the ground as bullets danced and whined over his head.

He lay there, breathing hard, pulling himself into a tighter hole. The last shell went into the Sharps, and he peered through the scope. He could see the Texan's boots; the man never moved. Letting the telescope move over the terrain below, Matt spotted two dead horses, another man in the middle of the road, and there was Wilson, still twisting, rolling. Moving back, Matt found the hot barrel of the Winchester, and pulled it forward.

Damn, he thought, *I could use a drink of water.* Silently, Matt laughed. Water. *Ain't that something, Jeff? Matt Johnson, wanting water. Not whiskey.*

That's right, he heard Jeff Hancock tell him. *You've come far.*

And he could picture Bounce McMahon shaking his head, and hear his voice: *This time,* the Ohioan said, *they won't be able to say you shot these sons-of-bitches in the back.*

You done us proud, Kim Buchman chimed in: *Stopped another range war on the Picketwire. Stopped a land grab in the Ute country. Solved a murder or two. Avenged a deputy marshal's death.*

And don't forget, Jeff Hancock said, *you kept that railroad strike from turning ugly.*

Matt tried to find the best spot where he could

344

see those riflemen off to the east, and the fools down below. Eventually, he would have to worry about the two that circled wide to the west.

Four men down, dead, wounded, or dying. That left six. Maybe eight.

He didn't stand a chance. Unless the cavalry under Captain Stotz came galloping up. Which could happen. But if it didn't, Matthew Johnson would still win. He had made the right decisions.

He tensed, envisioning Jean McBride. For a moment, he could even smell her perfume.

But he knew something else. He had made the right choice regarding her, too. Women could get divorced these days. Especially from drunkard husbands. As for John Kimbrough? Yeah, that rancher would take care of Jean. Love her as much as Matt did. Take better care of her than Matt ever could.

He laughed out loud. *It takes a man to admit something like that,* Jeff Hancock had once said. Of course, Hancock had been conceding that Red Underwood was a better calf roper. But Matt saw Jean's smile, could hear her singing at Chandler's Automatic Phonograph Parlour. He felt his hand on her stomach. Stuck in these rocks, surrounded by people meaning to kill him, he felt as alive as he had been when he was with Jean.

The bullets rang out again from the east, showering Matt with dust and gravel. He brought the Winchester's stock to his shoulder, and fired once, twice, three times. Over the reverberating noise of bullets, echoes, and ricochets, while he pushed out shells from his cartridge belt to feed into the carbine, Matt heard something else.

He frowned, before finally understanding. Someone was singing. Now Matt laughed, then jacked another round into the carbine.

It was Matt. By thunder, he was singing. This time, he didn't stop. This time, he sang as loud as he could, bringing the Winchester up, waiting for Wilson's men to start the ball again.

Matthew Johnson,
United States marshal,
"Let bullets fly"
Is his battle cry.
Matthew Johnson,
United States marshal,
A living legend
Who can never die.

It was, he finally admitted, a catchy little tune.

AUTHOR'S NOTE

This is a work of fiction. There was no Matthew Johnson, and I've adjusted history to fit my narrative. A railroad strike in 1894 did spill violently into Colorado, but later in the year. I tweaked other things, too.

In 1999, the late Jon Tuska and Vicki Piekarski took me on as a client for Golden West Literary Agency, and *The Lonesome Chisholm Trail* was published late in 2000. So when Vicki told me in 2019 that she had decided to retire, I had to figure out what novel would be my last for her after a twenty-one-year run. Since the inspiration for *The Lonesome Chisholm Trail* came from a story I had written in my early teens—the only similarities being the title and the names of some characters—I thought that to end this era I should return to my early writing attempts back in the swamps of South Carolina.

Matthew Johnson, a U.S. marshal in Montana—not Colorado—was the hero of several short stories I wrote in elementary and middle school. I remember nothing about those tales, but I do recall Johnson had two loyal deputies named Liberty Rawlings (or something like that) and Strongo . . . Stephens/Stevens? Hey, it has been a while, and, thankfully, those early attempts at fiction no longer exist. But, except for adjusting the closing lines, that opening verse of the minstrel's song about heroic Matthew Johnson was the theme song to those stories.

This novel never could have been written if not for Mrs. Maynard, the teacher who gave my third-grade class this assignment: "Write a tale. Just make something up." Nor could it have been written without Vicki and Jon, who told me practically the same thing: Write a tale, but try to make it a good one. Good or not-quite-what-I'd-hoped, Vicki always made it better.

It has been a fun ride, but I look forward to the next tale, and wish Vicki all the best in her new adventures.

Johnny D. Boggs
Santa Fe, New Mexico
Late Winter, 2020

ABOUT THE AUTHOR

In 2019, Johnny D. Boggs won his eighth Spur Award from Western Writers of America—the most in the nonprofit association's 66-year history. *Booklist* has called him "among the best Western writers at work today," and Publishers Weekly said: "Boggs's narrative voice captures the old-fashioned style of the past."

A native of South Carolina and former newspaper journalist in Texas, Boggs has written historical Westerns (*Greasy Grass*; *Hard Way Out of Hell*); traditional novels (*The Big Fifty*; *MacKinnon*); comic novels (*East of the Border*; *Mojave*); baseball Westerns (*Camp Ford*; *The Kansas City Cowboys*); Civil War novels (*Wreaths of Glory*; *And There I'll Be a Soldier*); Colonial/Revolutionary War novels (*The Cane Creek Regulators*; *Ghost Legion*); Western mysteries (the *Killstraight* series); young-adult fiction (*Doubtful Cañon*; *South by Southwest*; *Taos Lightning*); and nonfiction (*Jesse James and the Movies*; *Billy the Kid on Film, 1911-2012*; *The American West on Film*); along with short fiction and short nonfiction. His Spur Awards came for his short story "A Piano at Dead Man's Crossing" (2002) and for his novels *Camp Ford* (2006), *Doubtful Cañon* (2008), *Hard Winter*

(2010), *Legacy of a Lawman* (2012), *West Texas Kill* (2012), *Return to Red River* (2017) and *Taos Lightning* (2019). He has also won the Western Heritage Wrangler Award from the National Cowboy and Western Heritage Museum for his novel *Spark on the Prairie: The Trial of the Kiowa Chiefs* (2004); the Arkansiana Award for Juvenile/Young Adult from the Arkansas Library Association for *Poison Spring* (2015); and the Milton F. Perry Award from the National James-Younger Gang for his novel *Northfield* (2007).

In 2020, Boggs was named recipient of the Owen Wister Award for Lifetime Contributions to Western Literature and inducted into the Western Writers Hall of Fame. He has also written for more than fifty newspapers and magazines, and is a frequent contributor to *Wild West* and *True West* magazines.

He lives with wife Lisa and son Jack in Santa Fe. His website is www.johnnydboggs.com.

| Books are produced in the United States using U.S.-based materials | Books are printed using a revolutionary new process called THINKtech™ that lowers energy usage by 70% and increases overall quality | Books are durable and flexible because of Smyth-sewing | Paper is sourced using environmentally responsible foresting methods and the paper is acid-free |

Center Point Large Print
600 Brooks Road / PO Box 1
Thorndike, ME 04986-0001 USA

(207) 568-3717

US & Canada:
1 800 929-9108
www.centerpointlargeprint.com

Fulton Co. Public Library
320 W. 7th Street
Rochester, IN 46975